S. Weir (Silas Weir) Mitchell

The adventures of François

S. Weir (Silas Weir) Mitchell

**The adventures of François**

ISBN/EAN: 9783337056964

Printed in Europe, USA, Canada, Australia, Japan

Cover: Foto ©Andreas Hilbeck / pixelio.de

More available books at **www.hansebooks.com**

# The Adventures of
# François

Foundling, Thief, Juggler, and Fencing-
Master during the French Revolution

By

## S. Weir Mitchell, M.D.

L.L. D. Harvard and Edinburgh

New York
The Century Co.
1898

THE DE VINNE PRESS.

## XIII

## XIV

## XV

## XVI

## XVII

## XVIII

## XIX

# LIST OF ILLUSTRATIONS

# THE ADVENTURES OF FRANÇOIS

### FOUNDLING, THIEF, JUGGLER, AND FENCING-MASTER
### DURING THE FRENCH REVOLUTION

## I

*Of how François the foundling was cared for by the good fathers of the Benedictine Asylum for Orphans, and of what manner of lad he was.*

IN the summer of the year 1777 a lad of about ten years, clad in a suit of gray, was playing in the high-walled garden of the Benedictine Asylum for Orphans in Paris. The sun was pleasant, the birds sang overhead, the roses were many, for the month was June. A hundred lads were noisily running about. They had the look of being well fed, decently clothed, and kindly cared for. An old priest walked to and fro, at times looking up from his breviary to say a pleasant word or to check some threatening quarrel.

Presently he paused beside the boy who was at the moment intently watching a bird on a branch over-

head.   As the priest turned, the boy had thrown himself on the grass and was laughing heartily.

"What amuses thee, my son?" said the father.

"I am laughing at the birds."

"And why do they make thee laugh, François?"

"I do not know."

"And I," said the priest, "do not know why the
birds sing, nor why thou dost laugh. Thou hast a
talent that way. The good God grant thee always
cause"; and with his eyes on his breviary, and his
lips moving in prayer, he walked away.

The lad fell back again on the grass, and laughed
anew, as if overcome with some jest he shared with
no one but the birds overhead. This was a kindly
little waif brought hither from the Enfants Trouvés,
nameless except for the card pinned on the basket
in which he lay when the unknown mother left him,
a red-faced baby, to the charity of asylum life.

His constant mirthfulness was a sad cross to some
of the good fathers, for neither punishment, fast, nor
penance got the better of this gaiety, nor served to
repress its instinctive expression. He had, too,—
what is rare in childhood,— quick powers of ob-
servation, and a certain joy in the world of nature,
liking to lie on his back and watch the birds at work,
or pleased to note the daily changes of flowers or the
puzzling journeys of the ants which had their crowded
homes beneath the lilacs in undisturbed corners of
the garden. His nearest mother, Nature, meant the
boy to be one of those rare beings who find happiness in the use of keen senses and in a wakeful
mind, which might have been trained to employ its

powers for the partial conquest of some of her many
kingdoms. But no friendly hand was here to guide,
no example present to incite or lift him. The simple
diet provided for the intellect of these little ones was
like the diet of their table — the same for one and
for all.

His head was high, his face long; all his features
were of unusual size, the mouth and ears of dispro-
portionate magnitude; altogether, a quaint face, not
quite of to-day, a something Gothic and medieval in
its general expression.

The dull round of matins and vespers, the routine
of lessons, the silent refectory meals, went on year
after year with little variation. The boy François
simply accepted them as did the rest; but, unlike
some of his comrades, he found food for mirth, silent,
gentle, or boisterous, where no other saw cause for
amusement.

Once a week a sober line of gray-clad boys, with
here and there a watchful priest, filed through the
gay streets to mass at St. Eustache or Notre Dame.
He learned, as he grew, to value these chances, and
to look forward with eager anticipation to what they
brought him. During these walks the quick-minded
François saw and heard a hundred things which
aroused his curiosity. The broad gardens of the Luxembourg, the young fellows at unrestricted play, the
river and the boats, by degrees filled him with keen
desire to see more of this outer world, and to have
easy freedom to roam at will. It was the first flutter
of wings longing for natural flight. Before they set
out on these journeys, a good father at the great

gateway said to them as they went by : " Look neither
to the right nor to the left, my children. 'T is a day
of prayer. Remember ! " Alas ! what eyes so busy
as those of François ?  " Look at this — at that," he
would cry to the lads close to him. " Be quiet, there ! "
said the priests' low voices; and on this François's
droll face would begin to express the unspoken delight he found in the outer world of men and things.
This naughty outside world kept calling him to share
its liberty. The boy liked best the choir, where his
was the most promising voice. Here was happiness
such as the use of dexterous hands or observant eyes
also gave him. Religion was to him largely a matter
of formal service. But in this, as in secular education, the individuality of the creature may not be set
aside without risk of disaster. For all alike there
was the same dull round, the same instruction.
Nevertheless, the vast influence of these repeated
services, and of the constant catechism, he continued
to feel to his latest day.

He was emotional and imaginative, fond of color,
and sensitive to music ; but the higher lessons of the
church, which should control the life of action, were
without effect on a character which was naturally one
of exceptional levity. Such a mind has small power
to apply to the conduct of life the mere rules laid
down for its guidance, and is apt to accept as personally useful only what comes from the lessons of
experience.

## II

*In which François becomes a choir-boy, and serves two masters, to the impairment of his moral sense.*

E was about fourteen, and the best of the choir, when a great change took place in his life. He was sent, with a dozen others, to the vestry of Notre Dame, and there carefully tested as to the power and quality of his voice. The masters of the choir were exacting, but, to his great delight, he was thought the best of the four who were finally selected to fill vacancies among the boy choristers of the cathedral. This came about in the autumn of the year 1781.

The next day he received a long lecture on how he should behave himself; and thus morally provided, was sent, with his small belongings in a bag, to the house of certain of the choir-masters who lived in the Rue des Chanteurs. One of the priests who escorted the four boys stood at the door of the house of the choir, and saying good-by to them as they went in, bade them come, if they might, and visit their old home; and so, with a benediction, sent them forth into a larger world.

5

It was not much larger, nor was it as agreeable.
When the good father left them, one Tomas, who
was steward of the choir-house, took the lads in
charge.

"Up with ye, singing-birds!" he cried; "up! up!"
And this at each story: "It will soon be your best
chance of heaven; up! up!" until they reached a
large attic under the tiles.

It was a dismal place, and hospitable to every
wind that blew. Each of twelve choir-boys had a
straw mattress on the floor, and pegs where hung his
clothes and the white surplice he wore during service. The four newcomers took possession, and were
soon informed by Tomas of their duties. They must
be up at five to sing before breakfast with the second
chanter.

"Before breakfast!" cried one of the recruits.

"Little animal!" said Tomas. "Before thou dost
eat there is room to fill thy chest; but after, what
boy hath room? Breakfast at six and a half; at
seven a lesson. Thou wilt intone with Père Lalatte."

Thus the day was to be filled; for here were lessons a-plenty in Latin, and all must learn to read and
to write, for they might be priests some blessed day.

François reflected as Tomas packed the hours with
this and that as one packs a bag. He made his
face as grave as nature would let it be, and said
it was very nice, and that he liked to sing. Was
there anything else? Tomas replied that this first
day they might ask questions, but that after that he
(Tomas) had only one answer, because to have only
one saved thinking.

This amused François, who was prematurely capable of seeing the fun of things.

When a duller boy who did not apprehend asked to know more he received an illustration in the form of a smart smack, which proved convincingly instructive, and silenced all but François, who asked, "Please, monsieur, when may we play?" and "Is there anything more?"

Tomas replied that there was a free hour before supper, and a little while somewhere about noon in the garden; also, they must wait on table; and oh, he forgot the prayers; and then went on to complete the packing of the day with various small duties in the nature of attentions to the comfort of Tomas. With some last words as to the time of the next meal, the steward left them.

The lads, silent and anxious, arranged their small possessions. A little goldfinch in a wicker cage was François's most valued property; he had taught it many pretty tricks, and now he had been allowed to bring it with him. François put the cage on the window-ledge, and fed his brightly tinted bird from a small store of millet with which he had filled his pocket. Then he looked out to see what prospect the view from the attic afforded.

The home of the master-choristers was an ancient house of the days of Henri IV, and leaned so far over that as the boy looked out he had a sudden fear lest it should be about to tumble. The street was not more than twelve feet wide. The opposite dwellings were a full story below the attic from which the boy looked. The nearest house across the way had

an ancient stoop.  Others bent back from the line of
the street, and the open windows gave them a look of
yawning weariness which set the boy to gaping in
sympathy.

Above was a mottled wilderness of discolored tiles,
chimney-pots, and here and there gray corner turrets
with vanes which seemed to entertain diverse views
as to the direction whence the wind blew.  Below
was the sunless well of the street.  As he gazed he
saw the broad hats of priests hiding the figures beneath them.  It interested the boy.  It was new and
strange.  He was too intent to notice that all but he
had gone, obedient to an order of Tomas.

A woman at a window over the way let fall a skirt
she had been drying.  It sailed to and fro, and fell
on the head of a reflective abbé.  The boy broke into
laughter.  A cat climbed on to a chimney-pot, and
was met by a gust of smoke from the flue beside it.
She scrambled off, sneezing.

"What fun!" cried the boy, and laughed again.

"Little beast!" shouted Tomas.  "Must I come
for thee?  'T is not permitted to laugh.  It is forbid
to laugh.  It spoils the voice"— a queer notion
which, to his sorrow, the boy found to prevail in the
house of the choristers.

"How can that be?" said François, boldly.

The man gave him to understand that he was to
obey his betters without answering, and then, taking
the cage from the window, said: "Come — quick,
too!  Thou art late for the dinner, and must do
without it.  There is a singing-lesson.  Off with
thee!"

He was leaving the room when, suddenly, a strange fury of anger came on the boy. He snatched the cage from the man's hand, crying, "My bird! It is my bird!"

Tomas caught him, and began to administer a smart cuffing; but the lad was vigorous and of feline agility. He used nails, teeth, and feet. Then, of a sudden, he ceased to struggle, and fell on a mattress in an agony of tears. The man had set his foot on the fallen cage, crying:

"I will teach thee a lesson, little animal!"

There lay in the crushed cage the dead bird, still quivering, a shapeless mass of green and yellow with a splotch of red. It was the first lesson of that larger world toward which the foundling had been so joyfully looking.

He made no further resistance to the discipline which followed. Then came a dark cell and bread and water for a weary day, and much profit in the way of experience. It was a gentle home he had left. He had known there no unkindness, nor had he ever so sinned as to suffer more than some mild punishment. The new life was hard, the diet spare. As the winter came on, the attic proved to be cold. The winds came in from the tiles above and through the shrunken window-frames. Once within, they seemed to stay and to wander in chilly gusts. The dark suits worn by the choir-boys were none too warm. If the white surplice were clean, little more was asked in that direction. There were long services twice a day at the great cathedral near by, and three hours of practice under the eye of a junior chorister. The boys were abed at eight, and up at five; and for play, there were two uncertain hours — after the noon meal and at seven in the evening — when they were free to move about a small court behind the house, or to rest, if they pleased, in the attic. Four days in the week there were lessons in Latin and in reading and writing. Assuredly the devil had little of the chance which idle hours are presumed to give. But this fallen angel has also the industry of the minute, and knows how to profit by the many chances of life. He provided suggestive lessons in the habits of the choristers who dwelt in the stories above the wine-shop on the first floor. Sounds of gay carouses reached the small garret saints at night, and gay voices were heard which had other than masculine notes. At meal-times the choir-boys waited on their masters, and fetched their food from the kitchen. The lads soon learned to take toll on the way, and to comfort their shrunken stomachs with a modest share of the diet of their betters.

"Little rats!" said Tomas the steward, "you will squeal in purgatory for this; and 't were better to give you a dose of it here." And so certain of the rats, on account of temporary excess of feed, were given none for a day, and left in a cold cellar to such moral aids as reflection might fetch.

François sat with his comrades of mishap in the gloom, and devised new ways of procuring food and concealing their thefts.

"Rats we are," said François, gaily; "and rats had need be smart; and who ever heard that the *bon Dieu* sent rats to purgatory?" Then he hatched queer stories to keep up the spirits of the too penitent; and whether full or empty, cold or warm, took all that came with perpetual solace of good-humored laughter. It was not in him to bear malice. The choir-masters liked him, and with the boys he was the leader.

Most of the dozen choir-boys were dull fellows; but this sharp-witted François was of other make, and found in the table-talk of the choristers, and of the curés who came now and then to share their ample fare, food for such thoughts as a boy thinks. He soon learned, as he grew older, how difficult is complete sin; how many outlets there are for him who, being penitent, desires to create new opportunities for penitence. François was fast forming his character. He had small need to look for excuses, and a meager talent for regret. When his stomach was full he was good, and when it was empty he must, as he said in after years, "fill it to squeeze out Satan."

There were singular books about, and for his education, now that he read Latin fairly well, a manual on confession. It was not meant for half-fed choir-boys. More fascinating were the confessions of one Rousseau — a highly educative book for a clever boy of sixteen. At this age François was a long-legged, active fellow, a keen-witted domestic brigand, expert in providing for his wants, and eagerly desirous of seeing more of the outside world, of the ways of which he was so ignorant. The procession of closely watched boys went to church and back again to the old house at least once a day, and this was his only glimpse of the entertaining life of the streets. When left to himself, he liked best in good weather to sit at the open attic window and watch the cats on the roofs across the way. So near were the houses that he could toss a bone or a crust on to the roof opposite, and delight to see these Ishmaelites contend for the prize. He grew to know them, so that they would come at dusk to the roof-edge, and contemplate dietetic possibilities with eager and luminous eyes. Being versed in the Bible, as all good choirboys should be, he found names for his feline friends which fitted their qualities; for there, among the chimneys, was a small world of stirring life which no man disturbed. He saw battles, jealousies, greediness, and loves. Constancy was not there. Solomon of the many wives was king of the tiles; a demure blue cat was Susannah, for good reasons; and there, too, were the elders. It might have seemed to some pitiful angel a sad picture — this poor lad in the grasp of temptations, but made for better chances, finding his utmost joy in the distant company of these lean Arabs of the desert housetops.

## III

*Of the misfortunes caused by loss of a voice, and of how
a cat and a damsel got François into trouble — whereupon, preferring the world to a monastery, he ran
away from the choristers of Notre Dame.*

T was in the month of June, in the year
1784, that a female got him into trouble,
and aided to bring about a decision as
to his future. This was, however, only
one of the distressing incidents which
at the time affected his career, and was not his final
experience of the perils to which attention to the
other sex may expose the unwary. A few days before the sad event which brought about a change in
François's life, he was engaged in singing one of the
noble Gregorian chants. Never had he used his voice
with greater satisfaction. He was always pleased
and eagerly ambitious when in the choir, and was
then at his best. This day it seemed to him, as he
sang, that his clear tones rose like a bird, and that
something of him was soaring high among the reso-
nant arches overhead. Of a sudden his voice broke
into a shrill squeak. The choir-master shook a finger
at him, and he fell into a dead silence, and sang no

13

more that morning.  The little white-robed procession marched out, and when it reached the gray old
house there was wrath and consternation over the
broken treble.   He was blamed and beaten; but, after
all, it was a too likely misfortune.   If it chanced again
he must go to the Dominican convent at Auteuil, and
perhaps in a year or two would be lucky enough to get
back his voice.  Meanwhile let him take care.   Poor
François did his best; but a week later, amid the
solemnity of a mass for the dead, came once more
that fatal break in the voice.   He knew that his fate
was sealed.

Little was said this time, but he overheard the
head of the choir arranging with Tomas the steward
that the boy should go to Auteuil.   Until then he was
no longer to serve in the choir.

François had seen all this occur before, when, as
was common, some little singer lost control of his
changing voice.  His case was hopeless.  Yet here
was an idle time and no more singing-lessons.  But
a part of the small joys of a life not rich in happy
moments was gone, to come back no more, as he knew
too well.  Of late his fine quality of song had won
him some indulgence, and he had learned how much
a fine voice might mean.  Dim visions began to open
before him, as he heard of how choir-boys had conquered fame and wealth in France or elsewhere.  One
day the leader of the choir had praised him and his
diligence, and hoped he would never leave them.  He
was told what a great possession was a voice like his,
and had even been envied by the less gifted.  Now
this possession was taken from him, and he was at

once made sadly aware of his loss. His vanity, always great, was wounded to the quick. A little kindness would have led him to go to the convent and hopefully bide his time; but nobody cared, or seemed to care, for him, or to pity what to his active imagination was a fatal wreck of goodly chances.

For a day or two he went about disconsolate, and was set to serve in the kitchen or to wait on the man Tomas, who jeered at his squeaky voice, and called him "little pig," with additions of some coarser amenities of language, and certain information as to the convent life of a lay servant ill calculated to make Auteuil appear desirable.

In his leisure hours, which now were many, François took refuge from the jests of his fellows in the lonely garret. The people across the way in their rooms amused him. The cats were never long absent. He watched their cunning search for the nests of the sparrows, and very soon began to feel again the invincible lifting power of his comic nature. Some remembrance of the alarm in the choir-master's face when his voice broke came upon François, and he begana to laugh. Just then he saw Solomon on the roof opposite. The master of a populous harem was in the company of the two naughty elders. Susannah, behind a chimney, was making her modest toilet with a skilful tongue. He called her, and held up a tempting bone. The shy maiden hesitated. He called, "Suzanne, Suzanne!" to bring her to the edge of the tiled roof and near enough to make sure that the elders would not capture her desired prize.

As he called, a little grisette who was hanging out

clothes to dry kissed her hand to the boy. François
had seen her before. She was not attractive. He
liked his cats better. " Suzanne, Suzanne! " he
called, as the virgin, looking about her, daintily
picked her way to the edge. High on the roof-top,
Solomon exhorted the elders, and in a moment backs
were humped, and claws out, and there was bad language used, which may have been Hebrew, but at all
events appeared to be sufficiently expressive; for
the elders and Solomon, of a sudden rolling over in a
wild scuffle, disappeared on the farther side of the roof.
This was the maid's opportunity, and gratefully lick-
ing her anticipative chops, she crawled to the gutter.

" *Bonne Suzanne! Viens donc!* Come, come, Suzanne! " cried the boy.

Of a sudden a smart box on the ear broke up this
pretty love-affair. There stood Tomas.

" A nice choir-boy! Talking with that beast of a
grisette ! " Then there were more liberal whacks as
the boy, in a rage, was dragged away, and bidden to
come down-stairs and carry to market the nets used
in place of baskets. Tomas usually went alone to
buy provisions, but now the choir-boy was free and
could be made of use.

François uttered no complaint. It was literally
the only time he had had a chance to be in the
streets, except as part of the procession to and from
the church. He was sore, angry, and resentful of the
ill usage which in the last few days had taken the
place of the growing respect his talent had created.
He took the nets and his cap, and followed Tomas.
" What a chance ! " he thought to himself.

The boy concealed the delight he felt, and followed the steward, who went down to the river and across it to the open market on the farther bank. He stopped here and there to buy provisions and to chat with the market-women. When one of them, pleased with the odd-looking lad, gave him an apple, Tomas took it from him. François laughed, which seemed always to offend the saturnine steward. He could not destroy the pleasure of the gay market for François, who made queer faces at the mistresses of the stalls, teased the dogs and cats for sale in cages, and generally made himself happy until they came home again.

But from this time onward, except for these excursions, his life was made miserable enough. He was the slave of Tomas, and was cruelly reminded day after day of the misery of him who has a servant for his master.

At last he learned that the time was near when he must go to Auteuil. His voice had been tested again, and he had been told that there was small hope of its return. He began to think of escape. Once he was sent alone on an errand to a shop near by. He lingered to see some street-jugglers, and paid for it with a day in a damp cellar. Within this sad home he now found only reproaches and unthanked labor. The choristers laughed at him, and the happier boys mocked his changed voice. On the day after his last experience of the cellar, he was told by Tomas to be ready to go to Auteuil, and was ordered once again to follow the steward to market. He took up the nets and went after him. The lad looked back at

2

the choir-house. He meant to see it no more. He was now seventeen, and in the three years of his stay had learned many things, some good and some bad.

They went past Notre Dame to the *quai,* and through rows of stalls along the shores of the Seine. Tomas soon filled the nets, which were hung over François's shoulders. Meanwhile the chattering women, the birds and cages, the flowers, the moving, many-colored crowd, amused or pleased the boy, but by no means turned him from his purpose.

"Come!" cried Tomas, and began to elbow his way through the noisy people on the river-bank. Presently François got behind him, and noting his chances with a ready eye, slipped through between the booths and darted up the Seine.

# IV

*Of how the world used François, and of the reward of
virtue. He makes his first friend.*

HEN Tomas, having won his way out of
the press about a fortune-teller, looked
for François, there was a lost choir-boy
and two days' diet gone none knew
whither — least of all the fugitive. He
moved away with the speed of fear, and was soon in
the somber network of narrow streets which in those
days made a part of the Île de la Cité the refuge of the
finest assortment of thieves, bravos, gypsies, and low
women to be found in any capital of Europe.

His scared looks and decent black suit betrayed
him. An old fellow issued from a doorway like a
spider. "Ha, ha, little thief!" he said; "I will buy
thy plunder."

François was well pleased. He took eagerly the
ten sous offered, and saw the spider poke a long red
beak into the loaded nets as he passed out of sight
in the dark doorway. François looked at the money.
It was the first he had ever owned. He walked
away in haste, happy to be free, and so over a bridge
to the Île St. Louis, with its pretty gardens and the

19

palaces of the great nobles. At the far end of the
isle he sat down in the sun and watched the red
barges go by, and took no more care for to-morrow
than does a moth just out of its cocoon. He caught
up the song of a man near by who was mending a
bateau. He whistled as he cast stones into the water.
It was June, and warm, and before him the river
playing with the sunset gold, and behind him the
dull roar of Paris. Ah, the pleasure to do as he
would! Why had he waited so long?

Toward night he wandered back into the Cité, and
saw an old woman selling fried potatoes, and crying,
"Two sous, two sous!" He asked for thus much,
and received them in the top of his cap. The hag
took his ten-sou piece, and told him to begone.
Amazed at this bit of villainy, poor François en-
treated her to give him his change. She called him
a thief, and when a dreadful man sallied out of a
wine-shop and made murderous threats, the boy ran
as fast as he could go, and never ceased until he got
to the river again. There, like Suzanne, he kept
watch for the foes of property, and at last ate his
potatoes, and began to reflect on this last lesson in
morality. He had stolen many morsels, many din-
ners, and his fair share of wine; but to be himself
robbed of his entire means was calculated to enlarge
his views of what is possible in life, and also unde-
sirable. The night was warm; he slept well in an
abandoned barge, but woke up early to feel that liberty had its drawbacks, and that emptiness of stomach
was one of the large family of needs which stimulate
the ingenuity of man or boy.

Quite at a loss, he wandered once more through the slums of the Cité, and soon lost himself in the network of narrow streets to the north of the cathedral, hearing, as he went, strange slang, which his namesake François Villon would have better understood than he. The filth of the roadways and that of the tongue were here comparable. Some boys, seeing his sober suit of the dark cloth worn by the choir, pelted him with stones. He ran for his life, and falling over a man who was sawing wood, received a kick for remembrance. Far away he paused breathless in a dark lane which seemed unpeopled, and where the houses leaned over like palsied old scoundrels who whisper to one another of ancient crime. Even to a boy the place was of a sudden terrible. There was murder in the air.

He felt, without knowing why, the danger of the place. A painted creature, half clad, came out of a house — a base animal whom the accident of sex had made a woman. She called to him to come in. He turned and went by her in haste and horror. A man in a red shirt ran toward him, crying out some ordures of speech. As he fled there was a sudden peopling of window and doorway with half-naked drunken men and women. He had never before seen such faces. He was in that pit of crime and bestiality which before long was to overflow and riot in a limitless debauch of blood. The boy's long legs served him well. He dodged and ran this way and that. At the mouth of the *cul-de-sac* a lank boy caught him by the arm. François struck him fiercely, and with a sense of joy in the competence of the first blow he had ever given one of his own years, he fled again; nor did he pause until, free from foes, he stood panting in the open sunshine below the great buttresses of Notre Dame.

He saw here that no one took notice of him, and, once more at ease, crossed from the Cité to the right bank of the Seine. Thus wandering he came at last to one of the low bridges which spanned the broad ditches then bounding the Place Louis XV, where now is the Place de la Concorde. The ducks and swans in these canals delighted him. He lingered, liking the gaiety and careless joy of the children with their nurses. The dogs, acrobats, musketeers, and the pomp of heavy, painted carriages rolling by with servants in liveries, the Swiss guards, the magnificence of the king's palace, were all to him as a new world might have been.

He went on, and at last along the Rue St. Honoré and to the Palais Royal, where, amid its splendid shops, cafés, jugglers, fortune-tellers, and richly clad people, he forgot for an hour his poor little stomach and its claims. By and by he took note of the success of a blind beggar. He watched him for an hour, and knew that he had in this time gathered in sous at least a franc. The shrunken stomach of the boy began to convert its claims into demands, and with this hint he put on a sad face and began to beg. It was not a very prosperous business; but he stated his emptiness so pitifully, and his voice had such sweet, pleading notes, that at last he thus acquired six or eight sous, and retired to the outer gate to count them.

The imprudence of estimating wealth in public was soon made clear to him. He was seated back of the open grille, his cap on his lap, when a quick, clawlike hand, thrust between the railings, darted over his shoulder, and seized two thirds of his gains. He started up in time to see that the thief was the blind beggar, who was away and lost in the crowd and among the horses and carriages, to all appearances in excellent possession of the sense of sight. Pursuit was vain. François's education was progressing. Most lads thus tormented by fate would have given way to rage or tears. François cried out, "*Sathanas!*" not knowing as yet any worse expletive, and burst into a roar of laughter. At least there were three sous left, and these he put into his pocket. His lessons were not over. The crowd thinned at noon, and he rose to go in search of food. At this moment a gentleman in very gorgeous dress, with ruffles, sword, and a variety of dazzling splendors, went by, and at the boy's feet let fall a lace handkerchief. François seized it, and stood still a moment. Then he put it in his breast, and again stood still. To take food is one thing; to steal a handkerchief is quite another. He was weak with hunger, but he had three sous. He ran after the gentleman, and cried:

"Here is your handkerchief!"

"A very honest lad," said its owner; "you will do well in the world"; and so went his way, leaving to virtue the proverbial reward of virtue. This time François did not laugh. In the Rue St. Honoré he bought some boiled beans for two sous, and retired to eat them in peace on the steps of St. Roch. Soon he saw a woman with a tin pan come out of a little shop and after her a half-grown black poodle. She set down the pan, and left the dog to his meal. François reconnoitered cautiously, and giving the dog a little kick, fled with the pan, and was shortly safe in an unfrequented passage behind the church. Here he found that he was master of a chop and a half-eaten leg of chicken. He had eaten the chop and some crusts, as well as the beans, when he became aware of the black poodle, which, being young, still had confidence in human nature, and now, with sense of ownership, thrust his black nose in the pan of lessening viands.

François laughed gaily. The touch of friendly trust gave the lonely boy a thrill of joy, and, with some reluctance doubtless, he gave the dog what was left, feeding him in bits, and talking as a comrade to a comrade. The poodle was clearly satisfied. This was very delightful society, and he was receiving such attention as flatters a decent dog's sense of his social position. The diet was less than usual, but the company was of the best, and inspired the extreme of confidence. There is a charm of equality as between dog and boy. Both are of Bohemia. The poodle stood up when asked to beg. He was invited to reveal his name. He received with the sympathetic sadness of the motionless tail the legend of François's woes.

When at last François rose, the dog followed him a little way, saying plainly, " Where thou goest I will go." But the unlicked pan needed attention; he turned back to the fleshpots. Seeing himself de-

serted, a vague sadness came upon François. It was
the shadow of an uncomprehended emotion. He
said, " Adieu, *mon ami!*" and left the little black
fellow with his nose in the pan.

An hour of wandering here and there brought
François to the palisades around the strong foundations of the new church of the Madeleine. Beyond
were scattered country houses, the Pépinières of the
king, and the great English garden of Monceaux
belonging to the Duc d'Orléans. This fascinating
stretch of trees and green and boundless country
was like a heavenly land to the boy. No dream
could be more strange. He set out by the Rue de la
Pologne, and at last went with timid doubt through
the *barrière*, and was soon in the open country. To
his surprise, he heard a yap at his side, and there
was the little black poodle, apparently as well pleased
as he. François had no scruples as to ownership.
*Mon Dieu!* had he stolen the dog, or had the dog
stolen him? They ran along happy, the boy as little
troubled as the dog by questions of conscience. The
country was not productive of easily won food, but
a few stolen plums were to be had. A girl coming
from milking gave a jug of milk, which François,
despite keen hunger, shared with his friend. When
a couple of miles from Paris, he sat down to rest by
the roadside. The dog leaped on to his lap, and the
boy, as he lay in the sun, began to think of a name
for this new friend. He tried merrily all the dog-
names he could think of; but when at last he called,
" Toto!" the poodle barked so cordially that François sagaciously inclined to the belief that he must

have hit upon the poodle's name. "Toto it shall be,"
he cried. All that day they wandered joyfully,
begged a crust, and at night slept in an orchard,
the poodle clasped to the boy's bosom — a pair of
happy vagabonds.

When, next day, the pair of them, half starved,
were disconsolately returning toward Paris, an old
woman bade François earn a few sous by picking
strawberries. But the dog must not range the garden;
he should be tied in the kitchen. François worked
hard at the matter in hand, taking good toll of the
berries, and at noon went back with the old dame to
her cottage.

"It is five sous, *mon garçon*, and a bowl of milk
thou shalt have, and a bit of meat; and how merry
thou art!"

Alas! as she opened the door the poodle fled past
her with a whole steak in his mouth. Hot it was,
but of such delicate savor that it gave him courage
to hold on. The old woman threw a stool after him,
and cried out in wrath that they were both thieves.
Then she turned on poor François with fury and a
broom, so that he had scarce time to leap the fence
and follow the dog. He found him at last with his
rather dusty prize; and seeing no better thing to do,
he went deep into a wood, and there filled himself as
he had not done for days. The brigand Toto had
his share, and thus reinforced, they set out again to
return to Paris.

# V

*Of the immorality which may come of an empty stom-
ach, and of how François became acquainted with a
human crab.*

HIS nomad life was sadly uncertain; but
Toto was a sharp forager, and what
with a sou begged here and there, and
the hospitality of summer, for a while
they were not ill contented. But at last
François passed two days of such lean living as set
his wits to work. There was clearly no help for it,
and with a rueful face he entered the shop whence
Toto had followed his uncertain fortunes.

The owner was a pleasant little woman who took
honesty for granted. Yes, it was her dog; and how
long he had been gone! Here was a great piece of
twenty sous; and where did he find the poodle?
François declared that he lived near by and knew
the dog. He had found him in the Rue du Faubourg
St. Lazare. And was it so far away as that? He
must be tired, and for his honesty should be well fed.
Thus, rich as never before, and with a full stomach,
he left Toto tied up, and went out into the world
again, lonely and sad.

27

Needless is it to describe his wanderings, or to relate how the lonely lad acquired the sharp ways of a gamin of the streets. For a while he begged or stole what food he required. Some four months later, a combination of motives led him into theft which was not mere foraging.

On a cold November day he was again in the crowded gardens and arcades of the Palais Royal. He was shabby enough by this time, and was sharply reminded by the cool nights of the need for shelter. By chance his eye lighted on the man who shammed blindness and had stolen his precious sous. The beggar was kneeling, cap in hand, with closed eyes, his head turned upward, entreating pity for his loss of sight. There were some sous in his cap. As François passed he made believe to add another sou, and as he did so deftly scooped up the greater part of the coins.

The blind man cried out; but the boy skipped aside, laughing, well aware that for the beggar to pursue him would be hardly advisable, as he might lose more than he could gain.

A few sous were of small account. They insured a meal, but not a lodging. As he was thus reflecting, he saw near by and presently beside him the gentleman who had so highly appreciated the return of his handkerchief. The coat pockets were large in those days, and the crowd was great. A little white corner of lace besought Master François, crying, "I am food and lodging for thee!" Whereupon it was done, and a lace handkerchief changed owners.

It cannot be said that these downward steps cost

François any moral discomfort. He grinned as he thought of the beggar's perplexity, and laughed outright as he felt how complete had been his own joy in the satisfaction of possession could he have made the owner of the kerchief understand that he had suffered not merely a theft, but the punishment of injustice.

François was now too well versed in the ways of the street-boy, too dirty and too ragged, to fear the Cité. Thither he went, and found a thieves' shop, where he sold the handkerchief, and got ten francs for what was worth thirty.

The question of a place where he could be sure of a bed was his first consideration on coming into his fortune. In the long, warm summers of France one who was not particular could find numerous roosting-places, but in winter a more constant home was to be desired.

In the Cité François had occasionally lodged here and there when he could afford to pay, and had been turned out when he had no more sous. Now, being affluent, and therefore hard to please, he wandered until he came upon the lodging-house of an old woman in the Rue Perpignan. He knew of her as a dealer in thieves' goods, and as ever ready to shelter the lucky — and, it was suspected, as willing to betray those who were persistently unfortunate.

What drew him to this woman's house it were hard to tell. She was repulsive in appearance, but, strangely enough, was clean as to her person, dress, and abode. Asylum life had taught François to be cleanly. He declares in his memoirs that he was by habit neat, and that it was the absence of dirt which first tempted him into a relation which was so largely to affect his after life.

When he became one of this woman's lodgers he took a step which was for him of moment. Now for the first time he was to be in the company of old and practised thieves; but he was not yet of an age to be troubled as to the future or to reflect upon the past. The horizon of youth is small.

He found plenty of masters to educate him in the evil business into which he had been driven by relentless fate. Never was pupil more ready. His hostess appreciated the cleverness of her new lodger, but it was long before he himself realized how strange was the aspect and how sinister the nature of this mother of evil.

Certain historical epochs create types of face. This was a period which manufactured many singular visages. None was more strange than that which Mme. Quatre Pattes carried on a body quite as remarkable. François speaks of her over and over in his memoirs, and dwells upon the peculiarities of her appearance. I recall well what he said to me, one evening, of this creature:

"You see, monsieur, I went to one den of thieves and another until I chanced upon the Crab. It is not to be described; for here in a little room was a witch, crumpled and deformed, sharply bent forward as to the back from the waist, and — ah, *diablement* thin! She was cleanly and even neat, and her room was a marvel, because over there in the Cité men were born and lived and died, and never saw a clean thing. And she was of a strangeness — consider, monsieur; imagine you a bald head, and a lean face below, very red, and the skin drawn so tight over the bones as to shine. Her eyes were little and of a dull gray; but they held you. Her lips were lean, and she kept them moving in a queer way as if chewing. I did laugh when first I saw her, but not often afterward."

When he confided to this clean and horrible creature what he wanted, she made him welcome. She rattled the two sticks which her bent form made needful for support. She would house him cheaply; but he must be industrious — and to sell a lace handkerchief for ten francs — *tonnerre!* He needed caution. She would be a *bonne maman* to him — she, Quatre Pattes, "four paws"; the Crab, they called her, too, for short, and because of her red leanness and spite; but what was her real name he did not learn for many a day. At first her appearance excited in his mind no emotion except amazement and mirth. A terrible old crab it was when she showed her toothless gums and howled obscenities, while her sticks were used with strange agility. The quarter feared her. M. François had a fortune in his face, she said; and did he know the *savate*, the art to kick? There was a master next door. And again, what a face! With that face he might lie all day, and who would disbelieve him? Better to fetch her what he stole. She would see that no one cheated him but herself, and that would be ever so little. One must live. When she laughed, which was not often, François felt that a curse were more gay. There were devil-women in those days, as the mad world of Paris soon came to know; and the Crab, with her purple nose and crooked red claws, was of the worst.

## VI

*Of how François regained a lost friend, and of his adventure with the poet Horace and another gentleman.*

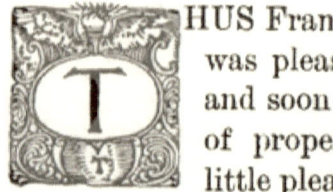HUS François was launched on what he was pleased to call the business of life, and soon became expert in the transfer of property. Strange to say, he had little pleasure in the debauchery of successful crime, and was too good-natured to like violence. When he had enough for his moderate wants he wandered in the country, here and there, in an aimless, drifting way. Simple things gave him pleasure. He could lie in the woods or on the highway half a day, only moving to keep in the sun. He liked to watch any living creature — to see the cows feed, to observe the birds. He had a charm for all animals. When the wagons went by, dogs deserted them, and came to him for a touch and a word. Best of all it was to sit beside some peasant's beehive, finding there no enmity, and smiling at the laborious lives he had no mind to imitate. Sometimes he yearned for the lost poodle, and had a pang of loneliness. That this man should have had gentle tastes, a liking for nature, a

32

regard for some of the decencies of life, will not surprise those who know well the many varieties of the
young criminal class; neither will these be amazed to
learn that now and then he heard mass, and crossed
himself devoutly when there was occasion. Children
he fascinated; a glance of his long, odd face would
make them leave nurse and toy, and sidle up to him.
In the Cité these singularities made him avoided, while
his growing strength caused him to be feared. He
sought no friends among the thieves. "Very prudent, that," said Mme. Quatre Pattes; "the more
friends, the more enemies."

He was quick and active, and a shrewd observer;
for the hard life of the streets had sharpened his naturally ready wits, and he looked far older than his
years. Of a Sunday in May he was walking down
the Rue St. Honoré, feeling a bit lonely, as was not
often the case, when he saw Toto. He whistled, and
the poodle ran to him, and would no more of the
shop or fat food he liked.

" Toto! *Mon Dieu !* " he laughed, hugging the dog,
his eyes full with the tears of joy. "Hast stolen me
again? Wilt never return me? 'T is no honest dog.
*Viens donc.* Come, then, old friend." Joyous in the
company of his comrade, who was now well grown,
he strolled out into the fields, where Toto caught a
rabbit — a terrible crime in those days.

During the next two years the pair fairly prospered. François, as he used to relate, having risen
in his profession, found a certain pleasure in good
clothes, and being of a dramatic turn, could put
on an air of bourgeois sobriety, or, with a sword

3

at his side and a bit of lace here and there, swagger as a lesser gentleman. If things were very bad, he sold Toto and all his fine tricks for a round sum, and in a day or two was sure to find the dog overjoyed and back again at the garret door. The pair were full of devices. There was Toto, a plated snuff-box in his mouth, capering before some old gentle or some slow-pacing merchant; appears François, resistlessly smiling.

"Has monsieur lost a snuff-box? My dog? Yes, monsieur. He is honest, and clever too."

Monsieur, hastily searching, produces his own snuff-box — the indispensable snuff-box of the day.

"No; thanks." And it is noted that the box he shows is of gold, and into what pocket it falls. In the next crowd Toto knows how to make a disturbance with some fat lap-dog, and in the confusion thus created the snuff-box changes owners.

"If the man be sorry, I at least am made happy," says François; "and he hath been the better for a lesson in caution. I got what I needed, and he what he required. Things are very even in this world." François had learned philosophy among the curés and priests of the choir-house. As he avoided great risks, and, as I have said, was averse to violence, he kept clear of detection, and could deceive the police of the king if by rare chance he were in peril of arrest. When the missing property was some minor article, such as a handkerchief, it was instantly hid in Toto's mouth. The dog skipped away, the outraged master was searched; the bewildered owner apologized, and the officers were shocked at such a needless charge. François talked about his offended honor, and as he looked at twenty to be a strong man of full age, the affair was apt to go no further.

Half the cleverness and thought thus devoted to an ignoble pursuit would have given him success in more honest ways. But for a long while no angel chance tempted him, and it must be admitted that he enjoyed the game he pursued, and was easily contented, not eagerly caring to find a less precarious and less risky mode of life.

Temperament is merely a permanent mood. François was like the month of June in his dear Paris. There might be storms and changes, but his mental weather had the pleasant insurance of what was in the order of despotic nature. And yet to be owner of the continual sunshine of cheerfulness has its drawbacks. It deprives a man of some of the wholesome lures of life. It dulls the spurs which goad us to resolve. It may make calamity too easy of endurance. To be too consistently cheerful may be in itself a misfortune. It had for this vagrant all its values and some of its defects. His simple, gay existence, and his flow of effervescent merriment, kept him happy and thoughtless. Most persons of this rare type like company; but François was an exception. He was better pleased to be alone with his dog, and usually desired no other society. As the poodle could not talk, his master was given to making answer for him, and finding no one to his taste among the Crab's villainous lodgers, kept to himself, and was satisfied. Nor did he ever appear to have imagined what the larger world he knew not held of such human society as

would have comforted that sense of void in his heart
which he acknowledged at times, but had no way
to fill. When fortune played him some sorry trick,
he laughed, and unconsciously quoted La Rochefoucauld. "Toto, ah, my Toto, one can never be as cunning as everybody." This was apropos of an incident
which greatly amused him.

He was in his favorite resort, the Palais Royal, one
June morning, and was at this time somewhat short
of cash. The Crab had preached him a sharp sermon
on his lack of industry, and he had liked neither the
sermon nor the preacher. At this moment a young
fellow in fine clothes came by. François, producing,
as usual, a gaudy snuff-box worth some ten francs,
politely asked of monsieur had he lost this box.
Monsieur took it in his hand. Yes, yes; he had just
missed it, the gift of his god-father, and was much
obliged. He let it fall into his pocket, and walked
away. François looked after him. "Toto, *nous
sommes volés* — we are sold!" Then the fun of it, as
usual, overcame him, and he wandered away to the
garden of the Luxembourg, and at last threw himself
on a bench, and laughed as a child laughs, being for
moments quiet, and then given over to uncontrolled
mirth. Having feasted with honest comfort on all
the humorous aspects of the situation, his hand
chanced to fall on a little book left by some one on
the seat. He had long ceased to read, for no books
fell in his way, nor could he often have afforded to
buy them even had he had a keen appetite for their
contents.

The little vellum-bound volume opened to his

FRANÇOIS AND TOTO IN THE LUXEMBOURG.

touch, as if used to be generous of what it held.  It
was Latin, and verse.  He knew, or had known,
more than most choir-boys needed of this tongue,
and the talk of the choir-house was, by stringent
rule, in Latin.  But this book was not of a religious
kind; it half puzzled his mind as he read.  Unaccustomed to profane Latin verse, and yet wholly
pleased, he began to murmur aloud the rhythmic
measures:

> "Poscimus, si quid vacui sub umbrâ
>  Lusimus tecum, quod et hunc in annum
>  Vivat, et plures: age, dic Latinum,
>      Barbite, carmen.

" It hath a fine sound, *mon ami ;* and who was this
Quintus?"  He went on reading aloud the delicious
rhythms for the joy of hearing their billowy flow.
Now and then he smiled as he caught the full meaning of a line.

The keen-faced poodle sat on the bench beside
him, with a caressing head laid against his shoulder;
the sun was sweet and warm, the roses were many.
The time suited the book, and the book the man.
He read on, page after page of the beautiful Aldine
type, now and then pausing, vexed to be so puzzled
by these half-guessed beautiful riddles.

" Toto, my dog, I would thou didst know Latin.
This man he loved the country, and good wine, and
girls; and he had friends — friends, which you and
I have not."

Then he was lost for an hour.  At last he ceased
to read, and sat with a finger in the book, idly drift-
ing on the immortal stream of golden song.

"That must have been a merry companion, Toto.
I did hear of him once in the choir-house. He must
be dead a mighty while ago. If a man is as gay as
that, it must be horrid to die."

My poor thief was one of the myriad who through
the long centuries had come into kindly touch of the
friend of Mæcenas. For the first time in his uncertain life he felt the charm of genius.

Indulgent opportunity was for François always
near to some fatal enmity of chance. So does fate
deal with the unlucky. He saw coming swiftly toward him a tall, strongly built man of middle age.
He was richly dressed, and as he drew near he smiled.

"Ah, monsieur," he said; "I came back in haste to
reclaim my little Horace. I missed it only when I
got home. I am most fortunate."

François rose. He returned the small volume, but
did not speak.

"Monsieur of course knows Horace," said the gentleman, looking him over, a little curious and more
than a little interested. Too sure of his own position to shun any intercourse which promised amusement, he went on: "No; not know Horace? Let us
sit awhile. The sun is pleasant."

François, rather shy, and suspicious of a manner
of man he had never before encountered, sat down,
saying, "I was a choir-boy once. I know some Latin,
not much; but this sounded pleasant to the ear."

"Yes; it is immortal music. A choir-boy, you
said; and pardon me, but, *mon Dieu*, I heard you
laugh as I was searching for my book. You have a

fine gift that way, and there is little to laugh at nowadays in France."

"Monsieur will excuse me; I am so made that I
laugh at everything and at nothing. I believe I do
laugh in my sleep. And just now I laughed because
— because —"

"Well, why did you laugh?"

François glanced at the questioner. Something
authoritative in his ways made it seem needful to
answer, and what this or any man thought of him
he cared little — perhaps because in his world opinions went for nothing. And still he hesitated a
moment.

"Well?" There was a note of strong surprise in
the voice, as if the owner felt it to be unusual that a
query he put should not evoke instant reply.

"I laughed because I was cheated."

"Charming, that! May I ask how? But perhaps —"

"No," said François; "if it amuse monsieur, why
should I care?" He calmly related his adventure.

The gentleman threw himself back on the seat in
an ecstasy of amusement. He was out of humor
with the time and with his own world, and bored by
the incessant politics of the day; here was a pleasant
diversion.

"By St. Denis! my friend, you are like the great
Chicot that was fool to King Henry of merry
memory."

"And how, monsieur?"

"How? He had a long face that laughed ever,

long legs, and a shrewd way of seeming more simple
than he was."

"Monsieur flatters me."

"Ah, and a smart rogue, too.  I may conclude your
profession to be that of relieving the rich of their too
excessive luxuries."

François was enchanted with this ingenious and
unprejudiced companion, who had, like himself, a
sense of the laughable aspects of life.

"Monsieur has hit it," he said gaily; "I am a
thief."

No one had taught him to be ashamed of anything
but failure in his illegal enterprises.

"*Tiens!*  That is droll; — not that you are a thief:
I have known many in my own world.  They steal a
variety of things, each after his taste in theft — the
money of the poor, the character of a man, a woman's
honor."

"I scarcely comprehend," said François, who was
puzzled.

"They lack your honesty of confession.  Could
you be altogether honest if a man trusted you?"

"I do not know.  No man ever trusted me, and
one must live, monsieur."

The gentleman hesitated, and relapsed into the indifference of a too easy life.  He had been on the
point of offering this outcast a chance.

"*Enfin*, no doubt you are right.  I wish you every
success.  The deuce!  Have you my snuff-box and
my handkerchief?"

"Both," said François.

"Then don't run away.  I could never catch you.

Long legs must be of use in your profession. The snuff-box I will ransom. Let us say fifty francs. It is worth more, but it bears my name, and there are risks."

"Certainly," said François. "And the handkerchief. Monsieur is *enrhumé* — has a cold; I could not deprive monsieur."

The gentleman thanked him, paid over the money for the box, and, greatly pleased, rose, saying: "You are a dangerous acquaintance; but I trust we may meet again. *Au revoir!*"

François remained on the bench, Toto at his feet in the sun. This meeting affected him strangely. It had been the first touch of a world remote from his own. He did not recognize the fact that he had gifts which enable men to rise in life. At times he had had vague ambitions, but he was at the foot of a ladder, and the rungs above were broken or not to be seen. These moods were brief, and as to their cause not always clear to him. He was by nature social, and able to like or to love; but the people of the Cité were dreadful, and if now and then some broken refugee from a higher class delighted him for a time, the eventful hand of justice or what not was apt to separate them.

As he looked after the gentleman he felt his charm and the courtesy of his ways as something to be desired. His own form of attractiveness, the influence of joyous laughter and frank approach, he had often and usefully tested; and perhaps this sense of his own power to please made him intelligently apprehensive of what he had just experienced. Had he seized

eagerly the half-offered help the gentleman suggested
rather than offered, he had been wiser; but it was
literally true that, being when possible honest as to
speech, he had obeyed the moment's impulse. A better man than the gentleman would have gone further.
He had lazily reflected, and concluded that to help
this poor devil might be troublesome, and thus the
jewel opportunity lay lost at their feet. They were
to meet again, and then it was to be the thief's turn.

Now he sat in thought, kicking the ground with
his boot. Out of the past came remembrances of the
asylum, and how he had been told to be good, and
not to kill or to steal, or to do certain other naughty
things less clear to him then than now. But this
was a far-away time. At the choir-house were the
same moral lessons, but they who taught were they
who sinned. Since then no one had said a word of
reproach to the waif; nor had this great gentleman,
and yet he had left him in the rare mood of thought-
filled depression.

"Wake up, Toto," he cried; "thou art become too
fat. *En avant aux champs!*" And, followed by the
poodle, he went away up the Seine, and was gone so
long that Quatre Pattes began to think he had taken
to honest courses and would return no more.

He came back in a fortnight, the better for certain
prosperous ventures. And thus the days ran on. If
fortune were against him, and even diet hard to get,
Toto went with the Crab to some distant market
after dusk, and, while she bargained, knew to steal
a cutlet, and to run away with his prize, and make
for home or the next dark lane. But these devices

failed at times, and thus François's life consisted of a series of ups and downs. When lucky he bought good clothes, for which he had a liking; when unlucky he pawned them, and went back to garments no one would take in pledge.

It was in the year 1788 that this adventure occurred. He was, as far as was to be guessed, fully twenty-one years of age. His life of adventure, of occasional hardships, and of incessant watchfulness had already given him the appearance of being a far older person.

Always an odd-looking lad, as he grew to maturity his great length of limb, his long face, and ears of unnatural bigness, gave him such singularity of aspect as made disguises impossible.

The poodle was an added danger, and for this reason, when in pursuit of prey, François was forced to leave the dog with Mother Crab. Thus time ran on with such perils as attend the life he led, but with better fortune than could have been expected. As to these later years up to 1790, François, in his memoirs, says little. Once — indeed, twice — he left the Crab's house, only to be driven back by stress of circumstance. After 1790 his account is more complete, and here it is that we take up again the fuller story of his life.

The turmoil of vast governmental and social changes was disturbing all ranks of life. If the Revolution was nursed in the salons, as some say, it was born in the furrows of the tax-tormented peasant, and in the seething caldron of the Cité and the quarters of the starving poor.

François, who cared little what ruler was on top, or who paid taxes, was aware of the uneasy stir in his own neighborhood. Men were more savage. Murder and all violent crimes were more common. That hungry beast, the mob, began to show its fangs, soon to be red with blood. The clubs of all opinions were busy. The church was toppling to ruin, its centuries of greedy gain at an end. Political lines were sharply drawn. The white cockade and the tricolor were the badges of hostile ranks, still more distinctly marked by costume. The cafés were divided: some were Royalist, some Jacobin or neutral. Too many who were of the noble class were flying, or, if more courageous or less forethoughtful, were gathering into bitterly opponent camps. So much of that lower Paris as felt, yearned, hated, and was hungry, glad of any change, was pleased amid tumult to find its chance to plunder and to kill.

The fall of the Bastille in the preceding year had not seemed important to François. He had interested himself in the purses of the vast crowd which looked on and was too much taken up with the event to guard the contents of its pockets. The violence which came after was not to François's taste; but these street crowds were admirable for business until money became scarce, and the snuff-box and the lace handkerchief disappeared with armorial bearings, and with the decree of the people that great dames must no more go in fine carriages.

# VII

I N the early spring of this year François found himself, one day, in a crowd near to the Porte St. Denis. He stood high on his long legs, looking on, while men on ladders broke up the royal escutcheon on the stone archway. It amused him a little to see how furious they were, and how crazy were the foolish *poissardes:* these fishwomen, who had so many privileges under the monarchy, at every blow of the hammer yelled with delight; and behold, here was the Crab, Quatre Pattes, far away from her quarter, hoarse with screaming, a horrible edition of woman as she stood under the arch, careless of the falling fragments. On the edge of the more prudent crowd, an old man was guilty of some rash protest in the way of speech. François heard the cry, "*À bas l'aristocrate! à la lanterne!*" and saw the Crab leap on the man like some fierce insect, horribly agile, a thin gray tress down her back. Swift and terrible it was. In a moment he swung writhing from the chain of the street-lantern, fighting with vain hands to loosen

47

the rope. A red-haired woman leaped up and caught
his leg. There was laughter. The man above her
hung limp. François did not laugh. He tried to
get out of the crowd, away from this quivering horror. To do so was not easy. The crowd was noisy
and turbulent, swaying to and fro, intent on mischief.
As he moved he saw a small, stout man take, with
some lack of skill, a purse from the side-pouch of a
huge fishwoman. François, being close to the thief, saw
him seized by the woman he had robbed. In the press,
which was great, François slipped a hand into the
thief's pocket, and took out the purse. Meanwhile
there were again wild cries of "To the lantern!"
"Up with him!" the woman lamenting her loss, and
denouncing the man who had stolen. His life was
like to be brief. Surrounded by these she-devils, he
stood, white, shaking, and swearing he was innocent.
The man's anguish of fear moved François. "*Dame!*"
he cried, "search the man before you hang him! I
say, search him!" While one of them began to act
on his hint, François let the purse fall into the
pocket of the original owner — an easy feat for a
practised hand. "The man has it not. Look again
in thy pouch, *maman*," he cried. "The man has it
not; that is plain." When the dame of the market
found her purse, she turned on François, amid the
laughter of her friends. "Thou art a confederate.
Thou didst put it back thyself." Indeed, things were
like to go ill. The crowd was of a mind to hang
some one. A dozen hands fell on him, while the
man he had aided slipped away quietly. François
shook off the women, and with foot and fist cleared

a space, for he was of great strength of body. He
would have earned but a short reprieve had he not
seen the Crab. He called to her: "*À moi!* Quatre
Pattes!" The ring of red-faced furies fell back
for a moment before the rage and power, of a man
defending his life. Half dismayed, but furious, they
shouted: "Hang him! Kill him!" and called to the
men to help them. Again François was hustled and
struck as the crowd closed in on him. He struggled,
and called to Toto, whom nothing so disturbed as to
see a rude touch laid on his master. In an instant
the dog was busy with the stout calves about him,
biting, letting go, and biting again. The diversion
was valuable, but brief; and soon Toto, who was not
over-valiant, fled to his master, the crowd yelling:
"Kill him! Hang him and the beast!" Once more
François exerted his exceptional strength, crying,
"Not while I live!" and catching up the dog under
his arm. Then he heard the shrill voice of the Crab.
"*À moi!*" he shouted, and struck right and left as
Quatre Pattes, with her sticks, squirmed in under the
great arms of the fishwomen.

"*À moi!*" she cried, "François!" With her sticks,
and tongue of the vilest, she cleared a space as the
venomous creatures fell back from one more hideous
than themselves.

Meanwhile the accusing dame shook her purse at
the Crab, crying, "He put it back; I felt him do it."
But the rest laughed, and the Crab faced her with so
fierce a look that she shrank away.

"Off with thee!" said the Crab to François; "thou
wert near to the lantern."

"'T is a Jacobin of the best," she cried to the mob; "a friend of mine. You will get into trouble — you cursed fools!"

The crowd cheered her, and François, seizing the chance, cried, laughing, " Adieu, mesdames," and in a moment was out of the crowd and away. He turned as many corners as possible, and soon, feeling it safe to move more slowly, set down the dog and readjusted his dress.

A minute later he saw beside him the man he had saved. " Do not speak to me here," he said; " follow me at a distance." The man, still white and shaking, obeyed him. At the next turn, as François paused in doubt which way to go, he met Quatre Pattes.

" The devil nearly got thee, my little boy," she said; " but a smart thief is worth some trouble to save. Pay me for thy long neck, and quick, too." She was full of *eau-de-vie*, and, as usual then, savage and reckless.

" More!" she cried — " more!" as he gave her a franc. "More, more! Ungrateful beast, thou art good to feed me, and for little else. More, more! I say, or I will call them after thee, and this time I shall have a good pull at the rope. More, more!" and she struck him with her stick. " *Sacré*, waif of hell! More! more!" she screamed. "And that fellow who helped thee! I have seen him; I know him."

François turned without a word, and ran as fast as his long legs would carry him. Two blocks away he was overtaken by the other thief. They pushed on in silence.

At last François, getting back his somewhat scattered wits, said : "We can talk now."

"Ah, I understand," said the other; "thou didst steal her purse from me, and put it back in her pouch."

"Yes; I took it just as they caught thee; then I let it fall into her pouch."

"I thank thee, monsieur. *Dieu!* I am all in a sweat. We are of a trade, I perceive. Why didst thou help me?"

"To keep it was a risk. My turn might have come next. I pitied thee, too."

"I shall never forget it — never."

François laughed. The fat man looked up at him. "*Dame!* but thou hast a queer face, and ears like wings. 'T is a fortune. Let us have a little wine and talk. I have a good idea."

"Presently," said François; "I like not the neighborhood."

Soon they found a *guinguette*, or low liquor-shop, in the Rue Neuve des Petits Champs, and, feeling at last secure, had a long talk over a bottle of wine.

François learned that his new acquaintance was named Pierre Despard, and that he had, for the most part of his means of living, given up the business of relieving the rich of their purses. He explained that he did well as a conjurer, and had a booth near the Pont Neuf. He made clear to François that with his quick fingers, and a face which none could see and not laugh, he would be a desirable partner.

"Thou must learn to move those huge ears." Would he be his assistant? When times were bad

4

they might profit by tempting chances in their old line of life.

François was just now as near to penitence as his nature permitted him to be, and his recent peril disposed him to listen. The more he reflected as Despard talked, the more he liked it. He ended by saying, "Yes"; and before the Crab had reached home he had taken away his slender store of garments, and, with Toto at his heels, found his way to the room of his new friend, in a little street which ran into the Rue Basse du Rempart, not far from the Madeleine. Thus began a mode of life which he found fresh and full of satisfaction.

The pair so strangely brought together took a room in the fifth story, and, with Toto, set up domestic life on a modest scale. It was much to François's contentment. He had what I may call a side taste for the respectable, and this new business seemed to him a decided rise in life. It was varied enough to amuse him; nor was it so conventionally commercial as to lack such adventure and incident as this wild young reprobate of the Cité had learned to like. The new business soon gave the partners more than enough to live upon. After their lodging and diet were provided for, Pierre Despard took two thirds of what was left, and put it away in a stocking, at first with some doubt as to his comrade, but soon with the trust which François was apt to inspire. From early morn until noon, Pierre taught François to do tricks with cards, to juggle with balls, and to tell fortunes by the lines of the hand. Toto was educated to carry a basket and collect sous, to

"PIERRE TAUGHT FRANÇOIS TO JUGGLE WITH BALLS."

stand on his head with a pipe in his mouth, and to pick out a card at a signal. The rest of the day was spent in the booth, where they rarely failed to be well paid. At evening there was a quiet café and dominoes, and a modest *petit verre* of brandy. Meanwhile the peasants burned châteaux, and Protestant and Catholic hanged one another in the pleasant South.

Now and then the Paris mob enjoyed a like luxury, and amid unceasing disorder the past was swept on to the dust-heaps of history.

The little audience of children and nurses in front of the booth was as yet nowise concerned as to these vast changes; nor was Toto disturbed when it was thought prudent to robe him with a three-colored ribbon. The politics of the masters of the show varied as their audiences changed from the children of the rich at noon to the Jacobin workmen at the coming of dusk. François personally preferred splendor and the finery of the great. He was by nature a Royalist. Pierre was silent or depressed, and said little as to his opinions. But both had the prudence of men always too near to poverty to take risks of loss for the sake of political sentiments in which they had no immediate interest.

Despard was a somber little man, and nimble, as some fat men are. He was as red-cheeked as a Norman apple, and, at this time, of unchanging gravity of face and conduct. Not even François's gaiety could tempt him to relate his history; and although at times a great talker, he became so terrified when frankly questioned as to his past, that François ceased to urge him. That any one should desire to conceal anything was to François amazing. He was himself a valuable possession to his morose partner.

"I do not laugh," said Pierre; " nay, not even as a matter of business. Thou shalt laugh for two. Some day we will go to see the little girl who is at Sèvres, in a school of nuns. 'T is there the money goes."

This was a sudden revelation to François. Here was a human being, like himself a thief, who was sacrificing something for another. The isolation of his own life came before him with a sense of shock. He said he should be glad to see the child, and when should they go?

# VIII

*In which François discovers the mercantile value of laughter, and the Crab takes toll of the jugglers — with the sad history of Despard, the partner.*

ATE in the evenings, in the room they shared, the practice of the early morning was resumed, and, above all, Pierre was overjoyed to see what tricks of feature were within François's control. He had, in fact, some of the art of the actor, and was the master of such surprises of expression as were irresistibly comic. By and by the fame of his wonderful visage spread, and very often the young nobles, with their white cockades, came to see, or great ladies would pause to have their palms read. When palmistry was to be used, the booth was closed with black curtains, between which was seen only this long face, with the flaring ears and laughing eyes. Presently a huge hand came out below, the rest of the figure remaining unseen. Then, in the quaintest language, François related wonderful things yet to be, his large mouth opening so as to divide the merry face as with a gulf.

It was a time eager for the new, and this astonishing mask had a huge success. The booth grew rich, and raised its prices, so that soon these two pirates of the Cité sat in wonder over their gains, and Pierre began to store up a few louis for a bad day, and for the future of the little maid at Sèvres, where two or three of the Sisters of the Sacred Heart had found a new home, and taken again the charge of some of their scattered flock.

François was fast learning the art of the conjurer; but at times, sad to say, he yearned for a chance to apply his newly acquired dexterity in ways which were more perilous. He liked change, and had the pleasure in risk which is common to daring men. Indeed, he was at times so restless as to require the urgent counsels of Pierre to keep him tranquil. Once or twice he must needs insist on a holiday, and went away with Toto for two days. They came back dirty and happy, but to Pierre's relief. This uneasy partner was now essential, and more and more Jacobin and Royalist crowded about the booth to get a laugh out of the sight of the face which, appearing through the curtain with hair brushed up and long brown beard combed down, suddenly grew as broad as it had been long. The laugh into which it broke was so cheery, so catching, so causeless, that all who saw fell into fits of merriment such as were not common in those days of danger and anxiety.

Then the partner appeared in front of the booth. So many wished the man who laughed to read their palms that Pierre declared it must be for the highest bidder. A gay auction took place; and the winner heard his fate slyly whispered by the voice of many

tones, or it might be that it was loudly read for the
benefit of the crowd, and, amid cries and jeers, the
victim retired with promise of a wife with a negative
dowry in some unexistent section of Paris. Or,
again, it was an elderly dame who consulted the voice
of fate. She was to have three husbands, and die
young. Then another broad hand came forth, and
on it the black poodle upright, with a handkerchief
to his eyes, and his tail adorned with crape. It was
witty, innocent, and amusing, and delighted this
Paris, which was becoming suspicious, cruel, and
grimly devilish.

Very soon the business in which laughter was
sold for what it would bring in laughter, and for
what men were willing to pay for an honest grin,
began to have incidents which more than satisfied
François's taste for adventure and greatly troubled
Pierre. The little room of the two conjurers had
flowers in the window, and a caged bird. These were
François's luxuries. Pierre did not care for them.
He had begun to read books about the rights of man,
and bits of "The Friend of the People," by Marat.
When François first knew him he liked to gossip
gravely of what went on, as to the changing fashions,
or as to the new "baptism" of the streets, but of the
serious aspect of the tumbling monarchy was not
inclined to speak. At times, too, he let it be seen
that he was well educated; but beyond this, François still learned nothing of his past. One evening
François, gaily whistling, and with Toto after him,
turned the knob of their chamber door. There was some
resistance. He called, " Pierre ! " and the door yielded.

He went in. Two candles were burning on their little dining-table. Facing him, in a chair, sat the Crab, Quatre Pattes, the spine bent forward, the head tilted up to get sight of Pierre, who was leaning against the wall back of the door. Her eyes, a dusky red, were wide open to enlarge the view which the bend of her back limited. The beak between them was purple. Her mouth, grim and lipless, was set in deep, radiating wrinkles, and the toothless gums were moving as if she were chewing. Her two wrists rested on the curved handles of her short canes, and her outstretched hands, lean, eager, and deformed, were moving like the claws of some ravenous creature of the jungle.

François looked from her to his partner, Despard. He was standing as if flattened, his eyes upon the woman, his palms, outspread, set hard on the wall behind him, a pitiful image of alarm and hatred.

"*Mon Dieu!*" cried François, "what is all this? What does this she-devil want?"

"Want! I want money, vagabond thief! I saw thee in the booth yesterday. We are honest, are we? And I know him, too. Him!" and she pointed at Pierre, who murmured:

"Kill her! Take her away!"

François laughed. "Out of this, hag!" and he laughed again.

"I know that man," she cried. "*Sacré*, but he is scared, the coward! I remind him of old times. He must pay — pay, or I will fetch the police. He knows me. Out with the money! Empty your pockets!"

François shouted: "What, Mother Puzzlebones,

dost thou think to scare an old dog of the Cité? Art
fit to be mother-in-law of Satan.    Out with thee!
Out of this, I say!    Here is to buy flesh to cover thy
rattlebone carcass."    He threw two francs before her.

The Crab stood up, and beat with her sticks on the
table.    "No francs!    It is gold I will have — red
louis, or I will set the police on thee, and on the fat
fool yonder.    I will find that girl of his.    She must
be fit to sell by this time.    A beauty was her mother."

"Kill her!    Kill her!" said Pierre, wrath in his
words, fear in their tremor.    Of a sudden he seized
a stool, and, mad with some memory of wrong,
leaped forward.    The Crab faced him with courage,
as François tore away the stool, and pushed him
back.    "No murder here.    Keep quiet, idiot!    And
as to thee, thou gutter Crab, out of this!"

Upon this, Toto set up a dismal howl, and made
at the old woman.    A rousing whack from her stick
sent him howling under the bed, where he sat pen-
sive.    Then she turned on François.

"Look here," she said; "thou hast some sense.
That ass has none.    Let us talk.    Thou canst give
me money or let it alone.    You both know me.    A
word to the police, and up goes the little show."

"Very likely."

"Then make a bargain.    Pay me, and I hold my
tongue.    No use to call me names."

"Well, let us have peace, and talk," said François.
This threat of the Crab as to the officers of the law
might not be vain; she was quite too well informed;
and there was Pierre, white and furious.    François
foresaw tragedy; comedy was more to his taste.

"What wilt thou have, Quatre Pattes? We are poor. Why threaten thy old lodger?" He was eager to get her away, in order to understand matters. Too much was dark. Pierre said no more, but stood staring, angry and yet afraid.

"A louis a week," cried the Crab.

"Nonsense! These good geese would soon die of starvation, and then no more golden eggs. Here are ten francs. Each week thou shalt have five."

"*Nom de Dieu!*" groaned Pierre; "and to kill her were so easy!"

"Not for thee, coward!" shouted the Crab, knocking her sticks together for emphasis.

"Kill her!" said Pierre, faintly.

"Nonsense!" said François. "Come to the booth for it, Crab; not here, mind you, not here — not a sou here."

"Adieu, my jolly bankers," cried the hag. "For the day this will do; then we shall see." With this, the sticks rattled on the tiled floor, and she pattered out of the door, which François shut after her.

"Behold us, netted like larks!" he said, and broke into a laugh.

"It is not a thing to laugh at," said Pierre, the sweat rolling down his face.

"No; perhaps not. Let us take counsel. But what troubled thee? Shall a crippled old woman ruin two strong men?"

Pierre groaned, and let his face fall on his palms, making no reply.

"What is it, my friend?"

"I cannot tell thee now. It were useless; it would

not help. God has made the little one safe — safe. One of these days I may have the courage to tell thee."

His natural reticence and some too dreadful past combined to keep him silent. François was puzzled. He knew the man to be a coward; but his timidity, followed by this sudden outbreak of murderous fury, was inexplicable; nor did he comprehend it fully until later events revealed to him, as he looked back at this scene, the nature of the morbid changes which his partner's character had already begun to feel. "What does it all mean?" he demanded.

"Ask me no more," said Despard. "Not now — not now. She cannot hurt me or mine. It is hate, not fear, I have. But thou? Why didst thou pay?"

"For good enough reasons," said François; "but I can take care of myself." He was by no means sure of this. Nevertheless, he laughed as usual, and said: "Let us have supper; I cannot think when I am empty."

No more was said. They ate in silence, and then Pierre turned to his "L'Ami du Peuple," and François to a pipe and to his thoughts. Must he give up the booth, and wander? He knew the Crab well enough to fear her. The price of her silence would rise, and to deny her would bring about disaster. He began to wish he had been honest. It was too late now; but France was large, and, after all, he could laugh at his own embarrassment. There was time to think; he had bought that.

They spoke no further of the Crab; but from this time Pierre became depressed and suspicious at every

knock on the door. Quatre Pattes came to the booth
with her usual eagerness, and if she chanced to be
full of bad brandy, and too noisy and unappeasable,
François paid her something out of his own share of
their growing profits. Had he been alone, he might
have done otherwise; but Pierre was timid, watchful,
and talked sadly of the little one at Sèvres. How
should he manage if the show came to an end? It
had not been worth much until François joined him.
Before that he had been starving himself to keep
the child in careful hands. He became increasingly
melancholy, and this especially in the early mornings.
He was apt to say at night, "A day is gone, and
nothing has happened."

François was courageous, and mocked a little at the
jade Fortune. "What could happen?" And yet
this shrinking little man, fat, doleful, and full of
fears, sat heavily upon him; and there, too, was this
child whom he had never seen. *Peste!* The children
he had known at the asylum were senseless, greedy
little cattle, all of one make. Perhaps this girl at
Sèvres was no better.

## IX

*In which François tells the fortune of the Marquis de
Ste. Luce and of Robespierre, and has his own fortune
told, and of how Despard saw a man of whom he was
afraid.*

RANÇOIS was soon to be further amazed
by Pierre Despard. To the last of his life,
François remembered that day. A cool
October had stripped the king's chest-
nut-trees of their glory as clean as the
king himself was soon to be shorn. The leaves were
rustling at evening across the Place Louis XV, and
covering the water of the canals. Here, of late, the
tent-booth had been set up for the benefit of the better society, which still wore the white cockade of the
Bourbons. A merry group of the actors of the Comédie was waiting to see François, the maker of faces.
There were Chenard of the Opéra Comique ; Fleury
and Saint-Prix, whose gaiety no prison in after days
could lessen, and no fear of death abate. "Behold,
there is the great Talma," said Pierre, peeping out ;
"and the aristos are many to-day. Art ready, François ?"

François was delighted. The great Talma here,

65

and actually to see him — François! He had of late
been acquiring stage ambitions, and taking great
pains to improve the natural advantages of a face
quite matchless in Paris.

Despard peeped in again. "Yes, François; they
talk of thee, and there are many in the crowd. They
gather to see Talma. There are Jacobins, and thy
friends the aristocrats. Make thou haste. Art
ready?"

"Yes, yes," said François. He felt it to be a great,
an unusual occasion. He had a bright idea. He
struck with a stick three times on the floor of the
booth, the traditional signal at the Théâtre Français
for the curtain to rise. A roar of applause outside
rewarded his shrewd sense of what was due to this
audience.

"*Tiens!* That is good," said La Rive.

The slit in the curtain opened, and, framed in the
black drapery, appeared a face which seemed to have
come out of the canvas of Holbein. It was solemn,
and yet grotesque, strong of feature, the face, beard,
and hair white with powder; the eyes were shut.

"*Mon Dieu*," said Talma, "what a mask! 'T is stern
as fate." The crowd stayed motionless and silent.

"Look! look!" said Fleury. "'T is a study. To
smile with closed eyes! Didst thou ever see a man
smile in sleep, Talma?"

It was pretty and odd. Little curves of mirthful
change crawled downward from the eyes over the
large, grave features; the ears moved; the eyes opened;
and a storm of liberal laughter broke up the quiet
lines of cheek and mouth.

"'T IS A GARGOYLE COME DOWN FROM THE ROOF OF ST. JACQUES.'"

"Bravo! bravo!" cried Talma and the other
actors, while the crowd burst into a roar of applause
and responsive mirth.

"Angels of fun!" cried Saint-Prix, "what a face!
'T is a gargoyle come down from the roof of St.
Jacques de la Boucherie. Does it go back of nights?
I wonder what next will he do?"

"*Tiens!* Wait," said La Rive.

The white face seen above in the slit of the black
curtain became suddenly serious, with moveless eyes
looking past the audience as if into futurity. Below
appeared two large hands, scrupulously clean, while
the man's figure remained hidden. There was something impressive in this artful pose.

"Fortunes, fortunes, *messieurs et dames!*" cried
Pierre. "Who will have his hand read? *Avancez* —
come!"

A shrill voice on the outskirts of the crowd cried,
"Read Louis Capet's!" The white cockades turned
to look. "It were easy to read," said a tall Jacobin.
A gentleman in the black garments of the unprogres-
sive noblesse turned: "Your card, citizen, or monsieur,
as you like." The crowd was scarcely stirred by this
politely managed difference. It was the year of duels.

Two lads pushed forward their tutor, an abbé, as
was plain to see, although few clerics still ventured
to wear their old costume. He laughed awkwardly,
and timidly laid a fat, well-fed hand on that of François's. The grave face of the reader of palms fell
forward to see the fateful lines. For a moment
François was silent; then the voice which came from
his stolid visage was monotonously solemn, and the

words dropped from it one by one, as if they were the mechanical product of some machine without interest in the results of its own action. One long, lean forefinger traversed the abbé's palm, and paused. " An easy life thou hast had. A woman has troubled it." The two pupils were delighted; the crowd laughed. " The line of life is broken — broken " — François's hands went through the pantomime of the snapping of a thread — " like that." The abbé drew back, and could not be persuaded to hear further. Again there was a pause. A grisette advanced smiling, and was sent away charmed with the gifts a pleasant future held in store. Pierre exhorted for a time in vain. Presently the crowd made way. A slight man in breeches and silk stockings came forward; he was otherwise dressed in the extreme of the fashion still favored by the court party, but wore no cockade, and carried two watches, the heavy seals of which François greatly desired to appropriate. His uneasy eyes were covered with spectacles, and around them his sallow complexion deepened to a dusky, dull green. Altogether this was a singular and not a pleasant face, or so, at least, thought the palm-reader, a part of whose cunning was to study the expressions of those who asked his skill. The man who laid his hand on François's looked up at the motionless visage of the ex-thief. François said: " Is it for the citizen alone to hear, or for all ? "

" For me — for me."

François's voice fell to a low whisper.

" Let the past go," said the listener; " what of the future ? "

"It is dark. The lines are many. They are — citizen, thou wilt be a ruler, powerful, dreaded. Thou wilt have admiration, fame, and at last the hatred of man."

"I — I — what nonsense! Then?"— and he waited, — "then? What then? What comes after?"

"I will tell thee"; and François whispered.

"No more — no more; enough of such foolishness!" He was clearly enough disturbed by what he had heard. "Thou must think men fools."

"Fate is always a fool, citizen; but the fools all win, soon or late."

"That, at least, is true, Master Palmister." Then a pair of sinister eyes, set deep behind spectacles, sought those of François. "Thou hast a strange face, Master Palm-reader. Dost thou believe what thou dost make believe to read on men's palms?"

"Sometimes."

"Now — now? — this time?"

"Yes; I believe."

"I shall not forget thee."

François felt something like a chill between his shoulders. The Jacobin stepped aside after depositing an ample fee in the basket which Toto presented.

There was a murmur in the crowd. Several persons looked with curious eyes after the retreating man, and the conjurer heard some one say: "*Tiens! C'est drôle.* It is Robespierre." His was at this time not more than a well-known name. For a minute no one else came forward. François saw Pierre slip hastily into the tent; he knew not why. A gentleman came up gaily. He was dressed splendidly, with no regard for the leveling tastes of the day.

5

"The deuce!" he said quickly; "you are my thief!"

"*De grâce*, monsieur!" exclaimed François; "you will get me into trouble."

"Not I. Happy to meet you. I am myself fond of palmistry. Come, read me my hand."

François bent over the palm. He began aloud: "Ah, here have been many loves." Then his voice fell. "Monsieur is a good swordsman."

"So-so," said the gentleman.

"Monsieur has been unfortunate in his duels."

"*Mon Dieu!* Yes; I always kill people."

"Monsieur has one remorse."

"*Sapristi!* Thou art clever, and I lucky to have but one. Go on; 't is vastly amusing. Shall I live to be old? My people do."

"Monsieur will have troubles, but he will live to be old — very old."

"Will he, indeed? I hardly like that. If I were you, I would tell more agreeable fortunes. To out-live the joys of life, to be left a stranded wreck, while the world goes by gay and busy — pshaw! I like not that. You do it well. Let me read your own palm. I have a taste for this art."

François was at once interested. The gentleman's strong left hand took that of the thief, and with a wandering forefinger he ran over the lines of the palm. He let it fall, and looked downward at his own hand. "It is strange that we shall meet again, and in an hour of danger. You will be fortunate, and I shall not. You will have —"

"*Tenez*, monsieur — stop!" cried François; "I will

hear no more"; and he drew his hands within the tent-folds.

"*Dame!* and you are really a believer in it all, my good thief? Belief is out of fashion. I hope you did tell that cursed Jacobin he would go to a place he does n't believe in, but which is a little like France to-day. Come and see me if ever you are in trouble and this trade comes to an end. I like men who can laugh. 'T is a pretty talent, and rather gone out just now. I am the Marquis de Ste. Luce — or was. Come and laugh for me, and tell me your story." He let fall a gold louis in Toto's basket, and elbowed his way through the crowd, with " Pardon, monsieur," to white cockades, and scant courtesy to the Jacobins and the *demi-constitutionnels*, who were readily known by their costumes.

As the marquis ceased to speak, François heard a singular noise in the tent back of him. He withdrew his head to see the cause, and a moment later, reappearing, said he must be excused, because his friend was ill. The crowd broke up. Within the tent lay Pierre on the ground, in a fit. François, greatly alarmed and utterly at a loss, threw water in his face, and waited. In a few moments it was over, and the man, flushed and breathing deeply, lay with red froth on his lips, as if in a deep sleep. He was no longer convulsed; but what further to do the partner knew not, and sat beside him, not more competent to deal with this novel situation than was Toto, who walked about, and scratched his nose, and gave it up. An hour went by with Pierre's head resting on François's lap.

At last Despard opened his eyes. "Take him away," he said. The man was delirious.

"Who?"

"Take him away. Will he kill me? He killed her." A half-hour he wandered in mind, while François bathed his flushed face. Then he drew a deep breath, and said: "What is this? Where am I?"

François replied: "Thou hast had a fit."

"A fit? Yes; I have them — not often. I remember now. Has he gone, that devil?—that marquis?"

"Who? Ste. Luce? Was it he that troubled thee?"

"Yes; he."

"But what then?"

By and by Pierre sat up. Seeing him to be quite himself, but staring about as if in fear, François said:

"Come, now; I must have the whole story. What the mischief has this fine gentleman done to thee? I am out of patience with thy tiresome mysteries. I know him; we have met before. Perhaps I can help thee."

"Thou?"

Pierre lay back on the floor, and covered his face.

"*Mon Dieu!*" he cried, "why wilt thou force me to talk of it? Oh, to hate, and to be afraid!" He started up. "I am afraid."

"If I hated a man," said François, "*sacré bleu!* I would twist his neck."

"If I could! if I could! I am not like thee. I am — am a coward. That's the truth."

"*Dame!* that is curious." He regarded the fat

little man with attentive eyes. "Suppose we have
it all out, and get done with it."

"Done with it?"

"Yes; done with it! Hast thou often had these
fits before?"

"Yes; and then I am better for a while."

"Tell me all about this man. I will take care of
thee."

"No; God did not: thou canst not."

"Then we must separate. I am tired of thy nonsense, and I do not care a rap how soon this business
ends, what with your cursed melancholy and that
jade Quatre Pattes. Now, out with it!"

Pierre, seated on the floor of the booth, red-eyed
and dejected, looked up piteously at his questioner.
"If I tell thee all, thou wilt despise me."

"Not I. Go on! If thou canst speak out like a
man, I may be able to help thee; but if thou art of a
mind to hold thy tongue, it were better we parted. I
am tired of thy folly."

Thus urged, Pierre told his story, reluctant, with
bowed head, and at times in tears. François sat over
him on a stool, now and then asking a question, or
waiting patiently when Pierre, choked by overmastering emotions, was silent for a while.

"I have been unhappy and unlucky from the time
I can first remember," said Pierre. "My people belonged to the lesser noblesse, but my father was poor
—oh, very poor. We had been ruined folks away
there in Normandy for half a century, only a bit of
farm and vineyard left to us. My mother was of the
bourgeoisie, foolish and pretty. She died young, and

I was left the only child. My father treated me ill. I had no courage, he said. It was true. As I grew up, I was timid like a girl, and fearful of quarrels. When I was about twenty years old I had a trouble with a brother of this marquis. He struck me with his whip because of something I said. My father learned that I had excused myself, and was wild with rage. It was my bourgeois mother, he said; we had lost all but honor, and now that too was gone. He died not long after, and I, with a few hundred francs, was driven out to care for myself. The marquis had a mortgage on the farm. I went to a village near by, and lived awhile as I could until I was down to my last sou. I worked like a peasant in the fields; I was the servant at an inn. At last a mountebank company attracted me, and in despair I went with them to take care of the horses which served them in their performances. By and by I learned sleight of hand, and fared better. At last I married a girl who danced in our company. She was pretty,— oh, more than pretty,— and clever, too. When we came again to our town, a notary offered me a petty clerk's place, and I was well contented to settle down. My wife was too eager for the society of the bourgeoisie, and they would have none of that of the dancing-girl. Then, unhappily, this marquis saw my wife, and how I know not, but his fine clothes and cunning were too much for one who was eager for a society she could not have. I was busy, and often absent collecting small debts. No one warned me. I was satisfied, and even put by a little money.

"There was a woman in the village, Mme. Quintette,

a dressmaker, a shameless creature of bad life. She might have been then some fifty years old. 'T is now twelve years ago. At her house the marquis met my wife. One day my Renée was gone, and this Quin-tette with her. It is she who is this Quatre Pattes."

"The deuce!" cried François. "Now I see."

"More than a year went by. Thou wouldst have killed the man. I could not. I am a coward, François —a coward! God made me so; I can't help it. One day an infant was brought to my door, with a note. *Mon Dieu*, such a note! The dying mother in the hospital with her last money paid a good sister to take the child to me — to me, of all men! And would I pardon her? François, it was that devil's babe and hers. Would I forgive her, and keep it? Wouldst thou have kept it?"

"No," said François; "not I."

"I did! I did! It was like her, all but the eyes. I grew to love it. Then there was an accident, a fall, and the little maid is crippled for life. It seemed horrible, but now I thank God, because she is safe from the baseness of men. I wanted to die, but I must live; she has no other friend."

François sat still, pitiful, and deep in thought. At last he said: "Why were you so terribly afraid of that woman? She could do no worse than ruin our business."

"I — hast thou ever been afraid thou wouldst murder some one? I was. I would have done it in a minute hadst not thou come in."

"*Sac à papier!* Afraid of thyself! How queer! Thou wert afraid of thyself?"

"Yes; I am—I was—I am often afraid of myself."

"Let us forget it."

"I cannot.  What can I do?"

"Do?  Nothing."

"But that man—"

"Well, thou art helpless.  I should not be.  Forget.
Thy chance may come."  He was at the end of his wisdom.  He pitied this weak-hearted coward who so
frankly avowed his defect.  "We will speak of it no
more, Pierre, or not now.  But what brought you to
Paris?  Let us have it all, and get done with it."

"My poor little humpback was hardly six years old
when she came to me, crying, to know why the village
children would not play with her.  She was a humpback and a bastard.  What was 'bastard'?  I have
always fled from trouble.  One day I took the child
and what little I had, and was away to Paris.  God
knows how it hurt me to hear every evening how she
had been mocked and tormented; one is so foolishly
tender.  In this great city I sought work, and starved.
And when at last she was fading before my eyes, I
stole — my God, I stole!"

"*Dame!*  thou art particular.  Must a man starve?"

"When I got money out of a full purse I took, I set
up our little business, and then I found thee.  And
this is all.  I dare say I shall feel better to have told
some one.  I did not want to steal.  I did not steal
after I began with the booth, unless I was in need—
oh, sorely in need.  It was so on that fortunate day
when I was saved by thee.  In thy place I should
have kept the old fishwife's purse."

"And let me swing?"

"Yes—perhaps; I don't know.    I—it is well for
me thou wert not a coward."

"*Sacristie!*    It appears that not to be a coward has
its uses.    Now *bon jour* and adieu to the whole of this
business.    Let the miserable past go.    'T is bad company, and not amusing.    Have no fear; I will take
care of thee.    Come, let us go home."

"Thou wilt look about a little before we go?"

"Toto, he is mad, this man."

"I sometimes think I am.    At night, in my dreams,
I have him by the throat, and he laughs, and I cannot
hold him.    I wake up, and curse in the darkness because I cannot kill him.    And then I know it is a debt
never to be paid — never."

François had had enough of the small man's griefs.
Contempt and pity were strangely mingled as he listened to his story.

"I shall let thee talk no more," he said.    "But *mille
tonnerres!* I cannot help thee to go mad.    Let us go
and wander in the country to-morrow, thou and I and
Toto.    It will comfort thee.    But no more of this; I
will not stand it."

The advice was wholesome, and, as usual, Pierre
accepted the orders of his more sturdy-minded friend.

# X

*How Pierre became a Jacobin and how a nation became insane.*

LTHOUGH the marquis was not again upon the scene, as the months went by Despard became by degrees more gloomy. At night, in place of the gay little café, he went out to the club of the Jacobins, and fed full of its wild declamations against the *émigrés* and the aristocrats. It amused François, who saw no further ahead than other men. Despard came home loaded with gazettes and pamphlets, and on these he fed his excitement long after his partner was asleep.

When, as time went by, Pierre's vagaries increased, François found in them less subject for mirth. The fat little man sat up later and later at night. At times he read; at others he walked about muttering, or moving his lips without uttering a sound. What disturbed François most was that the poodle now and then showed fear of Pierre, and would no longer obey him as he had been used to do.

Meanwhile, as Pierre still attended sedulously to business, François could find no fault. He himself had become devoted to his art of palm-reading. He bought at the stalls old books, Latin and French, which treated of the subject, and tried to keep up the name his odd ways had made so profitable. Deceit was a part of his working capital; but deceit and credulity are apt to go together, as a great man has well said. Not for many louis would the conjurer have let any one read again the lines of his own hand. When Despard began to teach him the little he himself knew of palmistry, it had caused interest, and after a while a half-belief. This grew as he saw the evident disturbance to which the use of his art gave rise in certain of those who at first appeared to look upon it as an idle jest. The imaginative have need to be wary, and this man was imaginative, and had the usual notions of the gambler and thief as to omens and luck. I have said he had no definite working conscience. I have also said that he possessed an inborn kindness of heart; he had a long memory for benefits, and a short one for injuries. His courage was of fine quality: not even Quatre Pattes could terrify him.

The politics of the time were becoming month by month more troublous to such as kept their heads steady in the amazing tumble of what for centuries had been on top, and the rise of that which had been as long underneath. The increasing interest of Pierre in all that went on surprised François, and sometimes, as I have said, amused him. He could not comprehend why he should care whether the king ruled, or the Assembly. This mighty drama was nothing to him. He paid no taxes; he toiled not, nor spun, except nets

of deceit; and whether or not commerce died and the
plow stood idle in the furrow was to him of no moment.
Meanwhile, before the eyes of a waiting, wondering
world historic fate was shuffling the cards as neither
war nor misrule had shifted them for many a day.
Knave and king, spade and club, were now up, now
down. Every one was in a new place. The old sur-
names were replaced by classical appellations. Streets,
palaces, and cities were rebaptized with prenominal
republican adjectives. Burgundy, Anjou, Navarre,
and the other ancient provinces, knew no more their
great names heroically famous.

All men were to be equal; all men were free to be
what they could. But the freedom of natural or acquired inequality was not to be recognized. There
were new laws without end. The Jacobin added a
social creed. All men must *tutoyer*. "Your Majesty"
was no more to be used. Because the gentles said
"thou" and "thee" to one another and to an inferior,
all men must "thou" as a sign that all are on a level.

A bit of paper was to be five francs—and take care
of thy head if thou shouldst venture to doubt its value.
As to all else, men accepted the numberless and be-
wildering decrees of the Assembly. But the laws of
commerce no ruler can break. These are despotic,
changeless, and as old as the act of barter between
man and man. The assignats fell in value until two
hundred francs would scarce buy a dinner. There,
too, was a new navy and a new army, with confusing
theories of equal rights for sailor, soldier, and captain.

A noble desire arose everywhere to exercise the new
functions. What joy to cast a ballot, to act the part

of officials, to play at soldiering! All the cross dogs
in France are unchained and the muzzles off; and
some are bloodhounds. What luxury to be judge,
jury, and hangman, like the noble of long ago!

Even childhood caught the temper of the time. It
played at being officer and prisoner, built and tore
down bastilles, and at last won attention and a law all
to itself when some young ruffians hung one of their
number in good earnest for an aristocrat.

However indifferent was François at this time, the
shifting drama amused him as some monstrous bur-
lesque might have done. Its tragedies were as yet
occasional, and he was by nature too gay to be long
or deeply impressed. There was none he loved in
peril, and how to take care of François his life had
taught him full well.

"*Allons zi gaiement!*" he cried, in the tongue of his
old quarter; and kept a wondering, anxious eye on
Pierre.

## XI

*The juggling firm of Despard, François & Co. is broken up—Despard goes into politics, and François becomes a fencing-master.*

N January, 1791, François, having of late found business slack, had moved to the open *place* in front of the Palais Royal. He had taught Toto new tricks—to shoulder a musket and to die *pour la patrie.* Time was telling men's fortunes quite too fast for comfort. Neither his old devices nor Toto's recently acquired patriotism was of much avail. Moreover, Pierre was losing interest in the booth as he became absorbed in politics.

"Thou wilt not go to thy *sacré* club, Pierre," said François, one night late in February. "Here are two days thou hast left us, the patriot Toto and me, to feed thee and make sous for the poor little maid at Sèvres."

"She is not at Sèvres."

"Why not? Thou hast not said a word to me of this."

"No; I had more important matters to think of."

François, who was tranquilly smoking his pipe,

looked up at his partner. The man had lately worn a look of self-importance.

"Well, what else?"

"The sisters are aristocrats. A good *citoyenne* hath her. I shall give up the show. The country calls me, Pierre Despard, to save her. The great Robespierre hath asked me to go into Normandy, to Musillon, whence I came. I am to organize clubs of Jacobins." He spoke with excitement, striding to and fro. He declared that he was not afraid now of any one. To serve France was to have courage.

"And how as to money?" asked François.

He said his expenses would be paid by the clubs. Barnave, Duport, and the deputies of the Right must be taught a lesson. There must be no more kings. The people must rule—the people! He declaimed wildly.

"*Fichtre!*" cried François, laughing. "It does seem to me that they rule just now."

Pierre went on with increasing excitement; and would not François go with him?

"Go with thee? Thou sayest we shall be deputies in the new Convention. A fine thing that! And Toto too, I suppose? Not I. I am an aristocrat. I like not thy Robespierre. As to the show, it pays no longer, and I have greased the claws of the Crab until there is no more grease left. I shall take to the streets, Toto and I. And so thou art to be a great man, and to play poodle on thy hind legs for Pétion and the mob?"

Pierre was offended. He rose and stood glaring at François with wide-open eyes; then he said, as if to himself: "The marquis is near Evreux. Let him take heed!"

"*Mon Dieu!* He will eat thee as he would the frogs of his moat, that man! I am not of those who fear, but if I had angered him—"

"I have named him to the great Robespierre, the just, the good. He will remember him."

"Then go; and the devil take the whole lot of you!"

"I shall go. But do not say thou art an aristocrat, for then I must hate thee."

"*Grand merci!* Thou poor, fat little pug, canst thou hate?"

"Aye, as hell hates." Upon this Toto took refuge under his master's bed.

François rose, and, standing in front of the flushed, fat little man, set a hand on each of Pierre's shoulders and stopped his excited march.

"I cannot understand thee. I never could contrive to hate even a gendarme, and if hell hates, I know not. Thou art helpless as a turtle that is on his back. What use to kick? No; do not answer me. Hear me out. I shall go my way—thou thy way. I served thee a good turn once, and thou hast helped me to a living. Now I like not thy ways; thou art going mad, I think."

"Perhaps—perhaps," returned Pierre, gloomily. "Well, *c'est fini*—'t is done. Now to settle."

They divided their spare cash; and after that Pierre went to his club, and François to bed and a dreamless sleep.

In the morning he rose early, left his share of the rent on the table, and with a little bag of clothes, and

"HE PAID IN ADVANCE THE CUSTOMARY DENIER à DIEU."

Toto after him, walked away across the Seine, and soon found a small room under the roof. He paid in advance the customary *denier à Dieu*, and settled down to think.

He was tired of the show, and meant to resume his old trade. His conscience, or so much as he had, was at peace; all France was plundering. Now the nobles were robbed, and now the church.

"The world is on my side," he laughed, as he sat with Toto on his knees, looking over a wide prospect of chimney-pots and tiles.

Thus began again the life of the thief; but now, thanks to his long training as a juggler, he was amazingly expert. He took no great risks, but the frequent tumults of the streets were full of chances, although it must be said that purses were thinner, watches and gold snuff-boxes rarer, and caution less uncommon than it had once been. If business prospered, he and Toto took long holidays in the country, and did a little hunting of rabbits; for the gamekeeper was no longer a person to be dreaded. Sometimes, lying on the turf, he thought how pleasant would be a bit of garden, and assurance of good diet and daily work to his taste. I fear it would scarcely have been long to his taste. When something like a chance came, he could not make up his mind to accept the heaven-sent offer. He was to see many things and suffer much before his prosperous hour arrived.

One fine day in April, François, with whom of late fortune had quarreled, was seated in the sun on a bench in the now ill-tended garden of the Luxembourg. The self-made difficulties of the country were affecting

6

more and more the business of the honest, and of that uncertain guild which borrows but never returns. He had a way of taking Toto into his counsels. "What shall we do, little devil?" The poodle barked. "No. These accursed Jacobins are ruining France. What, knock a man on the head at night! Bad dog, hast thou no morals? *Va donc!* Go to. Thou hast not my close experience of the lantern, and stone walls for a home I like not. Work, thou sayest? Too late; there is work for no one nowadays. Thou wilt end badly, little monster."

Toto whined, and having no more to say, fell asleep. At this moment François, looking up, saw go by a young woman in black, and with her a boy of perhaps ten years. On the farther side was a tall, well-dressed man of middle age, whom, as he was looking away, François did not recognize. Some bright thing fell unnoticed from the woman's wrist, and lay in the sun. "Hist, Toto! Look there—quick!" In a moment the dog was away, and back again, with a small miniature set in gold and surrounded by pearls. It was the portrait of a young officer. François hastily put it back into the dog's mouth, saying: "Go to sleep! Down! down quickly!" The dog, well taught, accepted the trust, and dropped as if in slumber, his head on his paws, while his master studied the weathercocks on the old gray palace. A moment later both the man and the woman turned to look for the lost miniature. Then François saw that it was his old acquaintance the marquis. He had more than once seen him in the garden, where he was fond of walking; but the great seigneur had passed him always without notice.

The boy ran back ahead of his grandfather, and coming to François, said innocently:

"Monsieur, have you seen a little picture madame let fall? It is so big, and I saw it only just now on her wrist. Please to help us to look for it. It is my father; he is dead."

After the boy came the woman, looking here and there on the gravel.

"*Dame de Dieu!* she is beautiful," murmured François; "and that *sacré* marquis!"

The voice he heard was sweet and low, and tender with regret at her loss.

"Has monsieur chanced to see a little miniature?"

Monsieur was troubled, but his pocket and stomach were both empty. Monsieur was distressed. He had seen no miniature.

Next came the marquis.

"Ho, ho!" he said pleasantly. "Here is the citizen my thief again. Have you seen a small miniature?"

François had not.

"*Diable!* 'T is a pity, monsieur. Well, pardon a *ci-devant* marquis, but I do think monsieur knows a little too much of that miniature for his eternal salvation. Also, monsieur does not lie as well as might be expected from one in his line of life."

François rose. He was embarrassed as he saw the tearful face of the woman.

"I was about to say I would look—I would search."

Ste. Luce smiled. "Suppose we begin with you?"

"I have it not."

"Well, but where is it? I am not a man to be

trifled with.   Come, quick, or I must ask the gen-
darmes yonder for a bit of help."

François looked at him.   There was menace in those
cold gray eyes.   Should he trust to his own long legs?
At this instant he heard a sob, and glancing to the
right, saw the woman seated on the bench with her
face in her hands, the little fellow at her side saying:
"Do not cry, mama; the gentleman will help us."
The gentleman was ill clothed and seedy.   He had
seen women cry, but they were not like this woman.

"M. le Marquis does me injustice.   Permit that my
dog and I search a little."

The marquis smiled again.   "*Pardieu!* and if you
search, and meanwhile take a fancy to run, your legs
are long; but now I have you.   How the deuce can I
trust a thief?"

The little lad looked up.   "I will go with monsieur
to look—and the dog; we will find it, mama."

"Monsieur may trust me; I will not run away," said
François.   "If monsieur desires to search me?"

"I do not search thieves."

François looked at this strangely quiet gentleman
with the large, light-gray, unpleasant eyes, and then
at the woman.

"Come, Toto; we must take a look."

The marquis stood still, quietly watching thief, dog,
and boy.

"Renée," he said, "don't make a fool of yourself."

Then from a distance the boy cried, "We found it,
mama!" and ran to meet her.

The marquis took it as François rejoined the group.

"Ah, Master Thief, you are clever; but it is a little

wet, this trifle, and warm too. The dog had it all the
while in his mouth. He is well taught. Why the
deuce did you give it up?"

The boy began to understand this small drama. He
had the courage of his breed, and the training.

"Did you dare to steal my mama's picture?"

"Yes; when she let it fall."

"I know now why you were glad to give it back.
It was because she cried."

"Yes; it was because she cried."

"*Ventre St. Gris!*" exclaimed the marquis, who was
pleased to swear like Henry of Navarre. "You are a
poor devil for a thief. You have temptations to be
good. I never have them myself. I thank Heaven
I have reasonably well used my opportunities to be
agreeably wicked."

"Father!" said the young woman, reproachfully;
and then to François: "If you are a thief, still I
thank you; I cannot tell you how much I thank you."

"And how many louis do you expect, most magnani-
mous of thieves?" said the marquis.

The woman looked up again. "Come to me to-morrow; I will find a way to help you."

Something of yearning, some sense of a void, some
complexity of novel distress, arose in the thief's mind.

"*Mon Dieu!* madame," he said, turning toward her,
without replying to the marquis, "you are a saint. I
—I will think. I am not fit for such as you to
talk to."

"Quite true," said the marquis. "Hast thou thy
purse, Renée? I forgot mine."

"No, no," she said. "Come and see us—Rue des

Petits-Augustines—a great house with a gilded gate. You will come? I will say they are to let you in. Promise me that you will come."

"And bring that poodle," added the marquis; "I will buy him."

François laughed outright—that merry laugh which half Paris had learned to like, till Paris tired of it and of its owner.

"Monsieur will pardon me. I cannot sell my only friend. Good day." And he walked away, the boy crying after him: "You will come? Oh, you must come, because my mama says so."

The marquis muttered: *"Animal!* If I had your carcass—no, if I had had you awhile ago in Normandy, your manners would have been bettered. But now the world is upside down. He will come, Renée. If thou art quit of him for two hundred francs and a few lost spoons, thou mayest rest thankful."

François moved moodily away. Something was wrong in his world; an angel coming into his crude life would not have disturbed him as this lady's few kind words had done, and yet he had left her unanswered. He knew he had been a fool, but knew not why. He had, too, a notion that he and this marquis would meet again, but for this he was not eager. He recalled the palm-reading. Had the woman been alone, he would probably have said a glad "Yes"; but now his inclinations to obey her were sadly diluted by feelings which he did not analyze, or perhaps could not have analyzed. He did not accept the hand thus stretched out to save him, but for many a day her tender eagerness and the pleading face which had so

attracted him came before him at times with a look of
reproach.   Is it strange that this glimpse of a nobler
nature and a better life than his own should have
had an influence on this man quite the reverse of
that which its good will sought to effect?   He cannot
be said to have been refined, but he had in him tastes
which are the germs of refinement, and which, when
I knew him, had no doubt produced results.   Probably he was in 1791 a coarser person, but he must
always have been a man who could be forced by
circumstances to think.

It may have been that the sense of a great gulf between him and a world he was by nature inclined to
like caused one of those rare spells of despair to
which the gay and over-sanguine are liable.   Of course
he had seen and for brief seasons shared the profligacy
of the Cité,—his memoirs confess this with absolute
frankness,—but these gross lapses had been rare and
brief.   Now he plunged headlong into the worst vileness of the most dissolute quarter, where few lived
who were not saturated with crime.   I have no desire
to dwell on this part of his life.   A month passed
away, and he was beginning to suffer in health.   This
amazed him.   He had not hitherto known a pang save
that of hunger.   He began to drink *eau-de-vie* to relieve his sense of impaired strength, and being off his
guard and under the influence of the temporary mood
of rashness which drink is apt to cause, he twice narrowly escaped arrest.

Under the vivid impression thus created he was
wandering homeward late at night to some low resort
in the Cité, when in the Rue aux Fèves he heard a cry

in front of him.   The moon was bright, and he saw a man set upon by two fellows.   The person assailed was staggering from the blow of a club, and fell with the cry which the thief heard.   Both bandits threw themselves upon him, and, as he unwisely struggled, François saw the glitter of a knife.   Clearly this was no easy prey.   As the three tumbled over in the mud of the street there was small chance for a decisive use of the blade.   François, as I have said, had been always free from crimes of violence, but this affair was none of his business, and had his pocket been full he might have left the ruffians and their prey unmolested. His purse, however, was down to the last sou, and here was a chance.

He called, "Catch them, Toto!" and, leaping forward, seized one of the men by the throat and threw him on his back.   The poodle took a good nip of the other rascal's leg, and when the man broke away and, stumbling, ran, pursued him until recalled by François's whistle.   Meanwhile the assaulted man sat up, a bit dazed.   The other fellow—it was he of the knife—was on his feet again, and at once turned furiously on the rescuer.   François darted to one side, and, catching him by the neck, throttled him savagely.   His great length of arm made it impossible for the scamp, who was short and strong, to reach any vital organ. But he stabbed François's shoulder over and over. François's grip on the throat was weakening, when the victim, now on his feet, struck the man under the ear, and thus knocked him clean out of François's failing grip.   He fell headlong, but was up and away in a moment, while a crowd began to collect.

"Hi! it is François!" some one cried.

"Quick!" said the thief. " Room there! Let us get out of this." Seizing the man he had saved, he hustled his way through the crowd and hurried him toward the bridge. In a few minutes they were standing alone by the river, amid the tombs back of Notre Dame. Then the man spoke:

"By Heaven! thou hast saved my life. Hallo! thou art bleeding. Here!" and he tied a handkerchief about his shoulder. "We shall be in luck to find a chaise. Wait!" and he ran away.

François's head was dizzy. He sat on a tombstone, well sobered now, but bleeding freely. It was long before he heard a horse; and when in the chaise, where Toto promptly followed him, he fell back, and knew little more until they stopped in the Rue St. Honoré. Here his new acquaintance got out, and soon returned with a glass of *eau-de-vie*. With this aid, and the arm of his host, François was able to reach a large room in the second story. He fell on a couch, and lay still while the other man ran out to find a surgeon.

On his arrival, François was put to bed in an adjoining room, and for two weeks of care and good diet had leave to meditate on the changeful chances of this wretched world. For a while he was too weak to indulge his customary keenness of curiosity. His host, M. Achille Gamel, paid him brief visits, and was singularly unwilling to talk one day, and the next sufficiently so for the patient to learn that he had been in the army as a *maître d'armes*, and was now, in his own opinion, the best fencing-master in France.

Through the partitions could be heard the click, click
of the foils, and now and then the crack of pistols.
After a fortnight François's wounds were fairly
healed, and he began to get back his rosy complexion
and his unfailing curiosity.

One pleasant evening in June, Gamel appeared as
usual. It was one of his days of abrupt speech.

" Art well ? "

" Yes."

" Thou art soon mended."

" Yes." His brevity begot a like form of answer,
and François was now somewhat on his guard.

" I pay my debts."

" That is true."

" Now thou art well, what wilt thou do ? "

" I—I—I shall go away."

" Why didst thou help me ? "

" My pocket and paunch were empty. It seemed a
chance."

" Thy two reasons are good. Who art thou ? "

" Who is every one in the Cité ? A thief."

" *Diable!* but thou art honest—in speech at least."

" Yes, sometimes. I was a conjurer too—for a
while."

" Yes, yes, I remember now. Thou art the fellow
with a laugh. I see not yet why thou hast helped me.
Thou mightest easier have helped the rascals and
shared their gains."

François began to be interested, and laughed a
laugh which was the most honest of his possessions.

" I dislike clumsiness in my profession," he said.
" Why should the brutality of war be brought into a

peaceful occupation?"   He was half in earnest, half in jest.

"That is a third reason, and a good one."   It was difficult to surprise Gamel.   "Suppose we talk business," he added.

"Mine or thine?"

"Mine.   A moment, Citizen François—permit me. Pray stand up a moment."

François rose as the fencing-master produced a tape-measure.   "Permit me," and with no more words he set one end of the tape on François's shoulder and carried the length of it to his finger-tips.

François stood still, wondering what it all meant.

"The deuce!" said Gamel, slowly rolling up the measuring-tape.

"Well, what is it?   What is wrong?"

"Wrong?   Nothing.   It is astonishing!"

"What?"

"This arm of thine."

"Why?"

"It is one and a half inches longer than mine."

"Well?"

"A gift!   To have the longest arm in Paris!   *Mon Dieu!*"

"What of that?"

"A fortune!   Phenomenal!   Superb!   And a chest —and muscles!   By Hercules, they are as hard as horn!"

"Well?"

"*Diable!*   Thou art dull for a thief."

François had a high opinion of himself.   He said: "Perhaps.   What next?"

"I need help. I will teach thee to fence and to shoot. Canst thou be honest? I ask not if thou art."

"Can I? I do not know. I have never tried very long." Then he paused. To fence like a gentleman, to handle a sword, had its temptations. "Try me."

"Good! Canst thou be a Jacobin to-day and a Royalist to-morrow?"

"Why not?"

"The messieurs and their kind fence here in the morning; after our breakfast come the Jacobins about two. I ask not thy politics."

"Why not?" said François, who was the frankest of men—"why not? I am an aristocrat. I am at the top of my profession. I like naturally the folks who are on top."

"France is like a ball now, no top, no bottom, rolling. Let us be serious."

"*Dieu!* that is difficult. I want to quit thieving. It does n't pay at present. I accept the citizen's offer. Does it include my dog?"

"Yes, indeed! Toto—a treasure! He will delight our pupils."

"Good! He must have a little sword and wear a white cockade till noon, and then a tricolor."

"And will five francs a week suffice until thou art fit to teach? And thy board and lodging—that goes without saying. After a while we will talk again."

"'T is a fortune!" said François; and upon this agreement the pair fell to chatting about the details of their future work.

"One moment," said François, as Gamel rose. "What are thy own politics?"

"I will tell thee when I can trust thee," said the fencing-master. "Now they vary with the clock."

"I see. But I have told thee mine."

"Thou wert rash. I am not."

François laughed merrily, "Good night." He was happy to be at rest, well fed, and with something to do which involved no risk. Gamel went away, and François fell to talking to the poodle.

"Toto! Sit up, my sleepy friend! Attention! What dost thou think of M. Achille Gamel?" The poodle had been taught when questioned to put his head on one side, which gave him an air of intelligent consideration. "Ah, thou dost think he is as long-legged as I! Any fool of a cur can see that. What else?

"He has great teeth—big—the better to eat thee, my dear! Curly hair, like thine, and as black; a nose —of course he has a nose, Toto. Art perplexed, little friend? Oh, that is it! I see. Thou art right. He smiles; he never laughs. 'T is that bothered thee. Thou dost like him? Yes. Thou art not sure? Nor I. We must laugh for two. The bones are good here. That is past doubt. We will stay, and we will keep our eyes open. And listen now, Toto. We are honest. Good! Dost thou understand? No more purses, or out we go. No stealing of cutlets. Ah, thou mayest lick thy chops in vain, bandit!"

A few days later Gamel began to fence with François, who liked it well. He was strong, agile, and like his old friends the cats for quickness of foot. Gamel was charmed.

"We must make no mistakes. The foil held lightly

—so, so! If you grasp it too strongly you will not feel the other's blade. That is better. 'T is the fingers direct the point. Thy hand a little higher—so, so!"

They fenced before the pupils came and in the intervals when none was on hand. François was tireless.

It was June now, and Robespierre was the public prosecutor, with Pétion at his side. Gamel read aloud the announcement with a coldly stern face. François heard it with indifference.

"*Tiens!*" he cried. "What matters it? *Dame!*" as he lunged at the wall, "I do believe my arm is an inch longer." He was thinking, as he tried over and over a new guard, of what a queer education he had had. Gamel walked away into his own room. He was a man who often liked to be alone. Apt to be monosyllabic with his pupils, he could at times become seriously talkative at night over a pipe and a glass. François began to like him, and to suspect that he in turn was liked—a matter not indifferent to this poor devil, who had himself an undeveloped talent for affection.

"*Mon ami*, Toto! Let us think. I might have been a priest. What an escape! Or a great chorister. That is another matter. A thief, a street-dog, a juggler, a *maître d'escrime*. *Parbleu!* What next? We are getting up in the world. My palm, little rascal? Thou wouldst read it. Ah, bad dog, not I! Let us to bed; come along. It seems too good to last."

# XII

*In which Toto is seen to change his politics twice a day
—the mornings and the afternoons quarrel—In which
Jean Pierre André Amar, "le farouche," appears.*

HE fencing-master took great pains with
his promising *débutant*, and now at last
thought he could trust him to give lessons. He gave him much advice, full
of good sense. He must dress simply,
not in any marked fashion. And here were the two
cockades, and two for Toto, who was fitted with a toy
sword, and had been taught to howl horribly if François said, "Citizen Capet," and to do the like if he
cried, "Aristocrat!"

François, gay and a little anxious, followed Gamel
for the first time during the lesson-hours into the
*salle d'armes.* Toto came after them in full rig, with
a cap and a huge white cockade. A dozen gentlemen,
most of them young, were preparing to fence.

The poodle was greeted with "Bravo!" and strutted
about on his hind legs with evident enjoyment of the
approval.

"Wait here," said Gamel to François. "I will by
and by give thee a chance." François had, of course,

been constantly in the room when the patrons were absent, and it was now familiar. It had been part of the old hotel of some extinct nobleman, and was of unusual height, and quite forty feet square, with tall windows at each end; a cushioned bench ran around the walls, and above it hung wire masks, foils, sabers, and a curious collection of the arms of past ages and barbarous tribes. Chiefly remarkable were the many fine blades, Spanish or Eastern. At the side of the hall, a doorway led into the shooting-gallery, a late adjunct since the English use of the pistol had been brought into the settlement of quarrels made savage by the angry politics of the day. On one of the walls of the fencing-room was a large sign on which was painted: "Achille Gamel, *ci-devant* Maître d'Armes, Régiment du Duc de Rohan-Chabot. Lessons in the small sword, saber, and pistol." The word "Duc" was chalked over, but was still easily to be made out.

Presently Gamel came to François in his shirt and breeches, foil in hand. "This way, François." As they slowly crossed the room, Gamel went on to say in a low tone of voice: "Don't be too eager. Take it all as a matter of course. Don't be nervous. One must have had a serious affair or two before one gets over the foil fever. Remember, you are here to teach, not to triumph. There are few here you cannot touch, but that is not business."

"I understand," said François.

"I will give you for your lesson the best blade in Paris. You can teach him nothing. He is my foster-brother, the Marquis de Ste. Luce."

"Ste. Luce!"

"Yes; he is here often."

As they approached, the great gentleman came to meet them, separating himself from the laughing group of younger men.

"*Ma foi!*" he exclaimed. "Is this your new blade, Gamel?" He caught François's appealing eye, and showed no sign of having known the thief until they were apart from the rest and had taken their foils. Then he said quietly, "Does Gamel know?"

"Yes, monsieur. I saved his life in a row in the Cité, and he gives me this chance."

"Good! I shall not betray you. But beware! You must keep faith, and behave yourself."

"Monsieur may trust me."

"And you can fence?"

"A little, monsieur."

"Well, then, on guard!" The marquis was pleased to praise the new teacher. "He has a supple wrist, and what a reach of arm!" At last he went away to Gamel's room, where they were absent a half-hour. These private talks, François observed later, were frequent, especially with certain of the middle-aged gentlemen who took here their morning exercise.

After this first introduction to business, François sat still when the marquis had left him. By and by the gentleman came back, and saying a word of en-couragement to François, went away.

"Take M. de Lamerie, François," said Gamel; and turning to a gentleman near by, added, "*À vous*, monsieur." Others began to select foils and to fence in couples, so that soon the hall rang with the click,

7

click of meeting steel. François was clever enough to let his pupil get in a touch now and then, and meanwhile kept him and those who looked on delighted with his natural merriment. He was soon a favorite. The dog was made to howl at a tricolored cockade, and proved a great success. As to the fencing-lessons, Gamel was overjoyed, and as time ran on came to trust and to like his thief, who began speedily to pick up the little well-mannered ways and phrases he heard about him. He liked well to be liked and to be praised for his skill, which week by week became greater, until none except M. Gamel and the marquis were able to meet him on equal terms. The master of arms was generous; the wages rose. The clothes François now wore were better, and when Gamel asked him to choose a rapier for wear in the street, which was not yet forbidden, the poor thief felt that he was in the full sunlight of fortune.

The afternoons were less to his taste. If a new pupil arrived, the cook, an old woman, let him in, and Gamel saw him in an anteroom and settled terms and hours. The Jacobins came after two o'clock. Then the room was unusually full. The poodle howled at the name of Louis Capet. Tricolored cockades were everywhere. The talk was of war and the frontier, the ways of speech were guarded, the manners not those of the morning. These citizens were awkward, but terribly in earnest. The pistol-gallery was much in favor; but at this deadly play François was never an expert. He did not like it, and was pleased when the Vicomte de Beauséjour, a favored pupil, said: "'T is a coarse weapon, François. Ah, well

enough to enable bulldog English to settle their dis-
putes over a bone; but, *dame!* quite unfit to be the
arm of honor of gentlemen." This uncertain property
of honor seemed to François a too insecure kind of
investment. It was enough to have to take care of
one's pocket; and his being now well lined, François
began to resent the possibility of those sudden changes
of ownership which under other conditions he had
looked upon as almost in the nature of things.

During this summer, and in the winter of '91 and
'92, Gamel was at times absent for days. Whenever
he returned he was for a week after in his monosyllabic mood. François, who was keenly alive to his
present advantages, and who saw how these absences
interfered with their business, began to exercise his
easily excited inquisitiveness, and to meditate on what
was beneath Gamel's frequent fits of abstraction. His
own life had known disappointments, not always of
his own making. He dreaded new ones. The past of
the Cité, Quatre Pattes, Despard, those haunting eyes
of the marquis's widowed daughter, the choristers, the
asylum, the mad street life—all the company of his
uncertain days—were gone. Now, of late, he began
to have a feeling of uneasy belief that things were
once more about to change. Nor was the outer life
of the capital such as to promise tranquillity. A nation was about to become insane. It was at this time
like a man thus threatened: to-day it was sane, to-
morrow it might be reeling over the uncertain line
which separates the sound from the unsound. Had
François been more interested and more apprehensive,
he was intelligent enough to have shared the dismay

with which many Frenchmen saw the growth of tumultuous misrule. Indeed, the talk of the morning
fencing-school should have taught him alarm. But
he had formerly lived the life of the hour, even of the
minute, and as long as he was well fed, housed, and
clothed, his normal good humor comfortably digested
anxiety.

I should wrongly state a character of uncommon
interest if I were to give the impression of a man who
had merely the constant hilarity of a happy child.
He was apt to laugh where others smiled; but, as he
matured, cheerful contentment was his usual mood,
and with it, to the last, the probability of such easily
born laughter as radiated mirth upon all who heard
it, like a companionable fire diffusing its generous
warmth. He was at this time doing what he most
fancied. The company suited him. He liked the
tranquil ways of these courteous gentlemen. In a
word, he was contented, and for a time lost all desire
to seek change or adventure. His satisfaction in the
life made him more quiet and perhaps more thoughtful. He had every reason to be cheerful, and cheerfulness is the temperate zone of the mind.

At times, on Sundays, in the summer of '92, he
wandered into the country with Toto; but these holidays were rare. Now and then the habits of years
brought again the longing for excitement; with the
meal-hours he recovered his common sense, being a
big fellow of sharp appetite and a camel-like capacity
for substantial food.

The feud between the cockades broke out at this
time in duels, which it became the fashion to drive to

the Bois to see. Women of all classes looked on and
applauded, and few liked it if the affair failed to prove
grave. François found it entertaining. The duels
were, in fact, many in the years of grace '91 and '92.

The morning pupils wore their hair in curls, dressed
in short clothes, and defied the new-fashioned republican pantaloons, which were rising up to the armpits
and descending the legs. They carried sword-canes,
or sticks like the club of Hercules; a few still wore
the sword. Brown and gray wore the afternoon citizens, with long straight hair, short waistcoats, and
long and longer *culottes* above large steel shoe-buckles,
all that were silver having been given to aid the funds
of a bankrupt government. The morning, which knew
very well who came in the later hours, abused the
afternoon, and this portion of the day returned those
compliments in kind.

Now and then the morning had a little affair with
the afternoon, for the Terror was not yet. In cafés
and theaters there were constant outbreaks, and men
on both sides eager enough to sustain opinion by the
sword or the pistol. When one of what François
called "our little domestic difficulties" was on hand,
there was excitement and interest among Royalists
and Jacobins, with much advice given, and huge dis-
gust when monsieur was pinked by Citizen Chose of
the Cordeliers or of the Jacobin Club.

If the reverse obtained, and some gentleman of ancient
name condescended to run Citizen Chose through the
lungs, there was great rejoicing before noon and black
looks after it. Here were a half-dozen affairs in a
month, for these were the first blades in France.

There were laws against the duel, but the law changed too fast for obedience, and fashion, as usual, defied it. Hatred and contempt were ready at every turn. Two abbés fought, and what was left of the great ladies went to see and applaud.

This duel between morning and afternoon began to amuse Paris. But pretty soon neither the master of arms nor his assistant was as well pleased at the excessive attention thus drawn to the school of fencing. Gamel disliked it for reasons which he did not set forth, and François because he felt that his disturbing readiness to turn back to a life of peril and discomfort was like enough to be reinforced by coming events. He adored good living, yet could exist on crusts. He was intelligent, yet did not like to be forced to think. An overmastering sense of the ludicrous inclined him to take the world lightly. He liked ease, yet delighted in adventure. He distrusted his own temperament. He had need to do so. Excitement was in the air. The summer of '92 was unquiet, and pupils were less numerous, so that François found time to wander. The autumn brought no change in his life, but Gamel became more and more self-absorbed, and neglected his pupils. The gentlemen who fenced in the mornings began to disappear, and the new year of 1793 came in with war without and tumult within distracted France.

For several days before the 21st of January, 1793, strange faces were frequently seen in the morning hours, or more often late at night. These passed into Gamel's room, and remained long. The marquis, more thoughtful than usual, came and went daily.

Early on the 20th, Gamel told François that he should
be absent until after the 21st, the day set for the king
to die.  François asked no questions, and was not
deeply grieved to be left in the dark as to what was in
contemplation.  During the previous week there had
been sad faces in the morning hours.  The pupils
were fewer; they were leaving Paris—and too many
were leaving France.  The Jacobins, with whom
François fenced in the latter part of the day, were
wildly triumphant.  They missed Gamel when he was
absent, and asked awkward questions.  It was plain
enough to his assistant that the master of this turbulent school was a Royalist *enragé*, as men then said.
The assistant was much of his mind, but he was also
far more loyal to one François than to the unfortunate king.

He was not surprised that at the hour of opening
on the 21st no one appeared.  He sat thinking, and a
little sorry for the humbled Louis rumbling over the
crowded streets to his doom.  The prisons were already becoming crowded; the richer bourgeoisie had
become submissive.  The more able and aggressive
Jacobins were about to seize the reins of power from
the sentimental Girondists.

"Let us think a little," said François to his friend
and counselor Toto.  The poodle woke up, and sat
attentive.  "It is disagreeable to have to think, *mon
ami;* but there are our heads.  Without a head one
cannot eat or enjoy a bone.  Shall we go to the frontier,
and be shot at, and shoot?  *Dame!* a thousand bullets
to one guillotine.  We do not like that.  Let us change
our opinions, Toto, join the clubs, and talk liberty.

Yes; that is thy opinion. Must we go back to the streets? 'T is good nowadays to be obscure, and thou art becoming a public character, Toto."

He read the gazette awhile, practised with the pistol, and taught the dog a new trick. Still no one came, and the day wore on to noon. At this hour the bell rang, and the poodle barked, as was his custom. "Learn to hold thy tongue," said the master. The servant had gone, like all Paris, to see a brave man die.

François opened the outer door. A strongly built man he had never before seen entered, and, pushing by him, went without a word into the great room beyond.

"Hallo, citizen! What dost thou want?" said François, following him.

"Art thou Citizen Gamel?"

François was not; and what could he do for the citizen?

The man for a moment made no reply, but glanced searchingly about the hall, while the assistant looked him over as keenly. He was a personage not easily to be forgotten.

"No one else here?" he asked.

"No one."

The questioner was a man not over thirty-five, of colossal make, and with something about him which Toto resented. He began to bark, and then, of a sudden, fled under a bench, and watched the new-comer.

His features were out of keeping with his height and breadth. The Jacobin had small, restless eyes, a diminutive nose, perhaps broken, and a large-lipped mouth, which, as he talked, was drawn to one side as

"'AND SO A DOG IS SENT TO FETCH THE
SAFEGUARD THE PEOPLE PROVIDE?'"

though from some loss of power on the other half of
the face.

"I am Jean Pierre André Amar," he said, with an
air of importance.

"Will the citizen be seated?"

He would not. He desired to see Citizen Gamel.

François regretted his absence on business. Amar,
later known as *le farouche*, desired to see the list of
pupils, in order to select an unoccupied morning hour.
Unluckily, the master had the keys. The citizen
wished to fence, and could come in the morning only;
he was busy after that. François would mention his
name; perhaps the hours of the morning were full,
but Citizen Gamel would no doubt arrange.

The man with the wandering mouth stood in
thought, said he would return, and then asked
abruptly:

"Art thou his assistant?"

"Yes."

"And thy name?"

"François."

"Has Citizen François a *carte-civique*—a certificate
of citizenship?"

François knew better than to refuse. "Fetch me
the card, Toto. 'T is on the chair in my room. *Va*
—go!"

"Thou art careless, Citizen François."

François, on this, became short of speech. Toto
ran back. "Give it to the citizen."

Amar took it, saying: "It is correct. And so a
dog is sent to fetch the safeguard the people provide?"

François laughed. "The citizen is particular. But here we are good republicans, and have given our useful arms to the army, and think to go soon ourselves. Shall I give the citizen a lesson ?"

No; he would call again. The section wished the names of all who fenced here. As the citizen reached the door, he said, turning:

"Thou art the man who used to laugh in the show. Robespierre told me of what fortune was read on his palm. A great man. Take care of thy own fortune. Thou art not of the club. It may be thou wilt laugh no more." This while the distorted mouth went to left and came back, and the small eyes winked and wandered. François thanked him. He would join the club, the list should be ready, and so on.

When alone again, François began to reflect on what was likely to happen. At any time, Amar might return with a guard. On the 23d, as usual during this sad week, there were no morning pupils; and still Gamel came not, and François had to manage the turbulent afternoon pupils alone.

XIII

*Citizen Amar, meeting the marquis, is unlucky and vindictive.*

A FEAR vast and oppressive was upon the great city. The white cockades were gone. François burned all he could find. For a week no one came to fence in the morning. The afternoons were full, and there was much inquiry for Citizen Gamel. On the night of the 24th of this terrible January, 1793, François went out. Paris was recovering, and, as usual, forgetful, was eating and drinking and dancing, while all Europe was ringing with the news of this murder of a good man too weak for a mighty task.

When, later, François returned to the school of arms he smelt the odor of a pipe. "Ah!" he cried, "Toto, he has come. 'T is none too soon." Candles lighted dimly the large hall and the rooms beyond it. He heard no sounds, and, suddenly becoming uneasy, hastened to enter the little salon. It was empty, as were all the rooms. On the bedroom floor lay scattered clothes. Scorched leaflets were fluttering like black crows over the ashes of a dying fire. They were fragments of burnt paper. An open desk was on the table, and everywhere were signs of haste.

François ran out to the kitchen, and called their only servant, a shrewd old woman. She said: "I heard thee, citizen. I was coming to tell thee that Citizen Gamel has gone."

"Gone! *Mon Dieu!*"

"He has paid me, and well; and here is a box for thee, Citizen François. I hid it under the mattress. Oh, I have waited, but I am afraid."

François took the box and its key, and went to his room. The box contained some five hundred francs in gold, and as much more in assignats—the notes of the day, and really worth but little. In a folded package were papers and a letter. It read thus:

"I am sorry to leave thee. A business affair has failed, and I go westward. I risk this to warn thee to fly. For two days thou art safe, but not longer. If a gentleman calls whom thou knowest, and asks for *Monsieur* Achille Gamel, tell him all. I inclose for thee a passport. No matter how I got it. It is good. Use it soon. I divide with thee my small store. Thou hast been honest; stay so. We may meet in better times."

François laughed. "We must go, Toto. Well, it has a good side; thou wilt get thinner." Then he read the passport. It described him well: Jean François, juggler ("Good!"), returning to Normandy; affairs of family; a father dying. "Good! Now I have one parent at least." It was in due order.

"Thou hast no papers, Toto; but thy black head is secure."

At early morning on the 25th of January, he found a vender of antiquities, and quickly sold him, for two hundred francs, the antique arms in the fencing-room. He must remove them that coming night. Next he sought a maker of articles for the jugglers who were still to be found in every town; for neither at this time nor during the Terror did the people cease to amuse themselves. François bought a set of gaily tinted balls and the conjuring apparatus with which he was familiar. Once again in his room, he packed his clothes in a knapsack and his juggler's material in a bag that he could carry. A long cloak which his master had left he set aside to take, and, thus prepared, felt that on the whole he had better risk waiting until the dawn of the following day before he set out on his wintry journey. The old woman had already fled in alarm.

On the following morning, at 9 A. M., François went into the great hall to secure pistols and the fine Spanish rapier which Gamel had given him. Here he paused, and re-read the passport. A blank space had been left for the insertion of the special locality to which the bearer might wish to go in Normandy.

"Ah!" he exclaimed, "that must do. I will go to Musillon. Perhaps I shall find Despard. He will help me to recover that desirable papa." He went back to Gamel's room, and carefully completed the passport by inserting the name of the village Musillon.

After this he returned to the hall, talking to the poodle as he went. "Toto, thou art uneasy," he said;

"and I too, my friend. Remember to howl no more at Jacobins. Thou art of the Left, a dog of the Left. *Tiens!* the bell." He caught up his rapier, and opened the door. A powerful, broad-shouldered man entered. He was clad in gray, and wore the red bonnet the extreme Jacobins affected, and which Robespierre so much despised.

"Ah, no one here. That is well. I trust Gamel has gone."

"Ah!" exclaimed François to himself. "'T is my confounded marquis. Now for ill luck."

"Is Monsieur Gamel at home? *Monsieur* Achille Gamel?" He emphasized the title.

François understood, with no great amazement, that this was the man of whom Gamel's letter spoke. He replied, "This way, please, monsieur."

The gentleman followed without a word.

"Read this," said François; "and, pardon me, but read it quickly. My head appears to me to be less securely attached to my body than common."

"*Dame!* You are as jolly as ever, my delightful thief."

"I beg that monsieur will read this letter, and at once. *Nom de ciel!* there is no time to be lost." And still he laughed. "We are in a trap, monsieur."

The marquis was not to be hurried; it was not his way. "St. Gris! you can laugh. I envy you. In France men grin, for they must; but laughter is dead. Ah!" and he fell to considering the letter. Then he folded it deliberately. "Burn it," he said. "So; that is well; and now, my good thief, I came to warn Gamel. He has wisely fled. Of course there was a plot, and, as usual, it failed.  You, who are not in it, are like enough to pay other folks' debts.  I have a certain mild interest in honest rascality.  You are a marked man.  No cabbage of the field is more sure of the knife.  Go, and soon."

"I have heard from Gamel, monsieur.  He assured me that I was safe here for a day or two—I know not how he knew that."

"I do; but I scarcely share his confidence.  Go soon."

"I shall go at dawn to-morrow."

"No; go to-day—this evening."

"I will.  Monsieur will pardon me if I ask if madame, monsieur's daughter, is well and safe? There are few who have been kind to me, and—"

"My child is well," said the marquis, "and in Normandy; but if safe or not, who can say, while these wolves destroy women and children?  Safe!  I would give my soul to be sure of that."  His face showed the transient emotion he felt; and suddenly, as if annoyed at his own weakness, he drew himself up and said abruptly: "Go—and go quickly!  I shall leave at once—"

At this moment the bell rang violently.

"The devil!" cried the marquis.  "Go and see, and do not shut the inner door; I must hear."  With this he entered the pistol-gallery and waited.  François obeyed, and, with the sheathed rapier still in his hand, crossed the hall.  Again the bell rang.

"He is in a mischief of a hurry.  No noise, Toto!"

As he opened the outer door, the man of the warped face broke in, and, passing him at once, walked

across the little reception-room and into the great hall
beyond. Again his height and massive build struck
the fencing-master.

"Where is Gamel, citizen?—and no lies to me!
Where is Gamel, I say?"

"He has gone away. Why, I do not know. Will
the citizen search his rooms?"

"Search! Not I. I will call the municipals.
What are those rooms over there? And arms! Why
have they not been sent to the committee for our
patriot children on the frontier?"

"Perhaps Citizen Amar would kindly inspect them,
and then, if required, we can send them. Many have
been already sent. Behold, citizen, a war-club of
Ashantee, a matchlock, a headsman's sword. *Parbleu!*
the guillotine is better."

"I see, citizen; I see. But now of Gamel. He was
to be here to-day. I hear. I will return presently with
the officers; and, friend citizen, it will be well for thee
to assist, and heartily. This Gamel was in some plot
to save the Citizen Capet. Like master, like man.
Have ready the lists of those aristocrats who fence
here in the morning. Thou canst save thy head by
making a clean breast of it. I shall return in half
an hour. Have everything ready."

At this the dreaded Jacobin, having looked over
the arms and duly impressed the fencing-master,
moved toward the door of exit. Should Amar leave
the room, François felt that his own fate was certain.
He had been too much with Gamel. Less things
every day cost the heads of men. There was death or
life in the next five minutes. François was not one to

hesitate. Preceding the Jacobin, he quietly set his back to the door, and, locking it, put the key in his pocket. This action was so dexterous and swift that for a moment the Jacobin did not perceive that he was trapped. He was thinking if there was anything more to be said. He looked up. "Well, open the door, citizen." As he spoke, the two strangest faces in Paris were set over against each other. Here was comedy, with long lean features, twinkling eyes above, and below the good humor of a capacious mouth set between preposterous ears. And there was tragedy, strong of jaw, long hair lying flat in black, leech-like flakes on a too prominent brow, and small eyes, deep-set, restless, threatening, seen like those of a wolf in cave shelters—a face no man trusted, a face on which all expressions grew into deformity; not a mere beast; a terribly intelligent bigot of the new creed, colossal, alert, unsparing, fearless, full of vanity.

When the citizen commissioner said, "Open," François replied:

"Not just yet, citizen."

"What is this?" shouted Amar. "Open, I say, in the name of the law!"

"Not I." And François, with a quick motion, threw off the sheath of the rapier. It fell with a great clatter on the far side of the room.

"Open, I say!"

At this moment Ste. Luce came across the hall.

"What the deuce is all this, François?"

Amar turned his square shoulders, and looked at the marquis.

"I presume thee, too, to be one of this rascal

Gamel's band. If thou dost think I, Pierre Amar, am afraid of thee, thou art going to find out thy mistake. What is thy name?"

"Go to the devil!" cried the marquis. The Jacobin darted toward the window; but François was too quick for him, and instantly had him by the collar, the point of the rapier touching his back. "Move a step, and thou art a dead man." The face, crooked with passion, half turned over the shoulder.

"Misery! What a beauty! Didst thou think I valued my head so little as to trust thee, scum of the devil's dish-water?" For some reason this huge animal filled François with rage, and he poured out a flood of the abusive slang of the Cité as the marquis came up.

"Drop that window-curtain!" said the thief. "And now, what to do, monsieur?"

The captured man showed the utmost courage, and no small lack of wisdom. "Dog of an aristocrat! I know thee. It was thou didst kill Jean Coutier, last month. I saw thee, coward! We knew not thy name. Now we shall take pay for that murder."

The marquis grew white to the eyes, with a certain twitching of the lips to be seen as François again asked:

"What shall we do with him? Shall we tie him?"

"No; kill him. What! you will not? Give me your rapier. 'T is but one wolf less."

François was more than unwilling. The intense hatred of the noble for the Jacobin he did not share; indeed, he liked the man's fearlessness, but, nevertheless, meant to provide for his own security. His conscience, such as it was, refused to sanction cold-blooded murder.

"I cannot. Go away! I will take care of this rascal."

"There is no time to lose," said the marquis. "Kill the brute."

"Not I," said François.

"Thou art coward enough to kill a man in cold blood!" cried Amar. "This is the fine honor you talk of. Better go. All thy kind are running; but, soon or late, the guillotine will get thy hog-head, as it did thy Jew-nosed king's."

"The face and the tongue are well matched," said Ste. Luce, quietly. "It will take a good ten minutes to tie and gag him. You will not kill him? Then give the fellow a blade, and—I will see to the rest. Are you man enough to take my offer? Quick, now!"

"Try me. I am no weakling, like poor Coutier."

"Find him a blade, François. I will watch him. Be quick!" He took the rapier, and stood by the motionless figure, whose uneasy eyes followed the thief as he went and came again.

"The blades are of a length, François? Yes. Lock the door. Ah, it is done. Good! Now, keep an eye on him, François. Take care of yourself if he has the luck to kill me. However, that is unlikely. Ah, you have a sword, François."

"The citizen talks a good deal," said Amar, trying his blade on the floor.

"Yes," said the marquis, negligently untying his cravat. "It is so rare, in these democratic days,

that one has a chance to talk with one of you gentlemen."

" Bah ! " cried the Jacobin, " we shall see presently."
As he spoke, he laid his sword on a chair and began
to strip.  As he took off his coat and waistcoat, he
folded them with care, and laid them neatly on a
bench.

The marquis also stripped to his waistcoat, but it
was with more haste.  He threw his coat to François,
and took his place in the middle of the room, where
he waited until his slower antagonist, in shirt and
breeches, came forward to meet him.  Both believed
it to be a duel to the death, but neither face showed
to François any sign of anxiety.  The Jacobin said :

" The light is in thine eyes, citizen.  If we were to
move so as to engage across the room—"

" It is of no moment," returned the marquis.  " Are
you ready ? "

" Yes."

François saw no better method of disposing of an
awkward business.  Nevertheless, he was uncomfort-
able.  " What if this devil should kill the marquis ? "
He cried, " On guard, messieurs ! " and stepped aside.

The marquis saluted with grave courtesy ; but the
Jacobin, obeying the fashion of the schools of fence,
went through the formula of appearing to draw the
sword, and certain other conventional motions supposed to be exacted by etiquette.  The marquis smiled
as Amar led off in this ceremonious fashion.  These
preliminaries of the *salle d'armes* were usually omitted
or curtailed in serious combats.  The seigneur,
amused, and following Amar's lead, went through the

whole performance. Meanwhile François looked the
two men over, and was not ill pleased. This heavy fellow should prove no match for a practised duelist like
Ste. Luce. He was soon undeceived.

Both men were plainly enough masters of their
weapon, and for at least two minutes there was no
advantage. Then Ste. Luce was touched in the left
shoulder, and a distorted grimace of satisfaction ran
over the face of the Jacobin. The marquis became
more careful, and a minute or two later François saw
with pleasure that Amar was breathing a trifle hard.
He had half a mind to cry: "Wait! wait! He is
feeling the strain." He held his peace, and, with Toto,
looked on in silence. The marquis knew his business
well, and noted the quickening chest movements of
his adversary. He began to smile, and to make a
series of inconceivably quick lunges. Now and then
the point of either blade struck fair on the convex
steel shell-like guard which protected the hand.
When this chanced, a clear, sweet note as of a bell
rang through the great hall. The Jacobin held his
own, and François, despite his anxiety, saw with the
satisfaction of a master how lightly each rapier lay in
the grasp of the duelist, and how dexterously the fingers alone were used to guide the blades.

Of a sudden the strange face was jerked as it were
to left, and a savage lunge in tierce came perilously
near to ending the affair. Ste. Luce threw himself
back with the quickness of a boy. The point barely
touched him. "St. Gris!" he called out gaily.
"That was well meant. Now take care!"

"By St. Denis! 't is a master," muttered François.

The marquis seemed of a sudden to have let loose a reserve of unlooked-for power. He was here and there about the massive and by no means unready bulk of Amar, swift and beautifully graceful.

Then of a sudden the marquis's blade went out as quick as lightning, and just at the limit of a nearly futile thrust caught Amar over the right eye. "*Dame!* I missed those lanterns of hell!"

The Jacobin brushed away the blood which, running down his face, made his right eye useless for the time.

The marquis fell back, and dropped his point. "The deuce! The man cannot see. Tie a handkerchief around his head."

The Jacobin was not sorry to have time to breathe.

"Thou art more than fair, citizen," said Amar, getting his breath.

"Thanks," returned the marquis, coldly. "Make haste, François."

François took up a lace handkerchief which lay beside Ste. Luce's coat on the seat where he had cast his clothes. While François bound the handkerchief around the head so as to stop the flow of blood, Amar turned to his foe.

"Citizen," said the Jacobin, "thou hast been a gallant man in this matter. My life was thine to take. Let it end here. Thou art a brave man and a good blade."

Ste. Luce looked at him with an expression of amused curiosity.

"What else?"

"I will not have thee pursued—on my honor."

"Tie it firmly, François. You have just heard, my François, of the last Parisian novelty—a Jacobin's honor! Be so good as to hurry, François."

Had the stern Jacobin felt some sudden impulse of pity or respect? In all his after days he was unsparing, and certainly it was not fear which now moved him.

"As pleases thee," he said simply. Ste. Luce made no answer. Again their blades met. And now the marquis changed his game, facing his foe steadily, while François gazed in admiration. Ste. Luce's rapier was like a lizard's movements for quickness. Twice he touched the man's chest, and by degrees drove him back, panting, until he was against the door. Suddenly, seeming to recover strength, the Jacobin lunged in quarte, and would have caught the marquis fair in the breast-bone had he not thrown himself backward as he felt the prick. Instantly he struck the blade aside with his open left hand, and, as it went by his left side, drove his rapier savagely through Amar's right lung and into the panel of the door. It was over. Not ten minutes had passed.

"*Dame!*" he cried, withdrawing his rapier, and retreating a pace or two. "He was worth fighting."

The Jacobin's face moved convulsively. He coughed, spattering blood about him. His right arm moved in quick jerks. His sword dropped, and stuck upright in the floor, quivering.

"Dog of an aristocrat!" he cried. His distorted face twitched; he staggered to left, to right, and at last tumbled in a heap, a massive figure, of a sudden inert and harmless.

The marquis stood still and looked down at his foe.

"What the deuce to do with him?" said François.

"Take his head, and drag him into your room. We can talk then."

"Will monsieur take his feet?"

"What! *I* touch the dog? No, not I."

François did not like it; but making no reply, he dragged the Jacobin's helpless bulk after him, and, once in his room, pulled the mattress off the bed, and without roughness drew the man upon it.

Amar opened his eyes, and tried to speak. He could not; the flow of blood choked him. He shook his fist at Ste. Luce.

"Cursed brute," cried François, "be still! He will begin to howl presently. The sons of Satan are immortal."

"We must gag him, François."

"But he will die; he will choke. See how he breathes—how hard."

"*Diable!* it is he or I. Would he spare me, do you think? Don't talk nonsense. Do as I tell you."

François took up a towel. As he approached, Amar looked up at him. There was no plea in his savage face.

"Go on. What the deuce are you waiting for?" said Ste. Luce.

"I cannot do it," said François. "End it yourself."

"What! I? Strangle a dog! I! *Dame!* Let us go. What a fool you are!"

"Better go singly, then," said the thief. He had no mind to increase his own risks by the dangerous society of the nobleman.

"HE STAGGERED TO LEFT, TO RIGHT, AND AT LAST TUMBLED IN A
HEAP."

Amar was silent. The handkerchief had fallen from his head, but the wound bled no longer.

"What shall I do with the handkerchief, monsieur?"

"Do? Burn it. Faugh!" François cast it on the still glowing embers. "Now my clothes and my cloak," said Ste. Luce; "and do not lose any time over that animal."

He washed off the little blood on his clothes, and dressed in haste, saying: "Lucky that his point struck on my breast-bone. 'T is of no moment. The fellow has left me a remembrance. I am sorry I did not have the luck to kill him. Good-by, François. May we meet in better days." He was gone.

François locked the door after him, and went back to his room. He sat down on the floor beside the mattress.

"Now listen, Master Amar. Canst thou hear me? Ah, yes. Well, I have saved thy life. Oh, thou wilt get well,—more 's the pity!—and do some mischief yet. Now if I should kill thee I would be pretty safe. If I go away, and send thee a doctor, I am a lost man. What is that thou art saying? Ah!" and he leaned down to hear the broken whisper. "So thou wilt have my head chopped off. Thou art less afraid than I would be, were I thee. What shall we do, Toto?" and he laughed; somehow the situation had for him its humorous side.

"I can't murder a man," he said. "If ever I kill a man, I trust it may be one who hath not thy eyes and thy one-sided grin. To be haunted by a ghost like thee! The deuce! Not I! *Sac à papier!* I will take my chance." He sat down, and wrote a short note to a surgeon on the farther side of Paris, one whom he knew to have been much commended to his pupils by Gamel.

"My unforgiving friend," he said, "I shall lock thee in. Thou art too weak to move, and to try will cause thee to bleed. This note will get thee a surgeon in about six hours. I must leave thee. Be quiet, and be good. Here is a flask of *eau-de-vie*. Art still of a mind to give thy preserver to the guillotine?" The grim head nodded as the red froth leaked out over the lips. "'Yes, yes,' thou sayest. Thou art in a fine state of penitence. I hope we have seen the last of each other. One more chance. Promise me not to be my enemy. I will trust thee. Come, now."

But the Jacobin was past speech. As François knelt beside him, he beckoned feebly.

"What is it?" As he bent lower, a grim smile went over the one movable side of Amar's face, and, raising a feeble hand, he drew it across François's neck.

"*Mon Dieu!*" cried he, recoiling, "thou art ripe for hell. Adieu, my unforgiving friend; and as thou hast no God, *au diable*, and may St. Satan look after thee—for love of thy looks. Come, doggie!" He put his pistols in the back of his belt, set his rapier in the belt-catch, threw his cloak over all, and picked up his bag and knapsack. He took one last look at Amar, and saying, "By-by, my angel," left him, locking both doors as he went out.

François passed into the street, followed by the black poodle. In the Rue St. Honoré he paid the boy of a butcher with whom Gamel dealt to take his note when the midday meal should be over. And thus having eased his conscience and regulated the business of life, he set out to put between him and the Jacobin as many miles as his long legs could cover.

# XIV

*François escapes from Paris and goes in search of a
father.   He meets a man who has a wart on his nose,
and who because of this is unlucky.*

 E had been fortunate.   Not more than an
hour and a quarter had gone by since
Amar's entrance, and the mid-hour of
breakfast had probably secured them
from intrusion of foe or friend.   François, who knew Paris as few men did, strode on through
narrow streets and the dimly lighted passages which
afforded opportunity to avoid the busier haunts of
men.   The barriers were carelessly guarded, and he
passed unmolested into the country.   Once outside of
the city, he took the highroad to Evreux, down the
Seine, simply because the passport of Jean François,
juggler, pointed to Normandy as his destination.
Naturally a man of forethinking sense, he had assumed
that the village whence came Despard should be the
home of that father who was ill.   He knew from his
former partner enough of the village to answer questions.   It lay westward of Evreux.   France was then
less full of spies and less suspicious than it became in
the Terror; and until he arrived at a small town on the

136

north bank of the Seine, not far from Poissy, he had
no trouble. He saw no couriers. The post went only
once a week. He was safe, and, to tell the truth,
merry and well pleased again to wander. His money
was sewed in his garments. He wore his rapier under
his cloak, but with it he carried the conjurer's thin,
supple blade, which, when he feigned to swallow it, a
spring caused to coil into the large basket-hilt. His
pistols were strapped behind him, and on his back he
carried his knapsack and small bag of juggling apparatus. Thus, clad in sober gray, with the tricolor
on his red cap and a like decoration on the poodle's
collar, he was surely a quaint enough figure. Long,
well built, and wiry, laughing large between his two
wing-like ears, he held his way along the highroad on
the bank of the winding Seine.

He avoided towns and people, camped in the woods,
juggled and told fortunes at farm-houses for a dinner,
and, as I have said, had no trouble until he came at
midday to the hamlet of Île Rouge. Here, being
tired, and Toto footsore, he thought he might venture
to halt and sleep at the inn.

It was a little gray French town in the noonday
quiet, scarce a soul in sight, and a warmer sun than
January usually affords on street and steaming roof-
tiles. Hostile dogs, appearing, seemed to consider
Toto a Royalist. François tucked him under his arm,
and carelessly entered the stone-paved tap-room of
the "Hen with Two Heads." He repented too late.
The room was half full. One of the many commis-
sioners who afterward swarmed through France was
engaged with the mayor of the commune. François,

putting on an air of humility, sought out the inn-
keeper, and asked meekly to have a room.  As he did
so, a fat man in the red bonnet of the Jacobins called
out from the table where he sat, " Come here ! "

François said, " Yes, citizen," and stood at the table
where this truculent person was seated.

He was sharply questioned, and his papers and
baggage were overhauled with small ceremony,
while, apparently at his ease, he liberally distributed
smiles and the kindly glances of large blue eyes.  At
last he was asked why he carried a sword ; it was
against the law.  He made answer that he carried two
tools of his trade—would the citizen see?  And when
he had swallowed two feet of his juggler's blade, to
the wonder of the audience, nothing further was said
of the rapier.  At last, seeing that the commissioner
still hesitated, he told, with great show of frankness,
whither he was going, and named Despard as one who
would answer for him.  The mention of this name
seemed to annoy the questioner, who said Despard
was a busy fellow, and was stirring up the citizens at
Musillon.  He, Grégoire, was on his way to see after
him.  He should like to make the acquaintance of that
sick father, and, after all, François might be an *émigré*.
He must wait, and go with the commissioner to Musillon.

François smiled his best ; and, when the citizen
commissioner had done with business, might he amuse
him with a little juggling?  Citizen Grégoire would
see ; let him sit yonder and wait.  After a few minutes the great man's breakfast was set before him ; the
room was cleared, and the citizen ate, while François
looked him over.

"HE HELD HIS WAY ALONG THE HIGHROAD"

Grégoire was a short, stout man with long hair, a face round, red, chubby, and made expressionless by a button-nose, which was decorated with a large rugose wart. The meal being over, he went out, leaving a soldier at the door, and taking no kind of note of his prisoner. François sat still. He was patient, but the afternoon was long. At dusk Citizen Grégoire reappeared, and, as François noted, was a little more amiable by reason of the vinous hospitality of the mayor. He sat down, and ordered dinner. When it came, François said tranquilly:

"Citizen Commissioner Grégoire, wouldst thou kindly consider the state of my stomach? Swallowing of swords sharpens the appetite."

The commissioner looked up from his meal. He was in the good-humored stage of drunkenness.

"Come and eat," he said, laughing.

"He hath the benevolence of the bottle," thought François. "Let us amuse him."

The commissioner took off his red bonnet, poured out a glass of wine, looked at a paper or two in his hand-bag, and set it on a seat near by, while the juggler humbly accepted the proffered place. Then the poodle was made to howl at the name of Citizen Capet, and to bark joyously at the mention of Jacobins. François told stories, played tricks, and drank freely. The commissioner drank yet more freely. François proposed to make a punch,—a juggler's punch,—and did make a drink of uncommon vigor. About nine the commissioner began to nod, and François, who had been closely studying his face, presently saw him drop into a deep slumber. The open bag looked tempting. He swiftly slipped a dexterous hand into its contents, and feeling a wallet of coin, transferred it to his own pocket. The temptation had been great, the yielding to it imprudent; but there was no one else about, except the careless guard outside the door. François concluded to replace the wallet; but at this moment the great Grégoire of the committee woke up. "That was funny," he said. "I did not quite catch the end of it."

"No," said François; "the citizen slept a little."

Grégoire became angry.

"I—I asleep? I am on duty. I never sleep on duty." The citizen was very drunk. He got up, and, staggering, set a foot on Toto's tail. The poodle yelped, and the Jacobin kicked him. "*Sacrée bête!*" The poodle, unaccustomed to outrage, retorted by a nip at a fat calf. Then the great man asserted himself.

"Hallo, there! Curse you and your dog! Landlord! landlord!" The host came in haste, and two soldiers. "Got a safe place? Lock up this sc-scoundrel, and k-kill his dog!" The landlord kindly suggested a disused wine-cellar. "Now, no delay. I'm Grégoire. Lock him up!" Having disposed of the juggler, the citizen contrived to get out of the room and to bed with loss of dignity and balance.

A few minutes sufficed to set François in a chilly cellar, the poodle at his heels; for no one took seriously the order to kill Toto. Of the two soldiers, one, who was young and much amused, brought an old blanket, and a lantern with a lighted candle set within it. Yes, the prisoner could have his knapsack and bag—there were no orders; but he must give up his sword. It was so dark that when François promptly surrendered his juggler's blade it seemed to satisfy the soldiers; for who could dream that a man would carry two swords? With a laugh and a jest, François bade them to wake him early. He called to the young recruit, as they were leaving, that he would like to have a bottle of wine, and gave him sufficient small change to insure also a bottle for these good-humored jailers.

They took the whole affair as somewhat of a practical joke. All would be well in the morning. When Grégoire was drunk he arrested everybody. The young soldier would fetch the wine in an hour. Good night.

François was alone and with leisure to consider the situation.

"Attention, Toto!" he said. This putting of thought into an outspoken soliloquy, with the judicial silence of the poodle to aid him, was probably a real assistance; for to think aloud formulates conditions and conclusions in a way useful to one untrained to reason. To read one's own mind, and to hear one's own mind, are very different things.

'Toto," he said, "we are in a bad way. Why didst thou bite that fat beast's calf? It did thee no good, thou ill-tempered brute. 'T is not good diet; a pound of it would make thee drunk. I shall have to whip thee, little beast of an aristocrat, if thou dost take to nipping the calves of the republic."

Toto well knew that he was being scolded. He leaped up and licked the thief's face.

9

"Down, Citizen Toto! Where are thy manners?
I like better Citizen Grégoire drunk than Citizen
Grégoire sober. How about my poor papa? Oh, but
I was an ass to name Despard. Didst thou observe
that the commissioner's eyebrows meet? And, Toto,
he has a great wart on his nose. 'T is a man will
fetch ill luck. I knew a thief had a wart on his nose,
and he was broken on the wheel at Rouen. Besides,
there was the wallet. Toto, attention! Thou dost
wander. It is all the doings of that *sacré* marquis. *A
bas les aristocrates!* Let us inspect a little." Upon
this he pried about every corner, tried the heavy oaken
door, still gaily talking, and at last sat on an empty
cask and considered the grated window and the
limited landscape dimly visible between its four iron
rods. The end of a woodpile, about four feet away,
was all that he could see. This woodpile set him to
thinking.

An hour later the young recruit returned with the
wine. "I came to see if thou wert safe," he said.
"Like as not Grégoire will forget all about thee to-
morrow. Wine hath a short memory."

François laughed. "*Le bon Dieu* grant it. I can
tell fortunes, but not my own." And should he tell the
citizen soldier's fortune? With much laughter it was
told, and the gifts of fateful time were showered on
the soldier's future in opulent abundance. He would
be with the army on the frontier soon. He would
marry—*dame!*—a woman rich in looks and lands. He
would be a general one day. And this, oddly enough,
came true; for he became a general of division, and
was killed the morning after at Eylau. Seeing that

this young man had agreeable fashions, the thief
ventured to express his thanks.

"Monsieur—" he began.

"Take care! *Mon Dieu!* thou must not say that;
'citizen,' please. The messieurs are as dead as the
saints, and the devil, and the *bon Dieu*, and the rest."

As he did not seem displeased, François said:

"Oh, thou art no Jacobin. Hast a *De* to thy
name?"

This recruit's manners appeared to François a good
deal like those of the young nobles whom he had
taught to fence.

"What I was is of no moment," replied the young
fellow. "The *De's* are as dead as the saints. I *am*
a soldier. But, pardon me, the citizen may be as frank
as suits his appetite for peril. I have had my belly-
ful."

"Frank? *Dame!* why not? Up-stairs I was a
Jacobin; down here I am a Royalist. I was an aide
in Gamel's fencing-school, and, *pardie!* I came away.
Thou canst do me a little service."

"Can I help thee, and not hurt myself? We—my
people—are grown scarce of late. I am the last; I
take no risks."

"There will be none. Bring me a little steel fork
and a good long bit of twine."

"A fork! What for?" He had a lad's curiosity.

"To eat with."

"But there is nothing to eat."

"Quite true. But it assists one's imagination;
and, after all, there may be to-morrow, and to eat with
decency a fork is needed. A citizen may use his bare

paws, but a monsieur may not use the fingers of equality. Thou wilt observe how the thought of these tools of luxury reminds one of messieurs and the like."

The lad—he was hardly over twenty—laughed merrily. "Thou art a delightful companion. Gamel —thou didst say Gamel?"

"I did, monsieur. Gamel that was the master of arms in the Rue St. Honoré."

"My poor brother used to fence there. By St. Denis! thou must be François!"

"I am."

"Then thou shalt have the tool of luxury. But, good heavens! take care. Thou hast a tongue which —well, I have learned to bridle mine."

"My tongue never got me into trouble; like my legs, it is long, and, like them, it has got me out of a good many scrapes. I thank thee for the warning. One knows whom to talk to. I can be silent. Oh, you may laugh. I did not speak for a day after I first saw that juggler's tool, the guillotine, in the sun on the Place de la Révolution. *Dieu!* behold there is a man that talks and laughs; and, presto, pass! there is eternal silence."

"*Âme de St. Denis!* thou art not gay," cried the soldier.

"*Tête de St. Denis* were better. He was a fellow for these times—a saint that could carry his head under his arm when it was chopped off."

The young recruit laughed, but more uneasily. Not to laugh in some fashion was among the impossibilities of life when this face-quake of mirth broke out between those wing-like ears.

He would fetch the tools, and, in fact, did so in a few minutes. Then he bade François good night, and went away. As soon as he had gone, François retired to a corner with his lantern to inspect the wallet. There were three louis, a few sous, and no more. The risk was large, the profit small. In an inner pocket was a thin, folded paper. When opened it seemed to be a letter in due form, dated a month before, but never sent. It was addressed to Citizen de la Vicomterie of the Great Committee. François whistled. It was a furious attack on Robespierre and Couthon, and an effort to sum up the strength which an assault on the great leaders would command in the Convention—a rash document for those days. Clearly the writer, whose full signature of Pierre Grégoire was appended, had wisely hesitated to send it.

"It seems to have been forgotten. Was he drunk, Toto? Surely now we must get out and away. 'T is a letter of death; 't is a passport worth many louis, Toto." He pulled off a shoe, folded the paper neatly, and pulling up a tongue of leather on the inside sole, placed the letter underneath, and put on the shoe again. He took the louis, threw the wallet under a cask, and waited.

When the house was still he set to work. He had found behind a barrel a long staff used to measure the height of wine in casks. On the end of this he tied securely, crosswise, the steel fork, and then began to inspect the thin rods of the window, which were but ill fitted to guard a man of resources.

"Art still too fat?" he said, as he lifted Toto and managed to squeeze him between the bars. After that

he began to fish with his stick and fork for a small
log which had fallen from the woodpile and was just
a foot or two out of reach.   Twice he had it, and twice
it broke loose, but now Toto understood, and, seizing
the log, dragged it nearer.   At last François had the
prize.   The rest was easy.   He set the log between
the thin bars, and threw on this lever all the power of
one of the strongest men in Paris.   In place of breaking, the iron rod bent and drew out of its sockets.   A
second proved as easy, and at last the window-space
was free.   It seemed large enough.   He concluded to
leave his bag; but the knapsack he set outside, and
also his weapons and the conjuring-balls.   Next he
stripped off most of his clothes, and laid these too on
the far side of the window.   Finally his legs were
through, and his hips.   But when it came to the
shoulders he was in trouble.   It seemed impossible.
He felt the poor poodle pulling at his foot, and had
hard work to restrain his laughter.   "*Dame!* would
I grin at *Mère Guillotine?*   Who knows?   How to
shrink?"   He wriggled; he emptied his chest of air;
he turned on his side; and, leaving some rags and a
good bit of skin on the way, he was at last outside.
Here, having reclothed himself, he broke up the wine-
measurer and threw the fork over the wall.   In a few
minutes he was on the highway, and running lightly
at the top of his speed.   At dawn he found a farm-
house which seemed to be deserted—no rare thing in
those days.   He got in at a window, and stayed for
two days, without other food than the crusts he had
carried from the cellar.   The night after, weak and
hungry, he walked till dawn; and being now a good

ten leagues from that terrible commissioner, he ventured to buy a good dinner and to get himself set over the Seine. Somewhat reassured, he asked the way to Evreux, and, for once in his life perplexed and thoughtful, went along without a word to Toto.

He had been three weeks on the way, owing to his need to hide or to make wide circuits in order to avoid the larger towns. It was now the February of northern France, and there was sometimes a little snow, but more often a drizzling rain. He had suffered much from cold; but as he strode along, with a mind more at ease, he took pleasure in the sunshine. A night wind from the north had dried the roads. It was calm, cold in the shadows, deliciously warm on the sun-lit length of yellow highway. He had lost time,—quite too much,—but he still hoped to reach Musillon before that man with the wart arrived. If so, he would see Despard, warn him as to Grégoire, and, with this claim, and their old partnership, on which he counted less, he might get his passport altered, and lose himself somewhere. If he had to remain in the town, he must see, or be presumed to have seen, that sick father, and must be promptly adopted if by cruel circumstances he became unable to journey far enough from Paris to feel secure. The distorted face of Amar haunted him—the man who, to save his own life, would not even make believe to forgive. He had no power within him to explain a man like Amar; and because the Jacobin was to him incomprehensible, he was more than humanly terrible. What possessed that devil of a marquis to turn up? And was he now at his château? And why had Achille Gamel set down Normandy in the passport? And why had he himself been fool enough to fill up the vacant place for the name of his destination with that of the only small town he could recall in that locality? He had been in haste, and now a net seemed to be gathering about him. He must go thither, or take perilous chances. He was moving toward a fateful hour.

"Toto," he said, "let us laugh; for I like not the face of to-morrow."

## XV

*How François finds Despard and has a lesson in politics, and of what came of it.*

AT evening he ventured to enter an inn at Soluce. A good bed and ample diet restored his courage; but he learned that the citizen with a wart, and an escort of a dozen soldiers, had passed the day before, on their way to Evreux. Would he remain there, this friendly commissioner? No one knew. Evreux was Jacobin to the core. Then he thought of the marquis; it was well to be informed.

Yes; the Citizen Ste. Luce lived beyond Musillon.

The citizen juggler declared that he had once been in his service, but now that all men were equal, he could not lower the dignity of an equalized nation by serving him longer. He learned that the château of the marquis had not suffered, nor he, as he was never known to be absent, and no one molested him. This did not surprise François. In the South, at an earlier date, the peasants had burned hundreds of châteaux, but these riots had been mercilessly put down. The Jacobins meant to have peace in France, and at cost of blood, if that was requisite. To have peace at

home was essential to the success of national defense
on the frontier.   In many parts of France, throughout the whole of the Terror, very many large land-
owners were undisturbed.   In fact, the Terror, and its
precedent punishments, fell with strange irregularity
on the provinces.   The Dukes de Bethune-Charost, de
Luynes, de Nivernais, and others who had not been
active in politics, remained unhurt on their estates.
For the *émigrés* was reserved a bitter hatred.   Nor can
we wonder at this result of the vast exodus which
took place from '89 to '91—"*l'émigration joyeuse*," as it
was called by those who carried off means enough to
live gay lives in Brussels while their country was in
the convulsions of great social and political change.

François made haste to leave at dawn, and by night-
fall was close to the town of Musillon.   He found a
wood road, and was soon deep in one of the marquis's
forests.   In a quiet glade among rocks he put his
effects in security, and, charging Toto to guard them,
set out to inspect the town.   The poodle did not like
it.   He ran back and forth, whining.

"Oh, stop that!" cried François.   "Go back!
Dost thou hear?"

Toto lay down, and set himself to secure what comfort the situation afforded.

Meanwhile François took to the main road until
close to the village, and then left it for the fields, cautiously nearing the town, a small place of some twelve
hundred souls.   A monotonous double line of scattered
one-story stone houses lay along the highway.   Avoiding the village, François moved past and around the
red-roofed Norman farm-houses which lay off from

the main highway.  Mounds of earth set around the houses walled in an orchard and an inclosure of many acres, so that, seen from the exterior, they had the appearance of being fortified.  The lights were out, and François saw no one.  Now and then a sentinel dog barked as the wanderer went by the gateways, in wonder at this unusual style of fence.  At last he turned again toward the road.

The town was quiet.  It was after nine at night. Having purposely lingered thus long, François approached the back of the inn, and became sure that it was empty of guests.  A little beyond it was the village church, and as this was lighted, he approached it with care.  The crosses of the burial-ground were gone.  He stumbled over graves, and at last, standing on a tomb, got a fair glimpse of the interior of the church, for many of its windows were broken.  It was full of people, and the murmur of noisy debate came to his ears.  He felt that he must learn what was going on.  With this in view, he kept under the deep shadow of the wall, and soon saw that the outer porch was crowded with men and women, listening through the open door.  Favored by the darkness, he got unobserved into this mass of deeply occupied people, and was able at last to catch a little of what was going on.  Yes; this was the club of Jacobins which his partner Despard had been sent to organize, one of the hundreds which soon conquered and led opinion all through the provinces.

He caught the usual denunciation of *émigrés* and of the *ci-devant* aristocrats.  He had heard it all before; it did not help him.

Very soon an elderly man in peasant dress arose near the door. He spoke of something which they had considered as well to be done soon. He thought it better to wait until Citizen Commissioner Grégoire arrived. To arrest a *ci-devant* aristocrat like Ste. Luce was of course proper; but the people were excited, and might do mischief, and they knew that the Great Committee did not approve of riots. France must have rest. These outbreaks had ended elsewhere in the deaths of hundreds of peasants. He bade them wait, and, in fact, spoke with rare good sense. He was roughly interrupted. His speech was received with laughter and contemptuous cries, and, to François's amazement, there was Despard on his feet, not twenty feet away. His old partner was somber-looking and red-eyed, but seemed to have lost his shyness of speech. He broke out into violent invectives, charging the previous speaker with indifference to the good of France. This man was no doubt a traitor. He had been in the service of the *ci-devant.* He had advised the people to wait. Were they not the rulers? The Jacobin clubs would see to this rat of a commissioner; let him come. Then, leaping on a chair, he began to contrast the luxury in which Ste. Luce lived with the meager life of the peasant. He talked of the great noble's younger life, of his debauchery and hardness. All knew what he meant. Not he alone had suffered. How many of the children men liked to call their own were of noble blood?

His fluent passion, his ease of speech, his apparent freedom from his usual mood of fear, astonished François. At last Despard became more excited,

raved wildly, grew incoherent, paused, burst into horrors of blasphemous allusion, and, utterly exhausted,
reeled, and dropped into his chair, amid wild applaud-
ing cries and a dozen vain efforts of speakers eager to
be heard.   As if satisfied, the crowd waited no longer
to listen, and issued out in just the mood Despard
had desired to create.   François stepped aside, unnoticed.   Among the last, surrounded by a gesticulating group, came Despard, silent, exhausted, his head
bent down.   A voice cried out: "To-night!   Let us
do it to-night!"   Despard said slowly: "No, not to-
night.   He is not there—he is not there.   Perhaps
to-morrow; we shall see.   I must have rest—rest."

"Is he mad?" thought François.   "*Diable!*   How
he hates him!   Why is he not afraid?"   He had once
heard the choir-master tell of a feeble, timid nun who
had killed two people; and this man, he supposed,
might be, like her, crazed.   No matter; he must use
him.   The crowd dispersed, and, following Despard at
a distance, François saw him enter the house of the
village priest, who had long since said his last prayer
in the garden of the Carmelites.

For an hour, and until all was still, François
walked to and fro behind the house.   Suddenly a
door opened and closed.   François moved around the
house.   He saw Despard go out on the road.   After
looking about him, the Jacobin walked swiftly away,
and was soon past the farthest houses.

"*Dame!*" said François, "let us go after him.
What can he mean?   It becomes amusing."   Moving
with care in the shadows at the side of the road, he
followed Despard, who walked down the middle of

the highway, now and then stopping short and cracking his finger-joints, as he used to do when worried,
or clasping his hands over the back of his neck.

The thief smiled as he went. He was again the
savage of the streets, with all his keen wits in play,
and vaguely aware of pleasure in the use of his training. He looked about him, or stole noiselessly from
one depth of gloom to another across some less shad-
owed place. He put out with care one long leg and
then the other tentatively, like great feelers, and yet
got over the ground with speed, as was required, for
Despard walked at a rate which was unusual. The
great ears of his pursuer were on guard. Once, when
Despard stopped of a sudden, François was near
enough to hear him crack his knuckles as he pulled at
them. As Pierre stood, he threw up a hand as it were
in the eager gesture of a speech, or in silent, custom-
born attestation of some mentally recorded vow.
Then he went onward, silent, and was for a moment
lost to view in the aisles of the forest into which he
turned. François moved faster, dimly seeing him
again. The Jacobin hurried on. The man who followed him was smiling in the darkness, and was feeding curiosity with the keen satisfaction he felt in a
chase which was not without a purpose.

Despard seemed to know the great forest well. It
soon became more open. He came to a low garden
wall, and, climbing it, was heard to tumble on the
farther side with a crash of breaking earthenware.
He had come down on a pile of garden pots. The
thief reflected for a moment that his partner must
have lost the agility of his former business, and him-

self approached the wall with care. Moving to one side, he dropped to the ground, as quiet as a prowling cat.

There was no moon, but the night was clear, and over against the star-lit space he saw the silhouette of a vast château—angles, gables, turrets with vanes. The man whom he hunted moved across the garden, through rose-hedges, under trees, as if reckless as to being heard. Once he fell, but got up without even an exclamation; and so on and on in stumbling haste until he stood upon the broad terrace in front of the building.

François was for a little while at leisure to look about him. Despard, with a sudden movement, strode to the foot of the broad steps which led up to the lofty doorway of the château. Here again he stayed motionless. François, now used to the partial obscurity of the night, took quick note of the white gleam of vases, of a fountain's monotonous murmur, of statues, dim gray blurs seen against the dark wood-spaces beyond; the great size of the house he saw, and that three or four windows showed lights within.

What was Despard about to do? François waited. Then he heard now and then, rising and falling, the faint notes of a violoncello. At this moment he saw that Pierre was gesticulating, and at last caught sound of speech. He was too far away to be clearly seen or distinctly heard. François sat down, took off his shoes, tied them over his neck, and went down on all fours. It was one of his old tricks to amuse thus the children gathered before the show-booth. He could become a bear or an elephant, and knew how to

simulate the walk of beasts. Now he approached
Despard on his hands and feet, and, seen in the partial
gloom, would have seemed a queer-looking animal.
A closely clipped row of box lay between them and
bordered the broad roadway leading to the portal.

His approach was noiseless. Even if it had not
been, it is unlikely that Despard would have noticed
it. The quadruped knelt, and set his eyes to see and
his ears to hear, being now only six feet away. His
own fate was deeply involved. He cared little for the
marquis, but up out of the dark of memory came the
tender sweetness of the face of the widowed daughter.
No word of her brief pleading was forgotten by this
man who craved regard, affection, respect, consideration—all that he had not. It was only a flash of
thought, and again he was intently receptive.

Despard stood, shaking his arms wildly, looking
here and there, up and down. At last he spoke, and
so loud that François watched him, amazed at his unnatural lack of caution.

"To-morrow I, Pierre Despard, shall be master. I
shall no more be afraid. I shall see thee tremble on
the tumbrel. I shall see thee shudder at the knife."

François had an uncontrollable shiver, predictive,
sympathetic. Could he trust this creature? There
was no help for it. He recalled with a smile one of
the Crab's proverbs: "Monsieur Must is a man to
trust." She had many and vile sayings; this was one
of the few that were not swine-wisdom.

As the man went on speaking, his hands threatened
the silent house or snatched at some unseen thing.
He stood again moveless for a moment, and then

threw out his hands as if in appeal, and called aloud:
"Renée! Renée! art thou here? Oh, could he not
have spared thee to me—to me, who had so little?
And he had so much! Oh, for the name he should
have spared thee! For the shame—the shame. Renée, his own child's name. My Renée is dead, and
his—his Renée lives; but not long—not long."

"*Dieu!*" murmured François. "Let him have the
man. *Dame!* I should have killed him long ago."

Pierre was raving, and was only at times to be understood. He seemed to be seeing this lost Renée, and
was now rational and again incoherent or foolishly
vague.

François hesitated; but at this moment a window
on the second floor was cast open, and a man, who
may have heard Despard, showed himself. François
looked up, and saw a slight figure framed in the window-space clear against the light behind him.

Despard cried out in tones of terror: "The marquis! the marquis!" and, turning, fled down the terrace and along the avenue.

"Queer, that," muttered François. "He is afraid.
I must have him." He put on his shoes in haste, and
with great strides pursued the retreating figure, hearing, as he ran, the servant crying from the window,
"Who goes there?"

A hundred yards away from the house, Despard,
terrified at the nearing steps, turned into a side alley,
and at last tore through a thicket to the left.

In an instant François had him by the collar. The
captured man screamed like a child in a panic of alarm,
while François shook him as a terrier shakes a rat.

10

"*Mille tonnerres!* idiot, keep quiet! Don't kick; it is no use. Thou wilt have the whole house after thee. 'T is I—François. Keep quiet! Look at me—François. Dost not hear?" At last he was quieted.

"What scared thee, *mon ami?*"

"I saw him—I saw the marquis! I saw him!"

"Monsieur—the marquis? He is thrice that fellow's size."

They were now seated on the ground, Despard panting, and darting quick glances to right and left like a frightened animal.

"Come, Pierre, tell me what all this means. Art gone clean out of thy wits?"

"Why dost thou ask? Thou dost know well enough. I have waited—waited. Now I have him."

"*Dame!* Thou? Thou wilt never face him. Thou art afraid."

"I am now. I shall not be to-morrow night. There will be hundreds. I shall look! I shall see!"

"For Heaven's sake," cried François, "talk a little sense. A man who fears a mouse to talk of killing this terrible fellow!"

"The law will kill him, not I. The law—the knife."

"Stuff! A certain commissioner, Grégoire, is after thee, and, worse, after me. He hath a wart on his nose. I ran away to avoid those cursed Jacobins. Passport all right—name of Jean François. Mind thee! My father is old and failing. Thou wilt have to find me a papa. Grégoire has—he has doubts, this Grégoire. So have I. When I told him you were my friend, he shut me up in a cellar, and that I liked not. I was a fool to run away; but, *mon Dieu!* there was my errand—to see that poor father—all set out on my passport, and the man with the wart inquisitive. I had to get here and find my papa."

Another man's difficulties took off Pierre's mind from his own. He was clear enough now, and asked questions, some hard to answer, but all reasonable.

François related his story. The fencing-master had fallen under suspicion and run away. He, François, likewise suspected, had got a passport from a Jacobin fencing-pupil, and come hither to fall on the neck of his dear friend Pierre. It was neat, and hung together well. It had many omissions, and as a whole lacked the fundamental quality of truth, but it answered. When a man's head is set to save his head, it may not always be desirable to be accurate.

Pierre reflected; then he cried out suddenly: "This Grégoire! That for him! Let him take care. Art thou still a Royalist?"

François was a Jacobin of the best, unjustly suspected. He was eager to know what deviltry was in Pierre's mind as to this marquis; and there, too, was the daughter. If he meant to stir these peasants to riot in order to gratify himself and his well-justified hatred, that might sadly influence François's fate. The central power in Paris was merciless to lawless violence which did not aid its own purposes.

François talked on and on slackly, getting time to think. Pierre's speech had troubled him. He was puzzled as he saw more distinctly the nature of the man whom he was forced to trust. He did not analyze him. He merely apprehended and distrusted one who was to-day a shrinking coward and to-morrow a man to be feared less for what he might do than for what he might lead others to do when himself remote from sources of immediate physical fear. François did not—could not—fully know that he was now putting himself in the power of one who was the victim of increasing attacks of melancholy, with intervals of excitement during which the victim was eagerly homicidal, and possessed for a time the recklessness and the cunning of the partly insane.

"Come," said François, at last; "you must hide me until you can find me that papa, or until Citizen Grégoire has come and gone. I like him not."

"Nor I," said Pierre. "But let him take care; I am not a man to be played with."

François said he should think not, but that if he meditated an attack on that miserable *ci-devant* yonder, it were better to wait until Grégoire had come and gone.

This caution seemed to awaken suspicion. Pierre turned, and caught François's arm. "Thou art a spy —a spy of the Convention!"

"Thou must be more fond of a joke than was once thy way. Nonsense! I could go back and warn the marquis. That would serve the republic, and well, too; for, by Heaven! if thou art of a mind to burn houses, Robespierre will shorten thee by a head in no time."

"Who talks of burning houses? Am I a fool? I— Despard?"

"No, indeed. Thou—" François needed the man's help, and felt that he was risking his own safety. He

must at least seem to trust him. "Dost thou mean
to arrest Ste. Luce?"

"I do."

"But when?"

"Oh, in a day or two; no hurry."

François knew that he was hearing a lie. "Good,"
he said. "But I advise thee against violence."

"There will be none. I control these people. Thou
shouldst see; thou shouldst hear me speak."

"Let us go," said François, and they returned to
the village without a word on either side. The hamlet
was quiet. At the priest's door François said: "Wait
for me. I must fetch my bundle and Toto. I left them
in the wood." Pierre would wait. In an hour his ex-
partner came back, and before he could knock was
admitted by the anxious Jacobin.

When they were within the house, he told François
that he lived alone. An old woman cooked for him,
and came in the morning and went away at dusk.
He, François, should have the garret; and, this being
settled, they carried thither cold meats, bread, cheese,
wine, and water, so as to provision the thief for a few
days. There would be time to talk later. François
asked a single question, saying frankly that he had
heard Pierre speak to his club. Certainly he had
power over the people. What was it he had meant to
do, and when? Despard hesitated. Then the cunning of a crumbling mind came to his aid, and he replied lightly:

"We shall wait till Grégoire has gone. I told thee
so already. Thy advice was good. I do not know.
We shall see—we shall see." The door closed after

him. The man, descending the stair, paused of a sudden, the prey of suspicion. Why did François come hither? Was he a spy of the marquis—of the Convention? He feared François. To one in his state of mind little obstacles seem large, great obstacles small. He must watch him. He was in his power.

The man left within the room was not less suspicious. He hung a cover over the single window, locked the door, and lay down, with Toto at his feet, and at his side his rapier and pistols. He slept a tranquil sleep. Most of the next day he sat at the window, watching through a slit in the curtain the street below him. People came and went; groups gathered about the desecrated church; there was much excitement, but he could hear nothing. At dusk he saw a number of men, some with sticks and pikes, come toward the priest's house. Owing to his position, he lost sight of them as they came nearer, but from the noise below he presumed them to have entered. He was, for many reasons, indisposed to remain uninformed. He waited. The noise increased. Pierre had not come to visit him, as he had said he would; and where was that much-desired father? He laughed. "Ah, Toto, one must needs be his own papa." He had gone about all day in his stocking-feet to avoid being overheard. Now he bade Toto be quiet, and, opening the door, went cautiously down the stone stairway. It was quite dark. On the last landing he stood, intently listening. The hallway below was full of men, and evidently the two rooms on the ground floor were as crowded. He overheard Despard's voice, angry and strenuous. The words he could not catch, but the comments of those in the wide hall were enough. The commissioner was coming, and would interfere. Despard was right. The marquis was about to fly, to emigrate. He must be arrested. They poured out, shouting, tumultuous, to join the excited mob in the street.

François went quickly up the stair. He cared little for the marquis, but he cared much for the pale lady whose face was stamped in his memory. Moreover, all this ruin and threatened bloodshed were not to his mind. A day's reflection had enabled him to conclude that, between Grégoire and Despard, the situation was perilous, and that he had better disappear from the scene. Meanwhile he would warn the marquis, and then go his way.

He put on his shoes, took his bundle, his arms, and Toto, and, with his cloak on his shoulder, slipped quietly down-stairs. The house was empty. He went out the back way unseen, observing that the church was lighted, and seeing a confused mass of noisy peasants about the door.

## XVI

*How François warns the Marquis de Ste. Luce, and of the
battle on the staircase between the old day and the
new.*

T was now close to nine, and again a
bright, cold, starry night. A long cir-
cuit brought him to the highroad. A
mile away he struck into a broad avenue,
and, never pausing, pushed on. His
sense of locality was acute and like that of an animal.
Once or twice he was sure that he heard dull noises
behind him when the sharp night wind blew from the
village.

"Ah, Toto," he murmured, "keep thou close to heel.
This is our greatest adventure. I would we were out
of it. Ah, the château!" He ran across the flower-
beds, and with long leaps up the steps, and sounded
a strong summons on the knocker of the great door.

A servant opened it. "Where is the marquis?"
What the man said he did not wait to hear. The
lofty hall was dark, but the principal staircase was
lighted faintly from above. Without a word, François hurried past the servant and up the stairs. From
the broad landing he saw beyond him a lighted draw-

ing-room, and heard the notes of a violoncello. There
was the woman, pale and beautiful, in black, her face
upturned, the boy holding before her a sheet of music.
The human richness of the cello's tones sounded
through the great chamber. Where had he seen the
like? Ah, that picture in the vestry of Notre Dame
—the face of St. Cecilia! He had a moment of intense joy at having come. Till then he had doubted
if it were wise. As he stood, the marquis came toward him quickly from the side of the room, and two
gentlemen left a card-table and started up.

François went in at once, meeting the marquis
within the room. The music ceased; the woman
cried, "*Mon Dieu!*" Every one stared at this strange
figure.

"What is it, my man? *Ventre St. Gris!* 't is my
thief! This way," and he led him aside into a little
room, while the rest, silent and troubled, looked after
them.

"Monsieur, to waste no words, these cursed peasants
are on their way to do here what mischief the devil
knows. It is you they want. There is a fool, one
Despard, who leads them. But, *Dieu!* there is small
time to think."

François, breathless, panting, stood looking about
him, now as always observant, and curious as to this
wonderful room and this impassive gentleman. Toto,
as well blown as his master, recognizing the value of
a soft rug, dropped, head on legs, meaning to have at
least the minute's luxury and rest.

The marquis stood still in thought a moment. "I
am greatly obliged to you; and this is twice—twice.

I expected trouble, but not so soon. Come this way."

François followed. Toto kept one eye on him, and slept with the other. As they reëntered the great salon, the two gentlemen and Mme. Renée, all visibly agitated, came to meet them. "What is it?" they asked. The marquis forestalled further inquiry.

"My daughter, our kindly peasants will be here in an hour—no, half an hour, or less. Resistance is useless. To fly is to confess the need to fly; it is not to my taste. You gentlemen are better out of this. Go at once—at once!"

"Yes, go!" said madame. "You cannot help us, and can only make bad worse."

They wasted no time, and few words passed. The little drama played itself quickly.

"Adieu, madame!" Madame courtesied. The boy walked over and stood by his grandfather. He looked up at his clear-cut face, with its cold smile, and then at the backs of the retiring gentlemen. He had a boy's sense of these being deserters. They were gone in hot haste.

Mme. Renée came nearer. "We thank you—I thank you"; and she put out her hand. François took it awkwardly. A touch of the hand of this high-bred, saintly lady, *grande dame* and true woman, singularly disturbed the man. The tremor of a strange emotion ran over him. He let fall the soft hand, and drew himself up to the full of his unusual height, saying: "It is little—very little."

"And now you must go," she said; "and at once."

"Of course—of course," said Ste. Luce. "Out the

back way. Victor will show you." There were no
further thanks. All such common men had served
the great noble; it seemed of the nature of things.
But the woman said:

"God protect you! God will know to thank you.
I cannot fitly. Go—go!"

"I do not mean to go," said François. "Hark! it
is too late." He knew not then, or ever, why he stayed.
The boy looked up at him. Here was another kind
of man, and not a gentleman, either. Why did he
not go?

An old majordomo came with uncertain steps of
nervous haste, crying: "The servants are gone,
monsieur! The people are coming up the avenue!
*Mon Dieu!*"

"Indeed! Now be off with you, Master Thief."

"No." His head said, "Go"; his heart said,
"Stay."

"By St. Denis, but you are a fool!"

François muttered that he had been that always,
and then felt the hand of the boy touch his own. He
called: "Toto! Toto! We will stay." And the dog,
at ease in all society, selected a yet softer rug.

The marquis troubled himself no further as to François. He went out of the room, and was back in a minute, while the uproar increased, and Mme. Renée, at the
window, pleaded with the thief, urging him to fly, or
cried: "They are coming! Oh, a crowd—a mob—
with torches and arms! The saints protect us! Why
will you not go? Oh, *mon père*—father! thou hast thy
rapier. What canst thou against hundreds—hundreds?"

The marquis smiled. "*Costume de rigueur*, my dear. There will be no bloodshed, my child."

"And they will all run," cried the boy. "And if grandpapa has to surrender, he must give up his sword. When my papa was taken in America, he had to—"

"Hush!" said the mother. The lad was singularly outside of the tragic shadows of the hour.

François all this while stood near the window, his cloak cast back, his queer, smile-lit face intent now on the mob without, now on the woman, the boy, the man. "*Dame!*" he muttered. "We are in dangerously high society." He set his knapsack aside, cast off his cloak, loosened his rapier in its sheath, looked to the priming of his pistols, and waited to see what would happen when this yelling thing out yonder should burst into action.

"They must have made mad haste, madame."

"They are on the terrace. Mother of Heaven!" cried the woman. "They wait! A man is speaking to them. They have torches. Some go—some go to right around the house." A stone splintered the window-glass, and she fell back. "Wretches!"

The marquis turned to her. "Stay here. I go to receive our guests."

"No, no!"

"Do as I tell thee. Be still." She caught the boy to her, and fell into a chair, sobbing. The marquis called to the quaking majordomo: "Take those two candelabra. Set them at the foot of the staircase—the foot." The old servant obeyed without words. The marquis went by him. He seemed to have for-

gotten François, who glanced at Mme. Renée and followed the master of the house.

There had been a moment's lull outside. The double
stairway swept down to a landing, and then in one
noble descent to the great deserted hall, where the
faded portraits of lord and lady looked down among
armor and trophies of war and chase.

"Put those lights there—and there. Get two more
—quick! Set them on the brackets below. One must
see. Put out the lights in the drawing-room. What,
you here yet, Master Thief? What the devil are you
doing here? The deuce!" As he spoke they were
standing together on the broad landing, before them
the great stair which led down to the illuminated hall
below. The marquis had meant to meet these people
outside; he was quiet, cool, the master of many resources. Surprised at the suddenness of the outbreak,
he still counted, with the courage of habit, on his personal influence and address. As the marquis spoke,
the roar without broke forth anew. A shower of
stones clattered on door and wall and window with
sharp crash and tinkle of breaking glass. It was followed by an indescribable tumult—shouts, laughter,
the shrill voices of women, a multitudinous appeal to
fear, ominous, such as no man could hear unmoved.
The animal we call a mob was there—the thing of
moods, like a madman, now destructive, now as a
brute brave, now timid as a house-fly.

They beat on the great doors, and of a sudden
seemed to discover that the servants, in flying, had
not secured them. The doors gave way, and those in
front were hurled into the hall by the pressure of

those behind. In an instant it was half full of peasants armed with all manner of rude weapons. A
dozen had torches of sheep's wool wrapped about
pitchforks and soaked with tar. Their red flames
flared up, with columns above of thick smoke. There
were women, lads. None had muskets. Some looked
about them, curious. Those without shouted and
pressed to get in; but this was no longer easy. A
few of the boldest began to move up the lower steps
of the great staircase. At the landing above, in partial obscurity, stood the marquis and François. On
the next rise behind them were Mme. Renée and her
boy, unnoticed, unwilling to be left alone. The stairway and all above it were darker than the red-lighted
hall, where ravage was imminent. A man struck
with a butcher's mallet a suit of armor. It rang with
the blow, and fell with clang and rattle, hurting a
boy, who screamed. The butcher leaped on the ped-
estal and yelled, waving one of the iron gauntlets.
They who hesitated, leaderless, at the foot of the dark
ascent turned at the sound of the tumbled past.

The marquis cried aloud, "Halt, there!"

Some mischievous lad outside cast a club at the
side window of the hall, and the quartered arms of
Ste. Luce, De Rohan, and their kin fell with sharp,
jangling notes on the floor and on the heads of the
crowd.

"Halt, I say!" The voice rang out of the gloom,
strong and commanding. The marquis's sword was
out. "Draw, my charming thief. *Morituri te salu-
tant!*"

"What?" cried François—"what is that?"

"Nothing. We are about to die; that is all. Let us send some couriers to Hades. You should have gone away. Now you are about to die."

François drew his long rapier. He was strangely elated. "We are going to die, Toto." The dog barked furiously. "Keep back!" cried his master. Then he heard Pierre Despard's shrill voice cry out: "Surrender, Citizen Ste. Luce, or it will be worse for thee." The mob screamed: "Despard! Despard!" He was hustled forward, amid renewed shouts, cries, crash of falling vases, and jangling clatter of broken glass. The reluctant leader tried to keep near to the door. The mob was of other mind. He was thrust through the press to the foot of the stair, with cries of "Vive Despard! Vive Despard!" The people on the stair, fearing no resistance, were pushed up, shouting, "*À bas les émigrés!*"

"Now, then!" cried the marquis. "Get back there, dogs!" The two blades shot out. A man fell; another, touched in the shoulder, screamed, and leaped over the balustrade; the rest fell away, one man on another, with shrieks and groans. François caught a lad climbing on the outside of the gilded rail, and, with a laugh, threw him on the heads of those below. A joy unknown before possessed the thief—the lust of battle, the sense of competency. He took in the whole scene, heart, mind, and body alive as never before.

"*Sang de St. Denis!* You are a gallant man. But we are lost. They will be on our backs in a moment; I hear them." Amid a terrible din, stones and sticks flew. A pebble struck the marquis in the face.

"*Dame!*" he cried, furious, and darted down a step or two, the quick rapier mercilessly stabbing here and there. One madder than the rest set a torch to a priceless tapestry. It flared up, lighting the great space and the stair, and doing in the end no harm. Despard, terrified, was pushed forward to the edge of the fallen bodies on the staircase.

"Surrender!" he called out in a shriek of fear, for here before him were the two men he most dreaded on earth. The noise was indescribable. The butcher beat with the iron gauntlet on a shield beside him; then he threw the steel glove at François. It flew high. There was a cry from the space behind. The little boy screamed shrilly, "They have killed my mama!"

François looked behind him. There was now light enough, and too much. He saw the woman lying, a convulsed, tumbled heap, on the stair. The marquis glanced behind him, and lost his cool quietude. He ran down the stair, stabbing furiously. A half-dozen dead and wounded lay before him. In an instant he was back again beside François, his face bleeding from the stones and sticks thrown at him. François was standing, tall and terrible in his anger, a pistol in his hand.

"Shall I kill him, monsieur?"

"By Heaven, yes!"

The pistol resounded terribly in the vaulted space, and the brute who had thrown the gauntlet, swaying, screamed shrilly, and tumbled—dead.

"Give me your hand!" cried the marquis. "Thank you, monsieur; the devil hath a recruit. Now follow me. Let us kill and die. To hell with this rabble!"

"Wait," cried François, and, running down the steps, put out a long arm and caught Despard. He hauled him savagely after him, calling out, "Hold the stair a moment!" In an instant he was on the landing above, with his prey. His sword he let fall, and set a pistol to Despard's head. The terror of the trapped Jacobin was pitiful. He prayed for life. He would let them all go; he would—he would. François swung him round to face the suddenly silenced mob. "Keep still, or I will scatter your brains, fool! Tell them to go! Tell them to go, or, *sang de Dieu!* thou art a dead man!"

Pierre screamed out his orders: "Go—go—all of you. I order—go!"

The beast he had trained and led was of no such mind. A man called out, "Die like a man, coward!" A stone or two flew. . One struck him. The storm broke out anew.

"Say thy prayers. Thou art dead. Shall I kill him, monsieur?"

"No, no; not that man—not him!"

"Mercy!" screamed Despard.

"The deuce!" laughed François. "It gets warm, monsieur. What to do with this coward? Keep still, insect!"

The mob had for a little time enough of these terrible swordsmen on the stair. It was awed, helpless. Below lay, head down or athwart, three dead men, and certain wounded, unable to crawl. The mob shrank away, and, with eyes red in the glare, swayed

11

to and fro, indecisive, swearing. For a moment no more missiles were thrown. They awaited the expected attack from the rear of the house.

Pierre hung, a limp, inert thing, one arm on the balustrade, the thief's strong clutch on his neck, making his shivering bulk a shield against stick and stone.

"It will soon be over," said the marquis, quietly. "There! I thought so."

A dull roar was heard, and the crash of broken glass from somewhere behind them.

This signal set loose the cowed mob. Clubs and stones flew. Something struck Pierre. He squealed like a hurt animal, pain and terror in the childlike cry. More men crowded in, and the mass, with shout and cry, surged forward, breaking mirrors and vases, with frantic joy in the clatter of destruction.

"It is serious this time," cried the marquis. "Adieu, my brave fellow." Another tapestry flared up, slowly burning. "Let us take toll, François. Come!"

"Good, monsieur! But my fool here—"

At this moment the crowd at the door divided. A dozen soldiers broke in, and with them the man of the wart—Grégoire.

"*Dame!*" cried François; "the Commissioner Grégoire! The wart! It is time to leave."

"Order, here," shouted Grégoire, "in the name of the law!" The guard pushed in and made a lane. One or two persistent rioters were collared and passed out. A dead silence fell on all. The shreds of the tapestry dropped. The mob fell back.

"Help! help!" cried Pierre.

"*Morbleu!* dost thou want to die?"

"It is over," said the marquis. "I prefer my peasants."

Grégoire called out, "Where is the mayor?" A reluctant little man appeared.

"Commissioner, these men have slain citizens," he said.

"And they did well. France wants order. Out with you all, or I shall fire on you. Citizens indeed! See to that stuff burning."

The peasants, awed, slunk away. Grégoire coolly mounted the stairs.

"Hold!" cried the marquis.

"I arrest thee in the name of the law! Here is my order."

The marquis took it.

"The light is bad," he said; "but I see it is in good form. The law I obey—and muskets"; and then, in a half-whisper to François: "Run! run! I will hold the stairs."

Grégoire overheard him.

"The citizen *émigré!* I arrest him!" and he went up a step.

"Back!" cried the marquis, lunging fiercely at the too adventurous commissioner, who leaped down the stairway with the agility of alarm.

"Fire!" he cried.

"Thanks, monsieur; I can help you no more!" cried François. As he spoke, he hurled the unhappy Despard on top of the commissioner. They fell in a heap. The thief, catching up his rapier, was off and away through the drawing-room, seeing, as he went, the woman lying on the floor, her forehead streaming blood. He picked up his cloak and knapsack, and, followed by Toto, ran for his life down a long corridor to the left. At the end, he threw open a window, and dropped, with the dog under his arm, upon the roof of a portico over a side door. No one was near. He called the dog, and fled through the gardens and into the woods of the chase.

*Of how François, escaping, lives in the wood; of how he sees the daughter of the marquis dying, and knows not then, or ever after, what it was that hurt him; of how he becomes homesick for Paris.*

HE forest was of great extent, and inter-sected by wood roads. Along one of these François ran for an hour or more, until he was tired, and had put, as he believed, some miles between himself and the citizen with the wart. The way became more narrow, the forest more dense. At last there was only a broad path. Now and then he saw the north star, and knew that he was traveling southward. He came out at dawn on an open space, rocky and barren, a great rabbit-warren, as he knew by the sudden stampede of numberless rabbits. He turned aside into the woods, and a few hundred yards away found a bit of marsh, and beyond it a brook, with leaf-cov-ered space beneath tall plane-trees, now bare of foli-age. He drank deep of the welcome water, and sat down with Toto to rest and think.

"*Mon ami*," he said, "we like adventures; but this was a little too much." Then he laughed at the thought of Pierre's terror; but the man with the wart was not so funny, and the poor lady who was St. Cecilia, and that cold-blooded devil of a marquis— "What a man!"

Here were rabbits for food, and only a forest bed, but, on the whole, better than the Conciergerie or the Châtelet. He slept long, and was cold, fearing to make a fire. About eleven next morning he left Toto, and went with care to the edge of the wood. He heard noises, and saw boys setting traps; for now my lord's rabbits were anybody's rabbits. The traps pleased him. He slipped away. At evening, being dreadfully hungry, he went to the warren, took two rabbits out of the traps, and went back. The man's patience was amazing: not until late at night did he make a fire to cook his meat; but Toto, less exacting, was fed at once with the raw flesh.

A week went by, with no more of incident than I have mentioned. He explored the woods day after day, and a half-mile away found a farm, whence at night he took toll of milk, having stolen a pail to aid him. It was all sadly monotonous, but what else could he do? Once, after a fortnight, he was bold enough to wander in daylight within the woods near the château. It was apparently deserted; at least, he saw no signs of habitation; nor, later at night, when he went back, were there lights, except in one room on the ground floor.

François approached with caution, and, looking through a window, saw an old man seated by the fire. Making sure that he was alone, the wanderer tapped on the pane. The man at the hearthside looked up, and

"THE WANDERER TAPPED ON THE PANE"

François saw, as he had suspected, that he was the
majordomo. Again François tapped, and observing
the inmate move toward the door, he hurried thither.
As they met, François hastened to say that he was the
man who aided the marquis, having himself had the
luck to escape. Once reassured, the old majordomo
urged François to enter. But this he would not do.
He had had enough of house-traps. In the forest they
would be secure. To this the servant agreed, and followed him at once. When at last in the woodland
shelter, François asked: "What of the marquis?"
He had been taken by Grégoire toward Paris, but
was said to have made his escape. "A hard man to
hold is my master; and as to the village, it has had
to pay right dearly, too." Pierre had been arrested,
but was soon set free. And the little gentleman?
He had been taken to a cousin's house in eastern
Normandy. François hesitated over his final question;
he himself could not have told why.

"And Mme. Renée?" he exclaimed, and bent forward, intent.

"The countess?"

"I did not know. Is she a countess? Mme. Renée
—what of her?—she who was hurt. I passed her;
she lay on the upper stair. There was blood—blood.
The little boy cried to me to help her. My God! I
could not. I—tell me, was she badly hurt?"

"She is dying, monsieur. Something—a gauntlet,
they say—struck her head. She has known no one
since."

"Where is she?"

"In the château, with a maid and her aunt. She

was too ill to be taken away. She is dying to-night. They say she cannot last long. God rest her soul! 'T is the end of everything."

The thief stood still a minute; then he said resolutely, "I must see her." This the old servant declared impossible; but when François swore that he would go alone, he finally consented to show him the way, insisting all the time that he would not be let in.

In a few minutes they were moving down a long corridor on the second floor. All was dark until the majordomo paused at a door under which a line of light was to be seen. Here he knocked, motioning his companion to keep back a little. The door opened, and a gaunt middle-aged lady came forth.

"What is it?" she said.

"This man—this gentleman would see the countess."

"What do you want?" she said, facing François. "My niece is dying—murdered. You have done your cruel work. Would you trouble the dead?"

"Madame," said François, "I am he who held the stair with the marquis. I am no Jacobin. I shot the man who wounded the countess."

"You! He is dead."

"Thank God! May I see the lady?"

"She is dying; why should you see her?"

"Madame, I am a poor unhappy thief. Once this lady offered me help—a chance, a better life. I was a fool; I let it go by. I—let me see her."

"Come in," said the gentlewoman; and, with no more words, he entered after her, and approached the bed, leaving his dog outside. What he beheld he neither forgot nor, I believe, save in his memoirs, ever spoke of to any one.

He saw a white face on the pillow; a deep-red spot on each cheek; eyes with the glaze of swift-coming death. He fell on his knees beside her, and stayed motionless, watching the sweat on the brow, the breath quicken and then stop as if it would not come again. At last he touched the hand. It was cold, and he withdrew his own hand, shrinking back. He had seen death, but no death like this. He said, "Madame." There was no answer. He looked up at the older woman. "She is dying; she does not hear."

"No; nor ever will in this world."

He turned, bent down, and kissed the fringe of the coverlet. Then he arose, shaken by the strongest emotion life had brought to him.

"I thank you," he said, and moved to the door. He paused outside.

"Are you sure the beast is dead—the man who did that—that?"

"Yes."

"I am sorry—sorry." He shook his long arms in the air. "I should like now to kill him again—again!" He walked swiftly away, and, not waiting for the servant, left the house and found his way back to his forest shelter.

All night long he sat without a fire, indifferent to poor Toto's efforts to get a little notice, not feeling the cold, a sorely wounded man, with a scar on his memory which no after happiness could ever erase.

The next night he found the majordomo, and learned that the countess was dead. He took away blankets and the provisions bountifully supplied, and once more rejoined his dog.

In this manner the last days of February were passed; and in March the spring began to appear, but with it a new peril. The woodmen went here and there at work, and thrice he narrowly escaped being seen. Early in April his friend the majordomo disappeared, and the great château was infested with men who came and went—for what he knew not.

He began to be troubled with a feverish desire to see the streets of Paris. At last he made up his mind to leave his forest shelter; and sometime in April, having hesitated long, he set out. He hid all day in woods, and walked at night, until he reached the Seine. With this as a guide, he went on, robbing hen-houses of eggs, and milking cows, until he was close to Paris. How to enter it he did not know. The times were doubly dangerous. Spies and suspicion were everywhere to be dreaded. His papers had no certifications from the places he was presumed to have visited. Formidable in the background he saw the man Grégoire, the commissioner with the wart of ill luck.

How the thief and his dog lived near to Paris in woods and fields, there is no need to tell in detail. The month of June was come in this year of 1793. Marat was ill, and Charlotte Corday on her way to forestall the decree of nature. La Vendée was up. The Girondists had fallen, the great cities of the South were in uproar, the enemy was on the frontier, and the rule of France in the competent and remorseless hands of the Committee of Public Safety. All around

"HE SAW A WHITE FACE ON THE PILLOW."

Paris the country was infested with wandering people who, for the most part, like François, had good reason to fear. There were beggars, thieves, persecuted nobles, those who had no mind to face the foe as volunteers. Now and then François, ever cautious, picked up a little news on a scrap of gazette found by the wayside. He read that Citizen Amar was of the Great Committee of General Security. François laughed.

"Toto, dost thou think this will add to thy master's security? That was the gentleman with the emigrative mouth. *Ami*, he is still alive. They must be tough, these Jacobins. What fun, Toto! I can see him pinned to the door like a beetle, and that marquis with a face, Toto, like a white plaster cast those Italians used to sell.

"I like not M. Amar. Toto, we are unhappy in our acquaintances. But the man of the wart is the worst." This was François's black beast; why, he could not have said. Amar, *le farouche*, was really a more fatal foe. The citizen who dressed neatly, and wore spectacles over green eyes, and was in debt to the conjurer for a not desirable forecast of fortune, was a yet more sinister acquaintance. Yet it was Citizen Grégoire who came to François in dreams, and the bare thought of whom could chop short a laugh as surely as Mother Guillotine, the merciless.

## XVIII

*Wherein is told how François reënters Paris, and lodges with the Crab; and of how Toto is near to death by the guillotine. François meets Despard and the marquis, who warns him and is warned.*

 FEW days later, when lying behind a deserted hut at dusk, François heard a noise of military music, and ventured forth on the road leading to the barrier. Many hundreds of the wounded from the frontier were passing, in wagons or on foot. The communes and clubs were out to meet them. The cabarets outside of the gate poured forth a noisy company. The road was full. Who should stop the free citizens or the ladies of the fish-market, come to welcome patriot volunteers? Here was an escort of troops, wild, triumphant greeting of captured Austrian flags, many wounded in wagons, many more afoot, marching wearily. Those who walked the people must aid. The ranks were soon broken, and all was good-natured tumult. Here was help for heroes—wine, bread, eager aid of an arm. Some who were dragging along on crutches, to get a little relief from jolting wagons, were hoisted, to their dis-

190

comfort, on the shoulders of friendly patriots not eager to volunteer.

François, tucking Toto under his cloak, edged himself into the broken ranks of the heroes of Hondschoote and Wattignies. "We are many," he said to a man beside him, as tattered as he, for there was scarcely a rag of uniform. "Jolly to get home again!"

"*Sacré!* not if they guillotined thy father a week ago."

"*Dame!* is that so? But patience, and hold thy tongue, citizen. *Tonnerre!* my leg." He was limping.

"Thy shoulder, friend"—to a blouse. "*Tiens!* that is better. The Austrian bullets have a liking for one's bones. Crack! crack! I can hear them yet. They do not spare the officers any more than they do the privates."

Should they carry the citizen officer—take care of his sword? François thanked them; the citizens must be careful of his leg; and there was François on the shoulders of two big Jacobins, like a dozen more; for it was who should help, and a shouting, good-humored crowd. François was not altogether well pleased at his elevation; he dropped forward his too well-known face. There was a jam at the barrier. Had these citizen soldiers their passes, as provided? François was weak; he suffered, poor fellow! The Jacobins and the women roared derisively: "Passes for heroes?" All order was lost. They were through, and in the Rue d'Enfer. Would the good citizens let him walk? He was heavy, and they were pleased to be relieved of one hundred and ninety-five pounds of wounded hero.

Meanwhile there was some renewed order in the broken formation; yet now and then men fell out to meet sweethearts or friends, usually coming back again to the ranks.   The hint was good.

"*Ciel!* comrade, there is my mother!"   The crowd gave way as the hero hobbled out of the line.   He called out: "*Mère, mère*—mother!   Here!   'T is I —Adolphe.   The deuce! she is so deaf."

Where was she?   Citizens were eager to help him.

"Ah," he cried, "she saw me not"; and, turning into a side street near the asylum, limped painfully in pursuit of the mother who was afflicted with deafness. Toto followed.   Once around a corner, the lameness disappeared.   In the gathering dusk he set out for the Cité.

"It must be Quatre Pattes, Toto.   Come along.   A bad year, my friend, to have lost a father and a mother.   No matter; we are in Paris."

He loved the streets.   "Ah, there is Notre Dame and the river!"   He was happy, and went along laughing, and at last turned into a small café near to his old home in the Rue des Chanteurs.

He was tired and hungry, and, as he agreeably remembered, well off, having had small chance to spend the money with which he had been generously provided by Achille Gamel.   The bread and cheese were good, and the wine was not bad.   He asked for tobacco and a pipe.   Would the host find him "L'Ami du Peuple"?   He was a sublieutenant, wounded on the frontier; but, *dame!* to get home was happiness.

Two men sat down by him, and talked.   Good Jacobins were these, in the dirty uniforms of the

sansculotte army which kept Paris in order at the
rate of forty sous a day. "Bad wages, citizen lieutenant," they said.

The hero of the frontier was worse off—no pay for
three months. He related his battles; and now he
must go.

"Come, Toto." Toto had been wounded at Wattignies; he was well now, and would be promoted.
"*Bon soir*, comrades." In fact, he was wildly gay,
glad to be back in Paris.

He paused, at last, before a house of the date of
Henri II. Its heavy, narrow door, and a slit in the
wall for a window, told of days when every man's
house was a fortress.

"It is our best chance, Toto; but best may be bad.
We must do something." He jingled the bell. The
cord was drawn by the concierge within, so as to lift
the latch, and François entered the hall. To right
was the Crab's den, and there within was Quatre
Pattes. He saw the thin purple nose, the bleared red
eyes, the bearded chin, and the two sticks.

"*Mille tonnerres!* my child, it is thou. And where
hast thou been? There is no thief like thee. Come
and laugh for thy old mother." She welcomed him
in thieves' slang, vile, profuse, and emphatic. Had
he any money? Yes, a little; business was good in
the provinces; and would she house him? Here was
a louis d'or for *maman;* and what was this abominable
*carte de sûreté*, this new trap? She explained. He
need have no fear; she would get him one. He had
been in bad company, she had heard; for a Jacobin
had told her of the fencing-school, and thither, too

late, she had gone to get a little help. He had nearly killed Amar, *le farouche*, and that injured citizen was said to desire his society. But that was long ago; and Paris lived fast, and was gay, and forgot easily.

François had no wish to refresh Citizen Amar's memory. He asked lightly if she had ever seen Grégoire, the commissioner to Normandy?

Mme. Quatre Pattes had never seen him. He was of the Great Committee—a patriot of the best, like herself. Did he know Grégoire? He told her frankly that he had been arrested by Grégoire, and had escaped.

"Thou art the first, my child!" she cried, her jaws champing as if she were eating. "Thou hast a fine taste in the choosing of enemies. I would not be in thy skin for a hundred louis; and now a cat of the night thou must be. I can hide thee awhile; and if thou dost feed me well, the mama-crab will care for thee. No one need know thou art here. Come, get thee a few louis, and we will buy a fine card of safety, and christen thee to suit. Ha, ha! my little one!" and she beat with her sticks on the floor.

Our thief was now back in his garret, having lost as many fair chances of prosperity as did Murad the Unlucky. He reflected much in these late autumn months of 1793, being for his wants rich, and therefore in no necessity to give a thought to methods of getting his daily diet. During the daytime Quatre Pattes insisted on his secluding himself in his garret. At night he left Toto with the Crab, who fed him well, and was therefore liked by a revolutionary dog without prejudices. From these

QUATRE PATTES.

night prowls François returned with sad complaints
of the way the republicans guarded their slim purses;
in fact, at this time he avoided adventures, stole from
no one, and gave of his lessening store what barely
contented Mme. Quatre Pattes.   Were I to say that his
goodness came from newly acquired views of life, I
should mislead.   He was as honest as ever, which is
to say he took no thought at all as to ethical questions.
We are said to be children of circumstance, which
may be described as the environment of the hour.
This is true of the feeble; but character was the more
despotic parent in this resolute man, who could wrestle
strenuously with circumstance.   He was a Royalist
because he liked show and color and the fine manners
of the great; in the past he stole because he knew no
other way to live.   His admirable health was a contribution to his natural cheerfulness.   He still had
simple likings—for the country, for animals, and
would have had for books had they been easy to
get, or had he known how to get those which would
have fed his mind and had sauce of interest.

His surroundings would have surely and hopelessly
degraded a less permanent character, and a nature
without his ingrained gaiety would have taken more
steadily some thought of the far future.   He knew
too well how the thief's life ended: the galleys, the
wheel, the lonely death-bed in the hospital.   If he
reflected on it at all, as he seems to have done at this
time, it was because of his long, weary days in the
attic.   The immediate future at this period did dis-
turb him, but never long.   He liked to talk, and,
lacking society, talked more and more to himself

12

aloud, with Toto for an audience which never ceased to attend. He who is pleased with his own talk cannot easily be bored; and so he talked, until Quatre Pattes, who loved keyholes and to listen, thought he must be out of his head. She herself was always either silent or boisterous, and was as to this like other beasts of prey. When in calamity François was too busy to be serious. When at ease the mirthfulness of his natural man forbade argument as to what the dice-box of to-morrow would offer; for to laugh is to hope, and François, as we know, laughed much, well, and often.

There were many times in his life when to have been honestly loved by a woman capable of comprehending both his strength and his weakness would, I think, have given him the chance to live a better life. But how was this possible to one who lived as he lived— who was what he was?

To be merely liked was pleasant to François, and appealed with the most subtle form of flattery to his immense self-esteem. The man was sensitive, and in after days, when in an atmosphere of refinement, would never speak of the terrible women he had known too well in the Cité. Having no longer the distraction of the streets, he was at present condemned to live long hours with no society but that of Toto and the animal Quatre Pattes. He bought a small field-glass, and studied the habits of his neighbors far and near, and once more took interest in the feline owners of the roof-tops. Quatre Pattes fed him well, and brought him some of the old gazettes.

He read how, on that frightful 5th of September,

now past, one of the five complementary days of the
republican calendar, on motion of Barrère, "Terror"
was decreed by the Convention to be the order of the
day. It was indeed the birth-hour of the Terror. The
Great Committee was in power. The revolutionary
tribunals were multiplied. The law of suspected persons was drawn with care by the great jurist Merlin
of Douai. Behind these many man-traps was the
Committee of Public Safety, with despotic power
over the persons of all men, and in full control of the
prisons. To it the subcommittees reported arrests;
it secured the prisoners who were to be tried; it saw
to the carrying out of all sentences; it kept the peace
in Paris with an array of sansculottes, and fed the
guillotine daily. Of this stern mechanism, strong of
head and incapable of pity, was Pierre André Amar;
as, one day, François read with his full share of the
Terror. There was soon enough of it to supply all
France.

Before November came, François, pretending to
have been in luck, supplied the Crab with six louis.
She exacted two more, and how much she kept none
may know. He had very few left.

She was as good as her word. "Here, my little
one, is the *carte de sûreté* from the committee of this
section." The description was taken from his passport. He was no more to be François, but François
Beau. If he would denounce one or two people, the
committee would indorse his card as that of "a good
patriot who deserved well of the country." There
was the lame cobbler over the way, who talked
loosely, and to whom the Crab owed money; that

would be useful and convenient. François shivered all down his long back; he would see. Meanwhile, as he considered, Quatre Pattes twisted her bent spine, rattled her two sticks, and looked up at him sidewise with evil eyes, bidding him have a care, and not get his good mama into trouble, or else, or else—François felt that some night he might have to wring that wrinkled neck. He was uneasy, and with good reason.

He could bear the confinement no longer, and in December began to find his cash getting low. He had let his beard grow, and taken to long, tight pantaloons and a red cap. He felt that, come what might, he must take the risks of daylight.

The chances against him were small. The numberless denunciations of the winter fell chiefly on the rich, the rash in talk, the foes of the strong heads who were ably and mercilessly ruling France. The poor, the obscure, and the cautious bourgeoisie were as a rule safe until, in the spring, something like a homicidal mania took possession of Robespierre and others, who, although they were the most intelligent of the Great Committee, were never in control of a steady majority, and began to fear for their own heads.

Outwardly Paris was gay. The restaurateurs made money; the people were fed by levies of grain on the farmers; and the tumbrel, on its hideous way, rarely excited much attention. The autumn and winter of '93 were not without peril or adventure for the thief. The Palais d'Égalité, once royal, was his favored resort, and with his well-trained sleight of hand he managed to justify the name of the place by efforts to equalize the distribution of what money was left to his own advantage and to the satisfaction of the Crab.

The dark drama went on; but, except the *tricoteuses* who, like Quatre Pattes, went daily to see the guillotine at work, comparatively few attended this daily spectacle. Paris, wearied of crime and too much politics, was tired of the monotony of slaughter, which had now no shadow of excuse.

"Would the citizen miss the death of the Austrian, the ex-queen?" He would not; he knew better than to say no to Quatre Pattes. Would he go with her? She could get him a good place, and all Paris would be there. All Paris was not to his desire. He said he would go alone. A walk with this four-footed creature and the rattle of her becketing sticks he liked not. He called his dog, and, avoiding the vast assemblage on the Place of the Revolution, found his way to the Rue St. Honoré.

He stood in a crowd against a house. The tumbrel came slowly, and, because of the surging mass of people, paused opposite to him. He looked about him. In a group at a window on the far side of the street he saw a man apparently sketching the sad figure in the cart. It seemed devilish to this poor outcast of the Cité. His face flushed; he asked who that was in the window, at which many were staring. The man he addressed was in black, and looked to be an ex-abbé.

"My son," he said quietly, and with no evidence of caution—"my son, 't is David the painter, he of the Great Committee. He hath no heart; but in another world he will get it again, and then—"

"Take care!" said François. The shouting crowd
cried: "Messalina! Down with the Austrian!"

François looked, and saw the bent figure seated in
the cart. Pale it was, with a red spot on each cheek,
haggard; her gray hair cut close, pitiful; with pen-
dent breasts uncorseted, lost to the horrors of the in-
sults hurled at her abject state. François moved
away, and the tumbrel went rumbling on. An hour
later he was crossing the broad Elysian Fields amid
the scattered crowd. It was over, and few cared.
The booths were selling toy guillotines. Of a sudden
he missed Toto. He called him, and, hearing him
bark, pushed in haste into a large tent filled with
women and children and with men in blouses.

"The citizen has not paid," cried the doorkeeper.
François saw Toto struggling in the hands of a red-
bearded man who was crying out: "Enter! enter!
Trial and execution of an *émigré* dog. *Voilà*, citizens!
Range yourselves." There was the red guillotine,
the basket, the sawdust, and poor Toto howling. It
was a spectacle which much amused the lower class
of Jacobins. "*À bas le chien aristocrate!*"

François advanced with his cheerful smile. "The
citizen is mistaken; it is my dog."

"Where is his *carte de sûreté?*" laughed the man.
"Up with him for trial!"

Four monkeys were the judges. Jeers and laughter
greeted François: "No, no; go on!"

He caught the man by the arm. The fellow let fall
Toto, who made a hasty exit.

"I denounce thee for an enemy of the republic!"
cried the showman. "Seize him! seize him!" Fran-

çois broke away, and, using his long arms, reached
the entrance. There was no earnest desire to stop
him. The doorkeeper caught him by the collar. He
kicked as only a master of the *savate* knows how to
kick, and, free of the grip, called to Toto, and plunged
into a crowd which made no effort to recapture him.
He moved with them, and soon turned to cross the river.

Midway on the bridge he came face to face with
Despard. He was ragged and fleshless, the shadow
of the well-fed Jacobin he had last seen in the château
of Ste. Luce.

"*Ciel!*" exclaimed François, "thou art starved."
He had no grudge against his old partner, but he
fully appreciated the danger of this encounter.

He was comforted by the man's alarm. "Come,"
said François, and took him into a little drinking-shop.
It was deserted at this time of day. He easily drew
out all he desired to know. Mme. Renée was assuredly
dead; and he who threw the gauntlet, the butcher,
dead also; and three or more on the fatal stairway.
Grégoire had punished the village severely; heads
had fallen. Pierre's friend Robespierre had abandoned him, had even threatened him — Pierre! but he
had escaped any worse fate. He was half famished;
and would François help him? François ordered
bread and cheese and wine. He would see what next
to do. And what of the marquis? He had not appeared in the lists of the guillotined; but he might
readily have died unnamed, and escaped François's
notice.

"No," said Pierre, sadly; "he lives. Of course he
lives. The devil cannot die. He got away from

Grégoire. Who could keep that man? But for thee and the accursed commissioner, I should have had my revenge. We shall meet some day."

"Shall I find him for thee?"

"*Dame!* no. Let us go out. I am uneasy; I am afraid."

"But of what?"

"I do not know. I am afraid. I am accursed with fear. I am afraid as a man is in a dream. Somewhere else I shall cease to fear. Let us go." He was in a sweat of pure causeless terror, the anguish of an emotion the more terrible for its lack of reason. It was the inexplicable torment of one of the forms of growing insanity. François looked on, amazed and pitiful. The man's eyes wandered here and there; he got up, and sat down again, went to the door, looked about him, and came back. At last, as François began to consider how to be free of a dubious acquaintance, Pierre said drearily:

"Is it easy to die? I should like to die. If I were brave like thee, I should drown myself."

"Ah, well," laughed François, "there is the guillotine—short and comfortable."

"Thou wilt not denounce me?" he cried, leaping to his feet. "I have my *carte;* I will let thee see it." He was like a scared child.

"Nonsense!" cried François, with good-humored amusement. "I must go. Here is a gold louis. Why dost thou not rob a few Jacobins?"

"Hush! I dare not; I was brave once. Thou didst save me once; help me now. Thou wilt not let me starve?"

"No, indeed. I? Not I. Take care of thy louis; they are scarce. Meet me here at this hour in a week. Adieu. At this hour, mind."

"Art thou going to leave me alone?"

François was grieved, but could not remain, and hastened away, while Pierre looked after him with melancholy eyes.

"Come, Toto," he said, as he turned a corner. "The man is mad. Let us thank the *bon Dieu* we never have had a wife; and the rest of our relatives we have buried —papa and mama, and all the family."

It was not in the man to forget, and a week later he cautiously entered the little café to keep his engagement. It was noisy. To his surprise, he saw Pierre declaiming lustily to half a dozen blouses.

"Ah!" he cried, seeing François, "*mon ami*, here is a seat. There is good news from the frontier. A glass for the citizen." Clink, clink. "*À vous.* Death to royal rats!" He went on in a wild way until the workmen had gone, and François stopped him with:

"What the deuce has come to thee?"

"Oh, nothing. I have had one of the fits you know of; I am always better after them. *Diable!* no marquis could scare me to-day. I saw him last week, I did. I followed him. It is he who would have been scared. I—I missed him in a crowd. In a minute I should have had him, like that," and he turned a glass upside down so as to capture a fly which was foraging on the table—"like *that*," he repeated triumphantly.

François watched him, and saw a flushed face, tremulous hands, staring eyes.

"He is afraid; he can't get out"; and the man laughed low, pointing to his prisoner.

"And thou wouldst have denounced him?" said François.

"Why not? He is one of them. He is hell; he is the devil! I saw no officers to help me."

"Thou art cracked; thou wilt denounce me next."

Pierre looked at François with unusual steadiness of gaze, hesitated, and replied:

"I thought of it; you are all for these people."

François, in turn, looked his man over curiously. He had now a queer expression of self-satisfied elation. "A good joke, that," said François. "Wait a moment; I left Toto outside." He went to the door, and looked up and down the street. "Wait," he cried to Pierre. "Hang the dog!" And in an instant he had left the citizen to abide his return. Once in his garret, he cried: "Toto, thou hast no sense. The sane scoundrels are bad enough, but why didst thou fetch on me this crazy rascal? And so the marquis got away, Toto. The man with the wart is not as clever as I thought him. But some folks have luck."

The sad winter of the Terror wore on, while François continued to live unmolested, and pursued his estimable occupation always with an easy conscience, but often with an uneasy mind.

It was near the end of the pleasant month of May, 1794—the month Prairial of the new calendar. The roses were in bloom. The violets were seeking sunshine here and there, half hidden in the rare grasses of the trampled space of the Place of the Revolution. On the six bridges which spanned the canals, its

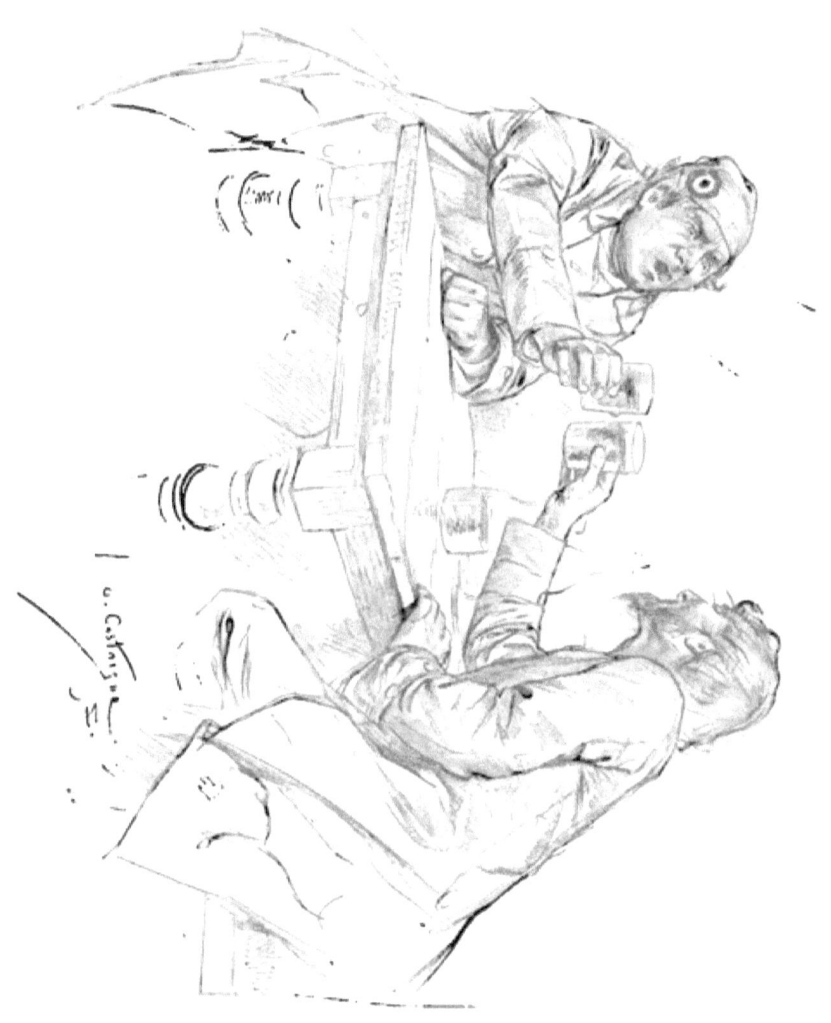

boundaries, children were looking at the swans. In the middle space, the scaffold and cross-beams of the guillotine rose dark red against the blue sky of this afternoon of spring. Two untidy soldiers marched back and forth beside it. The every-day tragedy of the morning was over; why should the afternoon remember? The great city seemed to have neither heart nor memory. The drum-beat of a regiment going to the front rang clear down the Quai des Tuileries. People ran to see; children and their nurses left the swans. The birds in the trees listened, and, liking not this crude music, took wing, and perched on the beams of the monstrous thing in the center of the Place.

François crossed the open ground, with Toto close to heel. The keeper of the little café where he liked to sit had just told him that the citizen with whom he had twice come thither had been asking for him, and that with this citizen had also come once a stout man, who would know where Citizen François lived. This last was of the fourth section, one Grégoire, a man with a wart.

"Thou didst notice the man?" said François, much troubled.

"Notice him? I should think so. *Dame!* I am of the Midi. A wart on a man's nose is bad luck; the mother of that man saw a cocatrice egg in the barn-yard."

"A cocatrice egg! What the mischief is that?"

"*Tiens!* if you were of the Midi, you would know. When a hen cackles loud, 't is that she hath laid a great egg; the father is a basilisk."

"*Tonnerre!* a basilisk?"

"Thou must crush the egg, and not look, else there is trouble; thy next child will have warts, or his eyebrows will meet, and then look out!" François's superstition was vastly reinforced by this legend.

"*Mon Dieu!*" he cried; "he hath both." This François was a bold man when he had to meet danger face to face, but, like a child as to many things, afraid where a less imaginative man would have been devoid of fear.

Just now he had been turning over in his mind the chance of the Crab's betraying him. She had been prowling about his garret, and had stolen a well-hidden score of francs. He dared not complain. What scant possessions he had would fall into her claws if at any minute she might choose to denounce him. Of late, purses were too well guarded. The display of luxury in lace handkerchiefs and gold seals no longer afforded an available resource. Except Robespierre, who defied popular sentiment, few men carried two watches. Quatre Pattes had the appetite of a winter wolf, and was becoming more and more exacting. She asked why he did not sell his rapier. If it were known that he withheld weapons such as the republic claimed, there might be trouble. Why had he not given up his pistols? They were gold-mounted, and had belonged to a grandee of Spain. Why not sell them? They would fetch a deal of money.

He was not inclined to part with his arms, and least of all with his rapier. At last he gave her one pistol, which she sold; the other he hung high up on a peg set within the chimney, having hidden in its barrel the precious little document he had captured from Citizen Grégoire in that pleasant inn on the Seine, where an agreeable evening had ended with such unaccountable abruptness.

Next to the Crab's treachery, he feared most to meet Despard when the Jacobin should chance to be in one of those aggressive moods which were so puzzling to François. But above all did he dread Grégoire, and grew terrified as he reflected on that business of the cocatrice egg and the basilisk.

It seemed as though he were doomed, and this most cheery of men became distinctly unhappy. "That *sacré* basilisk!" he muttered, and, less on guard than usual, wandered on, taking stock of his perplexities.

Near to the foundations of the Madeleine, where work had long since ceased, he paused to recreate himself with a puppet-show. The vanquished fiend was Citizen *Jean Boule*. He was soon guillotined. The crowd was merry, and François, refreshed, contributed his own share of appreciative mirth. In the throng he unluckily set his big foot on the toes of a little Jacobin dressed in the extreme of the fashions these gentry affected. The small man was not to be placated by François's abundant excuses, and demanded the citizen's card of safety. It was an everyday matter. No one dared to refuse. There were half-insane men, in those times, who satisfied their patriotism by continually exacting cards from timid women or from any well-dressed man. To decline was to break the law. François obeyed with the utmost civility. The little man returned the card.

" The citizen is of the best of the sections, but, *sacré!* he is heavy."

Much relieved, François went on.    In the Rue St. Honoré the corner of a lace handkerchief invited a transfer, and lace handkerchiefs were rare.    As there was a small, well-occupied group looking through a shop-window at a caricature of Mr. Pitt, the occasion appeared propitious, and the handkerchief changed owners.

A minute later a man touched François's shoulder.

" Thy card, citizen ! "

" The deuce ! " said the thief, as he turned.    " This gets monotonous.    *Mon Dieu*, the marquis ! " he exclaimed.

" Hush !    Your card.    You are followed—watched. There is this one chance."    François produced his card.    The marquis murmured, " Take care ; obey me."    Holding the card in his hand, he called authoritatively to a municipal guard who was passing.    The man stopped, but no one else paused.    Curiosity was perilous.

" This good citizen is followed by that man yonder —the one with the torn bonnet.    I know the citizen. Here is his card and mine.    Just tell that fellow to be careful"; and he slipped his own card of safety into the guard's hand, and under it three louis.    The guard hesitated ; then he glanced at the card.

" 'T is in order, and countersigned by Vadier of the Great Committee.    These spies are too busy ; I will settle the fellow.    Good morning, citizens."

They moved away quietly, in no apparent haste. As they were turning a corner, the thief looked back.

" I am a lost man, monsieur ! "    He saw, far away,

the man of the torn red bonnet, and with him Quatre
Pattes. She was evidently in a rage. He understood
at once. In the thieves' quarter denunciations were
not in favor. She knew too well the swift justice of
this bivouac of outcasts to risk being suspected as a
traitor to its code. The night before, he had been
unable to give her money, and had again refused to
sell his weapons. She had angrily reminded him that
he was in her power, and he had for the first time
declared that he would let the Cité settle with her. He
had been rash, and now, too late, he knew it.

He hastily explained his sad case to the disguised
gentleman, and was on the point of telling him that
this Quatre Pattes was that Mme. Quintette who had
once been his agent, and would probably be an enemy
not to be despised. He glanced at the marquis, and,
wisely or not, held his tongue.

"We must part here," said the gentleman. He had
hesitated when chance led him to the neighborhood of
the thief in trouble; but he was a courageous man,
and disliked to owe to an inferior any such service as
François had more than once rendered him. Vadier's
sign manual on his own card of safety was an unques-
tioned assurance of patriotism; it had cost him a
round sum, but it had its value.

When he said, "I must leave you," the thief returned:

"I am sorry, monsieur; I know not what to do or
where to go."

"Nor I," replied Ste. Luce, coldly. "Nor, for that
matter, a thousand men in Paris to-day." He had
paid a debt, and meant to be rid of a disreputable
and dangerous acquaintance. "Better luck to you!"
he added.

"May I say to monsieur, who has helped me, that Despard is in Paris, and has seen him?"

The marquis turned. "Why did not you kill him when you had the chance?"

"You forbade me."

"That is true—quite true. Had you done it without asking me, I had been better pleased."

"I had no grudge against him."

"Well, well, thank you, my man; I can look out for myself."

"Will monsieur accept the gratitude of a poor devil of a thief?"

"Oh, that is all right. One word more. It is as well to tell you, my man, how I came to speak to you. When first I observed you, as I fell behind, I saw that terrible old witch with two sticks pointing you out to the fellow with the torn cap; then he followed you."

"It was Quatre Pattes, monsieur. I lodge in her house."

"A good name, I should say. I wish you better luck and safer lodgings. Adieu"; and he went quietly on his way.

## XIX

*Of the sorrowful life of loneliness, of François's arrest,
and of those he met in prison.*

RANÇOIS stood still. He was alone,
and felt of a sudden, as never before,
the solitude of an uncompanioned life.
The subtle influence of the Terror had
begun to sap the foundations of even
his resolute cheerfulness. It was this constancy of
dread which to some natures made the terrible cer-
tainties of the prisons a kind of relief. He looked
after the retreating figure as it moved along the *quai*
and was lost to view in the Rue des Petits-Augustines.

"Toto," he said, "I would I had his clever head.
When 't is a question of hearts, *mon ami*, I would
rather have thine. And now, what to do?" At last
he moved swiftly along the borders of the Seine, and
soon regained his own room. The Crab would go to
the afternoon market; her net swung over her arm at
the time he had seen her; and, as she always moved
slowly, he had ample leisure.

He packed his bag, and taking from his pistol the
paper he had secured when in company with Grégoire,
replaced it under the lining of his shoe. Its value he

13

very well knew.   After a moment's reflection, he put
his pistol back on the peg high up in the chimney.
He had been in the house nearly an hour, and was
ready to leave, when he heard feet, and a knock at
the locked door.   A voice cried:

"In the name of the republic, open!"   He knew
that he was lost.

"*Dame!* Toto.   We are done for, my little one";
and then, without hesitation, he opened the door.
Three municipals entered.   One of them said:

"We arrest thee, citizen, as an *émigré* returned."

"*Émigré!*" and he laughed in his usual hearty way.
"If I had been that, no one would have caught me
back in France.   Ah, well, I am ready, citizen.   Here
is an old rapier.   The woman will sell it; better to
give it to thee or to the republic."   He took up his
slender baggage, and followed them.   When they
were down-stairs, he asked leave to see the Crab.
The guard called her out of her den.

"*Chère maman*," said François, "this is thy doing.
These good citizens have my rapier, and the pistol is
gone.   Not a sou is left thee.   Thou hast killed the
goose that laid the golden eggs.   Alas!"

The Crab rattled her claws on the sticks, and these
on the floor, and spat vileness of thieves' slang, declaring it a wicked lie.   Would they take the silver-
hilted sword?   It was hers, and he owed her rent.
At last, laughing, the guards secured the thief's
hands behind his back, and marched him away to
the revolutionary committee of the section Franklin.
Here no time was lost with the *émigré*, who was sent

off in a hurry to the prison of the Madelonnettes, with poor Toto trotting after him, much perplexed by the performance.

François was astounded at the celerity and certainty of the methods by which he, a free Arab of the streets, was thus caged. As usual, it acted on his sense of humor, and before the dreaded sectional tribunal and with the municipals he was courageously merry. When he heard that he was to be sent to the Madelonnettes, he said:

"But, citizens, I am not of the sex. *Mon Dieu!* the Madelonnettes! 'T is not respectable—'t is not decent"; and he laughed outright. As no man was ever so made as to be protected from the infection of such mirth as the thief's, the judges laughed in chorus. One of them, disturbed in his slumber, awoke, and seeing no cause for this long-visaged flap-ear so to mock the justice of the republic, he said:

"Thou wilt not laugh long, miserable aristocrat!"

This much delighted François. "By St. Jacobus, citizen, I swear to thee I am only an honest thief. I did not expect to be made of the fine nobility by a good democrat like thee."

"Off with him!" said the judge. "They laugh best who laugh last."

"No, no," cried the incorrigible; "they laugh best who laugh most. *Au revoir.*"

"Take him away! The next case."

The thief was gay, and amused the officers; but his keen senses were now all on guard, and, too, like others, he felt relieved at the ending of his life of suspense and watchful anxiety. His misfortune was plainly due to the avarice and needs of the Crab, and to her belief that he had ceased to be available as a means of support.

There was a little delay at the front of the old house of detention; some formalities were to be gone through with. François took careful note of it all. The prison stood in the Rue des Fontaines: a gray stone building, with a lofty story on the first floor, and, above, three stories and an attic; a high wall to left shut in the garden.

On entering a long, dark corridor, his bonds were removed, his bundle was searched, and what little money he had was scrupulously restored to him. He was stripped and examined, even to his shoes; but as the tongue of leather was loose only at the toes, the precious document escaped a very rigorous search. Poor Toto had been left outside, despite François's entreaties. In the cell to which he was consigned were eight straw mattresses. He arranged his small baggage, and was told he was free to go whither he would above the *rez-de-chaussée*, which was kept for forgers of assignats and thieves. The corridor was some fifty feet long, and smelt horribly. On the main floor was the common dining-room. A separate staircase led to a garden of considerable size, planted with box and a few quince- and other fruit-trees. At night two municipals guarded this space, while, outside, the steps of sentries could be heard when the hours of darkness brought their quiet. At 9 P. M. the prisoners, who assembled in the large hall, answered to their names; a bell rang, and they were locked in their

cells, or slept as they could in the corridors. The
richer captives were taxed to support their poor
companions, and even to buy and feed the mastiffs
which roamed at night in the garden.

Much of all this François learned as he arranged
his effects and talked gaily with the turnkey, one
Vaubertrand, a watchful but not unkindly little man.
Thus informed, François, curious as usual, went down
the corridor, and out into the garden. Here were
quite two hundred men and women, some in careful,
neat dress, many in rags. He saw, as he looked,
curés, ladies, seamstresses, great nobles, unlucky
colonels, and, as he learned later, musicians, poets;
and, to his surprise, for he knew the theaters,
actors such as Fleury, Saint-Prix, and Champville,
whose delicious laughter the Comédie Française knew
so well. Here, too, were Boulainvilliers, De Crosne,
and Dozincourt, the ex-kings and heroes of the comic
stage; and there, in a group apart, the fine gentles
and dames who had exchanged Versailles and the
Trianon for this home of disastrous fortunes.

"Yes," said the turnkey; "the citizen is right; 't is
a droll menagerie," and so left him.

François looked at the walls and chained dogs, and
knew at once that the large numbers in the prison
made impossible that solitude in which plans of
escape prosper. For a while no one noticed him so
far as to speak to him. The ill-clad and poor kept to
one side of the garden; on the other, well-dressed
people were chatting in the sun. Women were sew-
ing; a young man was reciting verses; and De Crosne,
with the child of the concierge on his lap, was telling

fairy-tales. Ignorant of the etiquette of the prison, François wandered here and there, not observing that he was stared at with surprise as he moved among the better clad on the sunny side of the yard. He was interested by what he saw. How quiet they all were! what fine garments! what bowing and courtesying! He liked it, as he always liked dress and color, and the ways of these imperturbable great folks. Beyond this his reflections did not go; nor as yet had he been here long enough to note how, day by day, some gentleman disappeared, or some kindly face of woman was seen no more. What he did observe was that here and there a woman or a man sat apart in self-contained grief, remembering those they had lost. The thief moved on, thoughtful.

At this moment he heard "*Diable!*" and saw the Marquis de Ste. Luce. "What! and have they trapped you, my inevitable thief? I myself was bagged and caged just after I left you. We are both new arrivals. Come aside with me."

François followed him, saying he was sorry to find the marquis here.

"It was to be, sooner or later; and I presume it will not last long. I was careless; and, after all, François, it was my fate—my shadow. A man does many things to amuse himself, and some one of them casts a lengthening shadow as time goes on. The shadow—my shadow—well, no matter. We all have our shadows, and at sunset they lengthen."

"'T is like enough, monsieur. 'T is like me. There is a man with a wart I am afraid of, and it is because of that wart. The man is a drunken fool."

"Despard is my wart," said the marquis, dryly. "As to being afraid, my good François, I never had the malady, not even as a boy."

"*Dame!* I have it now; and to get out of this is impossible."

"I think so. Did you mention Despard?"

"No; it was monsieur spoke of him."

"Quite true—quite true. He found me at last. Confound the fellow! I did not credit him with being clever."

"So this is his man with a wart?" thought François, but made no comment. He had not fully comprehended the simile with which this impassive seigneur illustrated the fact that but one of his many misdeeds had cast on his future a lengthening shadow of what he would have hesitated to call remorse.

"François," he said, "you and I are new additions to this queer collection. I may as well warn you that even here spies abound. Why? The deuce knows. Barn-yard fowls are not less considered than are we. It is the tribunal one day; then the Conciergerie; and next day, *affaire finie*, the business is over. Meanwhile, you are in the best society in France. There are M. de la Ferté, the Comte de Mirepoix, the Duc de Lévis, the Marquis de Fleury. I used to think them dull; calamity has not sharpened their wits. *Diable!* but you are welcome." The marquis had all his life amused himself with small regard to what was thought of him or his ways of recreation. "'T is a bit of luck to find you here in this hole." François could hardly agree with the opinion, but he laughed as he said so.

"Here comes my old comrade, De Laval Mont-morency. He is still a gay jester. He says we are like Saul and that other fellow, Jonathan, except that in death we shall both of us to a certainty be divided."

"*Ciel!* 't is a ghastly joke, monsieur."

"It has decidedly a flavor of the locality. I must not play telltale about you, or they will put you in the *rez-de-chaussée*, and, by St. Denis! I should miss you. I shall have a little amusement in perplexing these gentlemen. Your face will betray you; it used to be pretty well known. However, we shall see."

The nobleman last named threaded his way through the crowd, excusing himself and bowing as he came.

"Ah," he said, "Ste. Luce, another new arrival. The hotel is filling up. Good morning, monsieur. *Grand merci!* 't is our old acquaintance who used to tell fortunes on the Champs Élysées; told mine once, but, alas! did not warn me of this. Well, well, we have here some queer society. Take care, Ste. Luce; this citizen may be a spy, for all thou knowest. I assure thee we have to be careful."

"I—I a *mouchard*—a spy?"

"M. de Montmorency has no such idea," said Ste. Luce. "I shall ask him to respect your desire to be known by a name not your own. Permit me to add that I have less reason to thank some of my friends than I have to thank this gentleman. He is pleased to have mystified Paris for a wager, or no matter what. Just now he is—what the deuce is it you call yourself at present?"

François was delighted with the jest. "Allow me, monsieur, to pass as Citizen François. My real name— But you will pardon me; real names are dangerous."

"And what are names to-day," said the marquis, "thine or mine? My friend here—well, between us, Montmorency, this is he who held the stair with me in my *ci-devant* château. Thou wilt remember I told thee of it. A good twenty minutes we kept it against a hundred or so of my grateful people. He is the best blade in Paris, and, *foi d'honneur*, that business was no trifle."

"Who you are, or choose to be, I know not," said the older noble, "but I thank you; and, *pardieu!* Ste. Luce is free with your biography."

This was François's opinion.

No one knew distinctly who was this newcomer, concerning whom, for pure cynical amusement, Ste. Luce said so much that was gracious. Any freshly gay companion was welcomed, if his manners were at all endurable. The actors and actresses were pleasantly received. The few who remembered the long face, and ears like sails, and the captivating laugh of the former reader of palms, were so bewildered by Ste. Luce's varied statements that the poor thief found himself at least tolerated. He liked it. Nevertheless, as the days went by, and while seemingly the gayest of the gay, François gave serious thought to the business of keeping his head on his shoulders. He told fortunes,—always happy ones,—played tricks, and cut out of paper all manner of animals for the little girl, the child of the turnkey. Toto he gave up for lost; but on the fourth day the dog, half starved, got a chance when a prisoner entered. He dashed through the guards, and fled up stairs and down, until, seeing his master in the big hall, he ran to him, panting. The head jailer would have removed him, but there was a great outcry; and at last, when little Annette, François's small friend, cried, the dog was allowed to remain.

He was, as the marquis declared, much more interesting than most of the prisoners, and possessed, as he added, the advantage over other prisoners of being permanent. In fact, they were not. Every day or two came long folded papers. The *ci-devant* Baron Bellefontaine would to-morrow have the cause of his detention considered by Tribunal No. 3. Witnesses and official defenders had been allowed; but of late, and to *émigrés*, these were often denied. Also, witnesses were scarce and easily terrified, so that batches of merely suspected persons were condemned almost unheard. To be tried meant nearly always the Conciergerie and death. All cases were supposed to be tried in the order of their arrests; but great sums were spent in paying clerks to keep names at the foot of the fatal dockets of the committee. The members of this terrible government survived or died with much judicial murder on their souls; but countless millions passed through their hands without one man of them becoming rich. Elsewhere, with the lower officers, gold was an effective ally when it was desired to postpone the time of trial.

## XX

*Of how François gave Amar advice, and of how the
marquis bought his own head.*

T was now about May 26, when, at
evening, a commissioner in a cocked
hat, much plumed and scarfed, came
into the dining-hall. Toto was between
his master's knees, and was being fed.
François heard a gray-haired old lady exclaim to a
neighbor: "*Mon Dieu! chérie*, look! 'T is the Terror
in person."

The actor Champville cried out gaily: "I must
practise that face. 'T is a fortune for the villain of a
play. If ever I get out, it will be inestimable." Alas!
he was in the next day's list,—the *corvée*, they called
it,—and came no more to table. François looked up,
caught a glimpse of that relentless visage, and dropped
his head again over the slender relics of a not bounti-
ful meal. It was Jean Pierre Amar!

The marquis looked up from his plate, but made
no effort to conceal himself. Amar walked around
the table. Now and then his mouth wandered to
left. It was comical, and yet horribly grotesque. He
seemed to notice no one, and went out to make his

inspection. Presently a turnkey came and touched François's shoulder.

"The citizen commissioner would see thee."

"I am ruined—done for!" murmured the thief; and, followed by Toto, he went after the turnkey. In the room used as a registering-office, Amar, *le farouche*, sat handling a paper.

"Ah!" he said. "Citizen turnkey, leave the suspect with me, and close the door." The commissioner laid a pair of pistols on the table, and looked up at François.

"Well, citizen, we are met again. I am free to say that I had careful search made for thee, and now good fortune has brought hither not thee alone, but that infernal *ci-devant* who pinned me like a butterfly." As he spoke there was something fascinating in the concentration of emotion on the active side of this unnatural face. François felt the need to be careful.

"Why the devil don't you speak?"

"Will the citizen kindly advise me what answer it will be most prudent to make?" And for comment on his own words, which altogether pleased him, a pleasant smile drifted downward over his large features.

"*Sacré!* but thou art a queer one, and no fool," said the Jacobin. "Thou wilt be dead before long; a monstrous pity! I would give my place for thy laugh."

"'T is a bargain to my mind. Let us change. I shall set thee free at once—at once, citizen commissioner; I bear no malice."

Amar, silent for a moment, stroked his nose with thumb and finger.

"Thou dost not remind me thou didst save my life."

"No; what is the use?"

"Use? Why not?"

"Because men like the citizen commissioner do not lightly change. I have a too plain recollection of what I was promised in return for my benevolence. I should regret it except for—"

"For what?" said Amar.

Then François rose to the height of his greatness.

"I am a Frenchman, even if I am not of thy party. Had not the country needed thee, that day had been thy last. Citizen, as a man thou wouldst set me free; as a patriot thou wilt bow to the law of the republic. I am willing to die rather than soil the record of one to whom France owes so much." An overwhelming solemnity of aspect came upon this comedian's face as it met the gaze of the commissioner. "Alas! the country has few such citizens."

"*Tonnerre!* True—true; it is sad." The man's vanity was excelled only by that of the prisoner before him. François had personal appreciation of the influential value of the bait he cast. A great diplomatist of the older type was lost when François took to the war against society in place of that against nations.

"If the citizen commissioner has no more need of me, I will go. To waste his time is to waste the genius of France." Not for nothing had François been of late in the society of the Comédie Française.

"*Tiens!* Who told thee to go? I desire to do my own thinking. Why art thou here?"

François laughed, but made no other reply.

"Young man, art thou laughing at the Revolutionary Tribunal?"

"Thou art also laughing, monsieur." When François laughed, he who looked at him laughed also.

"*Diable!* yes. What right hast thou to make an officer of the Great Committee laugh? Thou wilt get into trouble."

"I am in it now, monsieur—up to the neck."

"No 'monsieur' to me, aristocrat! What brought thee here?"

"A greedy woman denounced me. Could not I denounce her in turn?"

"*Mort du diable!* that is a fine idea—to let the denounced also denounce. It would make things move. I will mention that to Couthon." The half of the face that was able to express emotion manufactured a look of ferocious mirth; but it was clear that he took the proposition seriously.

"It appears that we do not go fast enough, citizen," said François. "In April, 257; in May, so far, only 308. So say the gazettes. What if we denounce Citizens Robespierre and Vadier? We might go faster. Let us denounce everybody, and, last, the devil."

Amar set an elbow on the table, and, with his chin in his hand, considered this novel specimen of humanity.

François had a controlling idea that what chance of safety there was lay in complete abandonment to the natural recklessness of his ever-dominant mood of humor.

"AMAR CONSIDERED THIS NOVEL SPECIMEN OF HUMANITY."

"Art thou at the end of thy nonsense, idiot?" said the Jacobin.

"Not quite; the citizen might denounce himself."

"By all the saints! Art making a jest of me—me, Jean Pierre Amar? Thou must value thy head but little."

"*Dame!* it was never worth much; and as to saints, one Citizen Montmorency said yesterday that the republic hath abolished the noblesse of heaven and earth too. Droll idea, citizen"; and he laughed merrily.

"Oh, quit that infernal laughing! Thou must be of the Comédie Française."

"No; I am of the comedy of France, like the rest —like the commissioner; but the citizen has two ears for a joke."

"I—I think so"; and he made it manifest by a twisted, unilateral grin of self-approval. "That idea of the citizen—prisoners denouncing—I shall not forget that. Wilt thou serve the republic?"

"Why not?"

"These common spies in the prisons are useless. I will put an 'M' to thy name on our list; 'M' for *mouchard*—spy. That will put thee down at the bottom whenever the Committee of Safety comes to thy case. I am not ungrateful."

"Very good," said François, promptly. "I am as honest a Jacobin as the best. I will serve the republic, citizen, to the best of my ability."

"Then thou wilt report once a week, especially on the *ci-devants*. The head keeper will give thee pen, ink, and paper, and a chance to write here alone. I

will so order it.  But beware, citizen!  I am not a
man to trifle with; I do not forget."

"I should think not," said François, humbly.

"And when Grégoire comes, in June, thou wilt report to him."

"I—Grégoire—report—"

"Certainly.  What's the matter?  Off with thee
now.  Ah, that *sacré* Citizen Ste. Luce!  I forgot him.
Tell him his case will come on shortly."

"I am sorry."

"That is to lack patriotism."

"But he and De Crosne are the only people who
amuse me, and it is dull in this bird-cage.  He swears
thou art clumsy with the small sword."

"I—I clumsy!  I should like to catch him somewhere.  I was too fat; but now!" and he smote his
chest.  "Didst thou think me clumsy—me, Pierre
Amar?"

"I?  No, indeed.  These aristocrats think no one
else can handle a rapier.  Ah, if I could fence with
the citizen commissioner a little, and then—"

"Impossible."

"He swears thou art coward enough to use the
guillotine to settle a quarrel, and that thou dost fence
like a pigsticker."

Amar, *le farouche*, swore an oath too blasphemous
to repeat.  The great thick-lipped mouth moved half
across so much of his face as could move at all.  He
was speechless with rage, and at last gasped, as he
struck the table: "Me—Amar?  Ah, I should like
well to let him out and kill him; and I would, too,
but there are Saint-Just, and Couthon, and the rest.
Go; and take care how thou dost conduct thyself.

Go! The *sacré* marquis must take his chance. Pig-sticker indeed!"

Thus terminated this formidable interview; but, alas! it was now close to the end of May, and in the background of June was the man with the wart.

The next day, in the garden, François related to the marquis his interview with the dreaded Jacobin. The gentleman was delighted.

"*Mon Dieu!* François, you are a great man; but I fear it will do no good; my turn must be near. De Crosne and poor Fleury got their little billets last evening, and are off on a voyage of discovery to-morrow, along with M. de la Morne, and De Lancival, and more. They will be in good society. Did you think that Jacobin Apollo would be pricked into letting me out for the chance of killing me?"

"It came near to that, monsieur. I did say that you were not much of a blade, after all; that Citizen Amar was out of condition when you last met; and that if he and I could fence a little,—outside, of course,—M. le Marquis would regret the meeting."

"Delicious! And he took it all?"

"Yes, as little Annette takes a fairy-tale of M. Fleury's—who will tell no more, poor fellow!"

"But, after all, we are still here. I envy you the interview. *Parbleu!* these fellows do their best, but they can't take the jests out of life. I hope the next world will be as amusing."

As he ceased, François exclaimed:

"By all the saints! there is that crazy fool Despard."

"Despard—Despard?" repeated the marquis. "That is a contribution to the show. How the mischief did he get here?"

14

The unlucky Jacobin was wandering about like a lost dog, a shabby, dejected figure. Toto, at play, recognized his master's former partner, and jumped up in amiable recognition. Despard kicked him, and the poodle, unaccustomed to rude treatment, fled to François. The thief's long face grew savage and stern; to hurt Toto was a deadly offense.

"Pardon, monsieur," he said to the marquis, and went swiftly to where Despard stood against the wall.

"Look here, rascal," said François; "if ever thou dost kick that dog again, I will twist thy neck."

Despard did not seem to take in his meaning.

"It is thou, François. There is the *ci-devant*—the marquis. I followed him. I—Pierre Despard—I denounced him. I did it. I am not afraid."

"Stuff! Didst thou hear me? What have I to do with *ci-devant* marquises? Thou hast kicked Toto."

"I see him; I must speak with him."

"*Fichtre!* he is mad," said the thief, and went after him.

At the coming of Despard, ragged, wild-eyed, excited, the group about the tall gentleman turned.

Despard paused before him. "It is my turn now! I followed—I followed—I denounced thee—I, Pierre Despard. They will let me out when thou art to die; it will be soon. I will take thy child—thy bastard—my wife's child. We will go to see thee—I and thy hunchback—to see thee on the tumbrel at the guillotine. She hath thy own cold eyes—frozen eyes. Thou wilt know her by those when thou art waiting—waiting—shivering."

The marquis listened with entire tranquillity.

"One or two more in the audience will matter little"; and, smiling, he walked away.

A strange tremor seized on the chin and lower lip of Despard. He said to François, "Come with me," and then, in a bewildered manner, "He is n't afraid yet. I—I want him to be afraid."

"*Dame!* thou wilt wait then till the cows roost and the chickens give milk."

"No; it will come."

"Stuff! How camest thou here? Didst thou denounce thyself? I have heard of men mad enough to do that."

"No. Do not tell. I trust thee; I always did trust thee. I am a spy. I am to stay here till I want to be let out, when he—he is tried. I wanted to watch him. Some day he will have fear—fear—and—I—"

"Well, of all the mad idiots! A mouse to walk into a trap of his own accord! *Dieu!* but the cheese must have smelt good to thee."

"I shall go out when I want to go. Didst thou know his daughter is dead? I am sorry she is dead."

"Yes—God rest her soul!"

"I am sorry she is dead because she cannot be here. I wish she were here. If only she were here, it would be complete. Then he would be afraid."

"*Bon Dieu!*" cried several, "he will kill him!" The thief had caught Pierre by the throat, and, scarce conscious of the peril of his own strength, he choked the struggling man, and at last, in wild rage, hurled him back amid a startled mass of tumbled people.

"Beast!" muttered François, at his full height regarding angrily the prostrate man.

In an instant the jailers were at his side. "What is this?" said they.

"He—he kicked my dog!"

"Did he? Well, no more of this, citizen."

"Then let him be careful how he kicks my dog; and take him away, or—"

Pierre needed no further advice.

Presently Ste. Luce came over to François.

"What is wrong?"

"He kicked my dog!"

"Indeed? Do you know this man well? Once you warned me about him. Where have you met?"

"We juggled together, monsieur, when I used to read palms. He is a bit off his head, I think."

"'T is common in France just now, or else the reverse is. But he has a damnably good memory. We of Normandy say, 'As is the beast, so are his claws.' The fellow is of good blood in a way; but, *mon Dieu!* he is a coward to be pitied. To be through and through a coward does much enlarge the limits of calamity. If I or if you were to hate a man, for reasons good or bad, we would kill him. But a coward! What can he do? He has his own ways, not mine or yours. His claws are not of the make of mine. I have no complaint to make as to his fashion of revenging himself; but really, revenge, I fancy, must lose a good deal of its distinctness of flavor when it waits this long. It is, I should say, quite twelve years—quite. There is a child, he says, or there was. Do you chance to know anything about it?"

"Yes."

"Did you ever see it? Is it male or female?"

"A girl, monsieur. I never saw it."

"How old?"

"I do not know."

"Penitence becomes a question of dates, François. But it is true—true that I never had the least talent for regret; and if a man is not capable of regret, why, François, how the deuce can he achieve penitence? Don't think I am joking, my most accomplished thief. There are men here who—there is M. de— well, no matter. There are men here who are honestly bewailing their past—well, amusements—sins, if you please. I cannot. There are some here who, because they are noble by descent, are making believe not to be afraid, and will make believe until the knife falls. I am not penitent, because I am not; and as to the knife, I have had a most agreeable life, and should never have gone on living if life had ceased to amuse me."

He was now silent awhile, his strong, handsome features clear to see, as they lay on the scant grass in the sunshine. The thief had learned that at times this great seigneur would talk, and liked to do so; and that at other times he was to be left to the long silences which were difficult to secure where this morbidly gay crowd, of all conditions of men, was seeking the distraction of too incessant chat.

He rose quietly, and went away to talk with Domville of the Comédie, who himself was always glad of the company of François's cheery visage.

In the salon, which was now deserted, he saw Despard. Pierre stood at an open window, and was pulling at his fingers, as François had so often seen

him doing.   He was gazing at the people in the yard.
His eyes wandered feebly here and there, as if without
interest or purpose.   His attitude of dejection touched
some chord of pity in his partner's heart.

" *Dame!* he must have thought I was rough with
him for a dog—a dog."   He had no mind to explain.

Pierre turned to meet him.   He was not angry, nor
was he excited.   The shifting phases of his malady
had brought to him again the horrible misery of such
melancholy as they who are sound of mind cannot
conceive.   When this torture has a man in its grip,
the past is as nothing; the present a curse; duty is
dead; the future only an assurance of continued suf-
fering; death becomes an unconsidered trifle; life—
continued life—an unbearable burden.

Poor Pierre said no word of his ex-partner's recent
violence.   The tears were running down his cheeks.
The man at his side was, as usual, gaily cheerful.

"What is wrong with thee?" said François.   "I
was hard on thee, but thou knowest—"

"What is it?" replied Pierre.   "I—it is no matter."

François, surprised, went on: "Can I help thee?"

"No.   I cannot sleep; I cannot eat.   I suffer.   I am
in a hell of despair."

"But how, or why, *mon ami?*"

"I do not know.   I suffer."

"Rouse up a bit.   Why didst chance to come here?
I asked thee that before.   If thou canst get out, go at
once.   Thou art not fit to be in this place.   This devil
of a marquis excites thee.   To be a spy thou shouldst
be ashamed.   Canst thou really get out when it pleases
thee to go?"

"Why not?" said Pierre, in alarm. "Dost thou think they will not let me go? I did not want to be a spy, but I was half starved. All I could get I sent to keep my—his poor little hunchback. Vadier lent me some money. I kept none, not a sou. I asked him to let me come here as a spy. They say my reports are useless. I can't help that. I will go out. I want to see that man suffer; I want to see him afraid. He is not afraid. Dost thou think he is afraid?"

"No."

For a moment there was a pause, when Pierre, in a quiet, childlike manner, said: "Dost thou think he ever will be afraid?"

"No, Pierre; he never will be. What a fool thou art to have come here! 'T is not so easy to get out."

"*Mon Dieu!* don't say that. I—they said—"

"Dost thou believe a Jacobin—and Vadier, the beast, of all men?"

"Hush!" said Pierre, looking about him suspiciously. "I must go—I must go. I must walk; I cannot keep still."

He remained in this mood of subdued terror and the deepest melancholy for some days. Then for a few hours he followed the marquis about, proclaiming his own wrongs in a high-pitched voice. At last Ste. Luce complained to the keeper, Vaubertrand, who hesitated to interfere, being puzzled and fearful as to the amount of influence possessed by this spy of the Committee of Safety. He mustered enough courage at last to tell Despard that he must not speak to the marquis; and, as he luckily caught him in his mood of despair and depression, the man timidly promised to obey.

# XXI

*How François, having made a bargain with Citizen Amar, cannot keep it with the man of the wart— How Despard dies in the place of the marquis— Of François's escape from prison.*

HE second week of June was over. The keeper, who had taken a fancy to the merry thief, called him aside one afternoon, and said:

"Thou must write thy report, because to-morrow comes Citizen Grégoire. Thou canst use the office for an hour, as is permitted. But take care. Thou dost know how they are treated in the prisons who are suspected of making these reports to the committee. I will come for thee at dusk."

François thanked him, and at the time mentioned was locked up in the office; for despite Vaubertrand's amiability, he was careful as to the security of his prisoners. As it was now dark, the office table was lighted by two candles. He found pen and ink and paper, but no competent thoughts. What was he to say—whom to accuse? He had made a hasty contract with Amar, and was of no mind to fulfil his share of it. He got up from the desk, and walked

240

about. "The deuce!" he said to Toto, who never left
him. "'T is a scrape of our own making. I should
have told that scamp with the pretty face to go to
the devil with his spy business. *Sacristie!* doggie, I
am like that fellow in the play I once saw. He sold
his soul to the devil, and did n't want to pay up when
the time came. What to do?" He had told the
marquis, whom he trusted, of the difficulty he anticipated.

Ste. Luce, much amused, said: "Take me for a
subject. I am as sure to die as an abbot's capon. If
you have a conscience, it may rest easy so far as I am
concerned."

François took it seriously. "I beg of you, monsieur—"

"Oh, a good idea!" laughed the nobleman, breaking
in upon his remonstrance. "Tell them how you saw
me kill three good citizens that night on the stairs.
By Mars! François, those twenty minutes were worth
living for. I was in a plot to rescue the king; tell
them that."

"Not I," grinned the thief.

"Confound it! you are difficult."

And now, as François recalled their talk, his task
was not more easy. He nibbled the end of his quill,
and looked around him. At last, as he walked to and
fro, he began to exercise his natural inquisitiveness.
It was never long quiet. He stared at the barred
windows. A set of pigeonholes attracted him. He
glanced hastily over their contents. *"Tiens!"* he exclaimed.

Every day or two, about 3 P. M., a clerk of the

Committee of Safety brought a great envelop
stamped with the seal of the republic. Within was a
paper on which were clearly set out the names and
former titles of the citizen prisoners selected for trial
the night before in joint counsel by the Great Committee and that of Security. The keeper copied each
name on to the space in the blank summons kept for
this use, and these fatal papers were then duly de-
livered after supper.

François looked at the packet. It was sealed. He
knew well what it meant. It was labeled: "Mandate
of the Tribunals Nos. 4 and 5."

"Toto, we may be among them; we must see." He
looked about him. Here were all the writing-table
implements then in use. He heated a knife, and
neatly loosened the under wax of the seal. The
death-call lay before him. He ran over it with shud-
dering haste.

"*Dieu!* we are not there. But, *mon ami*, here is
the marquis!" His was the last name at the foot of
the first page. François sat still, his face in his
hands. At any moment he might be caught. He
did not heed.

"I must do it," he said. He saw, as it were
before him, the appealing face of the dead woman,
and felt in remembrance the hand the great seigneur
had given him on the stair. He had a glad memory
of a moment which had lifted him on to the higher
levels of self-esteem and manhood.

"I will do it, Toto; 't is to be risked; and, *mon
Dieu!* the rest—the rest of them!" Some he knew
well. Some had been kind to him. One had given

him clothes when these were greatly needed. He was profoundly moved.

"If I burn it, 't is but to give them a day, and no more—if I burn it!"

He took scissors from the table, and carefully cut off the half-inch at the foot of the paper. It was now without the name "Ste. Luce, *ci-devant* marquis." He tore up the strip of paper, and put the fragments in the fireplace, behind the unkindled logs.

Next he casually turned the page. "*Ciel!* this calls for eleven. I have left but ten. They will think it a blunder. One will be wanting; that is all."

He used a little melted wax under the large seal, replaced the warrant in the outer cover, and returned the document to the pigeonhole whence he had taken it. This done, he sat down again, and began to write his report.

He found nothing to say, except that those he would have spoken of had been already disposed of; and now he thought again that he would burn the fatal paper. He rose resolute, but at this moment the head keeper came back.

François was sorry, but he was not used to writing, and made excuses until at last the man said impatiently:

"Well, thou must settle all that with Amar and Grégoire. I gave thee time enough." Could he have another chance? He was told that he should have it; but now it was supper-time; better not to be missing. He went out and up-stairs to his place at table.

He had lost his gaiety. Here and there at the table were the doomed men and women. He could not eat, and at last left the room to wander in the corridors. Pierre soon found him. He was eager, anxious, and full of strange news.

"When will that brute marquis be sent for? I was to go out to-day. They have forgotten. There is trouble in the Great Committee. I hear of it from Vaubertrand. Robespierre and Vadier think things go not fast enough; and the rest—the rest, except little cripple Couthon and Saint-Just, are opposing our great Robespierre."

François began to be interested, and to ask questions. The gazettes were no longer allowed in the prisons. The outer world was a blank to all within their walls.

Despard, flushed and eager, told him how daily the exit of the prisoners for trial was met by a mob clamorous for blood. Then he began to exhibit alarm. Did François think that he, Pierre, might by chance miss the execution of the marquis? He would speak to Grégoire, who was coming next morning. They should learn not to trifle with a friend of Robespierre. When François left him he was gesticulating, and, as he walked up and down the deserted corridor, was cracking his knuckles or gnawing his nails.

After supper the varied groups collected in the salon. The women embroidered. A clever artist was busy sketching the head of a girl of twenty for those she loved, who were to see her living face no more. Some played at cards. Here and there a man sat alone, waiting, stunned by the sure approach of death. The marquis was in gay chat with the Vicomte de Beauséjour.

"Ah, here is my mysterious gentleman!" cried Ste.

Luce. "They have bets on you. Tell these gentlemen who you really are. They are puzzled."

François smiled. He was pleased to do or say
anything which would take his thoughts off the near
approach of the messenger of doom. He said:

"M. le Marquis knows that I am under an oath."

"*Pardie!* true, true; I have heard as much."

"The bets stand over," said a gray old man, M. de
l'Antilhac. "We knew you as a juggler."

"Yes, and a fencing-master," said Du Pin.

"You are both right. These times and the king's
service set a man to strange trades. Well, gentlemen, I am not to be questioned. Tales lose heads."

They laughed. "Pardon me," said a younger man.
"The marquis was about to tell us of the delightful
encounter you had on his staircase. 'T is like a legend
of the days of Henri IV of blessed memory."

"Tell them," said Ste. Luce.

"The marquis does me much—*Dieu!*" François
cried, and fell back into a chair, weak as a child. The
turnkey went by him with the fatal missives.

"Art thou ill?" said De l'Antilhac. "What is it?"

"Yes," said François. "Excuse me. He—he—"
And, as it were fascinated, he rose and went after the
keeper.

Vaubertrand paused behind a gentleman who was
playing piquet.

"Citizen Ste. Michel," he said, and passed on, as he
laid the summons before the player.

"At last!" said the man thus interrupted. "Quatre
to the king—four aces. Let it wait."

Vaubertrand moved on. François followed him.

The calls to trial and death were distributed.  A man rolled up the fatal paper without a word, and lighted his pipe with it.  One of those who sat apart took his summons, and fell fainting on the floor.

"Nothing for me?" said the marquis.

"Not yet, citizen."

"I was never before so neglected."

The game went on.  Here and there a woman dropped her embroidery and sat back, thinking of the world to come, as she rolled the deadly call to trial in her wet fingers, and took refuge in the strength of prayer.

François felt as if it were he who had condemned these people.  He went to his cell, and tossed about all night, sleepless.  Rising early, he went out into the garden.  After breakfast the keeper said to him:

"Thou shouldst have had thy report ready.  Grégoire is coming to-day.  He is before his time.  If he is drunk, as usual, there will be trouble.  That fool Despard is wild to-day.  He will be sure to stir up some mischief.  All the *mouchards* will be called."

"Despard is an idiot.  He is raving one day, and fit to kill himself the next.  Get him out of this."

"*Dame!* I should be well pleased.  He swears I keep him here.  He will—ah, *mon Dieu!* the things he threatens.  I am losing my wits.  My good François, I have been kind to thee, and I talk rashly.  I wish I had done with it all."

"And I too, citizen; but thou art safe with me."

As the jailer spoke, he looked over his list of those summoned.  "*Sacré bleu!* here is a list which calls for eleven, and there are only ten names!"

"Some one has made a mistake."

"No doubt. But Grégoire never listens. Pray God he be sober. Be in the corridor at nine; Grégoire will want to see thee."

François would be on hand. As to the report, he should wish to ask how to draw it up. He found a quiet corner in the courtyard, and began to think about the man with the wart—the man of whom he knew so little, and whom he feared as he had never before feared a man. The every-day horror and disturbance of the morning had begun. Officers were coming and going; names were called; there were adieus, quiet or heartrending. The marquis was tranquilly conversing, undisturbed by the scene, which was too common to trouble those who had no near friend or relation in the batch of prisoners called for trial. François had seen it all, day after day. It always moved him, but never as now.

He stood looking at a young woman who was sitting with the order in her lap, her eyes turned heavenward as if in dumb appeal. Now and then she looked from one man to another, as if help must come.

François glanced at the marquis; he was the center of a laughing group, chatting unconcerned.

"*Ciel!* has the man no heart?" he murmured. "Why did I save him even for a day? The good God knows. It must make life easy to be like him." The marquis would have been amazed to know that the memory of a white, sad woman's face, and of one heroic hour, had given him a new lease of life.

"Ah, Toto," said the thief to himself, "we held that

stair together, he and I." The thought of an uplifting moment overcame him. A sudden reflection that he might have been other than he was flushed his face.

"Ah, my friend Toto, we could have been something; we missed our chance in the world. Well, thou dost think we had better make a fight for it. Life is agreeable, but not here. Let us think. There is one little card to play. Art thou up to it? Yes! I must go now. Thou wilt wait here, and thou wilt not move. In an hour I shall be with thee; and, meanwhile, behold a fine bone. No, not yet, but when I come. Attention, now!"

He turned his back to the prison, took off a shoe, and extracted a paper, which he folded so as to be small and flat. Then he produced a bit of a kid glove he had asked from Mme. Cerise of the Comédie Française. In it he laid the paper, and put the little packet, thus protected, in the dog's mouth. "Keep it," he said. "It is death—it is life." The dog lay down, his sharp black nose on his paws, shut his eyes, and seemed to be asleep. He had done the thing before.

When François entered the corridor he found the keeper.

"Come," said Vaubertrand. "The commissioner is in a bad way, and drunk, too. He is troubled, I think, and the citizens who are outside reproach him that the supply for the guillotine is small, and the prisons full. What have I done to be thus tormented? There will be a massacre. *Ciel!* I talk too much. I have favored thee. Take care—and thou canst laugh yet." Whereupon François laughed anew, and went after him.

The large hall on the first floor was unusually full. There was much confusion. The great street door, as it was opened wide and shut again in haste, gave a not reassuring glimpse of men in red bonnets roaring the *Ça ira*. Over all rose the shrill tongues of the women of the markets. A new batch of prisoners was pushed in, the keeper declaring he had no room. Officers of the Committee of Safety untied the hands of the newcomers, and ranged them on stone benches to the left. On the right were those who were called to trial. François stood aside, watchful.

Pierre Despard was waiting, flushed and anxious. As a spy, he had leave from Vaubertrand to descend in order to state his case to Grégoire. He went hither and thither, noisy, foolish, gesticulating. He was now in his alternate mood of excitement, and soon began to elbow his way toward the office.

"Citizen La Vaque is summoned."

A tall man answered from the bench. Then another and another was called. The officers went down the line, and, paper in hand, verified the prisoners. They were taken, one by one, into a side room by a second officer, and their hands secured behind their backs.

At last the first officer said: "Here are but ten, Citizen Vaubertrand, and the list calls for eleven. The keeper must see the commissioner." The officer in charge reproached Vaubertrand for neglect. The man with the wart came out from the office.

"Silence!" he cried. "What is this?"

The matter was explained, or was being set forth,

15

when the door opened, and another half-dozen unfortunates were rudely thrust in, while the crowd made a furious effort to enter. Grégoire turned pale.

"Thou shalt answer for this. Find another. I shall hear of it, and thou, too."

Meanwhile, Despard, too insane to observe Grégoire's condition, and lost to all sense of anything but his own sudden wish to escape, was frantically pulling the furious commissioner by the arm.

"Citizen," he cried, "I must be heard! Dost hear? Thou wilt repent. I am the friend of Robespierre."

Grégoire paid no attention; he was half drunk, and raging at poor Vaubertrand.

"I will report thee," cried Despard. "I denounce thee!"

Grégoire turned upon him in a rage.

"Who is this?" he cried.

"I am Despard of the fourth section. I will let thee know who I am." In his madness he caught Grégoire by the collar and shook him.

Grégoire called out: "Take away this fool! What! threaten me—me—Grégoire! Ah, thou art the rascal who plunders châteaux. I know thee. Thou dost threaten an officer of the Committee of Safety. Tie this fellow; he will do for the eleventh. Quick, quick!"

There was no hesitation. The officers seized their prey, and Grégoire, growling, went again into the office.

Pierre fought like the madman he was, but in a minute was brought back screaming and added to the corvée. It was complete. He was carried out raving, amid the yells and reproaches of the mob, which broke up and went along with the wagons.

Again there was quiet in the hall, where the thief stood in wonder, horror-stricken. "It is I that have killed him—he who did long to see another die. And for him to die in the place of the marquis—*dame!* it is strange."

"*Ciel!*" cried Vaubertrand, wiping the sweat from his brow. "This is the second they took this way to make up for some one's blunder. Come, and have a care what you say. He is half drunk."

François entered the office.

"Who is this?" said Grégoire, facing him, with his large, meaningless face still flushed and angry.

Vaubertrand pushed forward the reluctant François. "It is one of the reporters, citizen commissioner."

"Ahem! One of Citizen Amar's appointments," said Grégoire. "Thou canst go, Citizen Vaubertrand"; and he looked up as he sat at the table.

"Thy name?"

"François," said the thief.

"Thy occupation?"

"Juggler."

The citizen commissioner was on the uncertain line between appearance of sobriety obtained by effort and ebriety past control. As he interrogated François his head dropped forward. He recovered himself with a sharp jerk, and cried sharply:

"Why dost thou not answer? I said, How didst thou get here, and who gave thee thy order to report?"

"Citizen Amar; he is a friend of mine."

"Is he? Well, where is thy *sacré* report?"

"I should like to tell the citizen commissioner

what I have to say. I—I did not know just how to frame it."

Meanwhile Grégoire was considering him with unsteady eyes. "Ah, now I have it; now I remember thee. Thou art an *ex-émigré*. I shall attend to thee. It was thou who stole my wallet of papers; and thou couldst laugh, too. *Ciel!* what a laugh! Try it now."

François replied that he was no *émigré;* as to the rest, he could explain; and leaning over, he said quietly:

"You will do well to hear what I have to say."

"' *You* will do well'! Idiot! Why dost thou say '*you, you*'? Cursed aristocrat that thou art! Say 'thou' when thou dost address me, or I shall—where is that report?"

"If the citizen will listen. There was in that wallet a little paper addressed to Citizen de la Vicomterie. *Dame!* it was good reading, and I have it still."

"Thou hast it? Thou wilt not have it long."

Grégoire was not over-intelligent, and had now the short temper of drink. The prisoner tried to get a moment in which to explain that another held the document.

Grégoire was past hearing reason. "Officers, here! here!" he cried. "Search this man! Search him. Strip him. Here! here!"

François did not stir. "When thou hast done we can talk."

"Hold thy tongue! Search him."

"*Ma foi*, marquis," said the thief, later, "they did it well. They even chopped up the heels of my shoes. And my coat! *Sacré!* The good keeper gave me another.   In our cell, as I learned, they went through the beds and Heaven knows what else.   I was well pleased, I can tell thee, when it was all over."

The commissioner had now cooled down.   "Put on thy clothes," said Grégoire, and himself shut the door. It was François's turn.

"Citizen," he said, "didst thou think me fool enough to leave within reach that little letter of thine to the good citizen of the committee—to—ah, yes, La Vicom-terie is his name.   I am not an *émigré*, only a poor devil of a thief and a juggler.   I do not love Citizen Robespierre any better than some others love him— some I could name.   But one must live, and the day I go out to thy infernal tribunal, Robespierre will have thy letter.   A friend will go himself and lay it before the committee."

Grégoire grew deadly pale, all but the wart, which remained red.   "I am betrayed!"

"Wait a little.   Thou art not quite lost, but thou wilt be unless—"

"Unless what?"

"Unless thou wilt open that door and set me free. I have no grudge against thee.   I will arrange to have for thee the letter, and must receive from thee a new *carte de sûreté*, and a good passport on business of the Committee of Safety."

The commissioner was partly sobered.   "How shall I know that thou wilt keep thy word?"

"Thou wilt not know until I do.   Why should I not?"

"But the letter may be lost."

"Well, what then?   Thou wilt be safe, and have

one less life to answer for to the devil when he gets thee."

"Talk business. There is no devil."

"I don't agree with thee. His name is Robespierre. The mischief is that it is I who do not trust thee. Thou hast a wart, citizen. Men who have warts are unlucky to meet. But take care, because I am a desperate man, and most extremely value my head. If thou shouldst fail to—"

"No, no; I promise."

"Good, then."

"Wait; I will write out the papers."

"I shall not hurry thee. I must pack up. I will be back in half an hour. Be so kind as to arrange that I may return without hindrance."

François went at once to the garden, and called Toto. Then he hastened to his *cachot*, or cell, and, finding himself alone, shut the door, took the little packet from Toto's mouth, and gave him the promised bone. He placed the paper inside his stocking, and secured it with a pin. Next he gathered up his small effects, left his mangled coat on the bed of a fellow-prisoner, and descended thoughtfully to the office.

He was glad to see that the man of the wart was sitting apparently inattentive to the piles of accounts before him. "Clearly, the citizen is worried," said François to himself.

"I have thy papers. One had to be sent out for a signature. Here is thy card of safety, and reapproved as that of a citizen who has denounced an *ex-émigré*. Also, behold a passport, and an order

from the Committee of Safety to leave Paris on business of the republic.   All are in the name of Citizen
François, juggler."

"The citizen has been thoughtful."

"*Sacré!* I never do things by halves; I am thor-
ough.   And now, as to the paper?"

"It will be best for thee to come, at twelve to-day,
to No. 33 *bis* Rue Perpignan.   There I will take thee
to my old room, or another, and make good my side
of the bargain.   After that, I have the agreeable hope
never to meet thee again."

"I will be there at noon."

François's watchful ear detected a certain emphasis
on the "I" of this phrase, which made him suspicious.
He said quietly:

"Citizen, thou hast sold me my head.   I shall give
thee thine.   Afterward I shall be in thy power."

"Yes, yes; that might be so with Amar or Couthon,
but not with André Grégoire."

"*Tiens!*" said the thief, "what is this?   'André'?
This order is signed 'Alphonse Grégoire.'   The citizen
must have been absent-minded.   Look!"

Grégoire flushed.   "True, true.   I will write a
second.   I was troubled."

François stood still, received the second order, and,
saying, "*Au revoir*, citizen," was about to leave, when
a thought seemed to strike him.   He paused.   "There
is here a *ci-devant* marquis you may recall—Ste. Luce."

"Well?"

"Put his name at the foot of the file of the accused
and keep it there.   Get a clerk to do it.   The citizen
is aware that it is done every day."

"Impossible! Art thou insane? I run risk enough with thy order and passport. But this I dare not do. There are limits."

"Do it, or I throw up my bargain. By Heaven, I am in earnest! Come, what will it cost? Will one hundred louis d'or do the business?"

Grégoire reflected. What more simple than to say yes, pocket the money, and let things take their course?

"I will do it for that—I mean I can have it done."

"Then give me ten minutes."

"I will wait."

The rich throughout these evil days were allowed to have in prison as much money as they could get from without. About March of this sad year they were told that they must feed the poorer captives, and were regularly assessed. François was aware that the marquis was well provided. He found him in the garden, and asked him to step aside.

"I am free, monsieur," he said. "No matter how. And I have bargained for your own head." He briefly related so much of his talk with Grégoire as concerned the marquis.

Ste. Luce looked at him. "*Pardie!* You are an unusual type of thief—or man. I would thank you if I considered my head worth much. But, after all, it is a natural attachment one's body has for one's head, or one's head for one's body, to put it correctly. Will it be wasted money, my admirable thief, or will the rascal keep his word?"

"Yes; he will keep his word—after we get through with the affair."

"You are a great man, François, but I have not
the money. I lost it last night to Delavigne. I will
get the loan of it. Rather a new idea to borrow one's
head! Wait a little." He came back in a few minutes.
"It pretty well cleaned out two of them. Good luck
to you; and if ever we are out of this hole, we must
fence a little. By the way, I hear they took that
poor devil Despard to-day. It is a relief. He bored
me atrociously."

"Yes; they took him in your place, monsieur. It
was to have been to-day—"

"To-day! In my place? *Tiens!* that is droll."

"Yes."

"But how—why?"

"No matter now. I will tell monsieur some day."

"Are you a magician, Master François?"

"I was. But I did not desire this man's death."

"And the guillotine will have him, and he will not
be on hand to see me scared. *Ciel!* but it is strange.
Alas! the disappointments of this mortal life! Good
luck to you, and *au revoir*. I thank you."

A few minutes later, Grégoire, having carefully
disposed of the gold about his ample person, escorted
Citizen François to the outer door. The look with
which the commissioner with the wart regarded the
retreating back and the big ears of François was un-
friendly, to say the least.

# XXII

*Wherein is told how François baits a crab-trap with
the man of the wart.*

RANÇOIS understood the risks of his
position. For a time he was safe. After
he gave up that precious paper he would
be at Grégoire's mercy. "More or less,"
muttered the thief, with a laugh which
set Toto to capering. He went toward the Seine,
looked in the shop-windows, and had a bite and a
good bottle of wine, for the marquis had insisted on
giving him ten louis for his own use. About half-
past eleven he turned into the Rue Perpignan, and
rang the bell at No. 33 bis.

"Come, Toto," he said, as he went in. "We owe
Mme. Quatre Pattes a little debt. Let us be honest
and pay." He closed the door behind him, and heard
the sharp voice of the concierge: "Who goes there?
Speak, or I will be after thee." He drew back, and
looked in through the glassed door of the Crab's room.
He knew she would not sally out. Why should she?
Her house was only a hive of thieves and low women,
who were driven away when they could not pay, and
who rarely plundered one another."

258

He had never before so carefully inspected his landlady. She was seated at a table, about to drink a cup of cocoa. The room, the table, the little well-swept hearth, were all as clean as care and work could keep them. The woman herself was no less neat than her surroundings, yet she seemed one who belonged to the sties of the Cité's lowest life. There was something strangely feline in the combination of animal appearance with the notable cleanliness of her patched clothes, her person, and her abode. Her back, bent forward from the waist, and rigid, forced her to turn her head up and to one side to attain a view of the face of man. The same need kept her red eyes wide open. The malady which caused this distortion had ceased to be active. It had scarcely affected her general health. Like many of those who have suffered from the more common forms of the disease which makes the hunchback, she possessed amazing strength.

Now, as François stood hesitating, watchful, she sat at table before him, intent on her meal, looking here or there for bread or salt, her head swaying from side to side.

"If she were to bite a man, he would be as good as dead," murmured the thief. "What is it she is like? Ah, 't is the vipers in the wood of Fontainebleau. *Bonjour, maman*," he cried gaily, as he went in.

Taken by a sharp surprise, she gripped at her two sticks on the table, but missed them. They fell clattering, and her shaky hands dropped on her lap. She lacked not courage. As she sat crouched, the bald head, red-eyed and vigilant, was held back to watch this enemy.

Toto ran in, and fawned at her feet.

"Enchanted to see you, *maman*." By this time she had her wits about her, and, hearing no accusing charges, felt more at ease.

"Come back again, art thou, my fine thief-bird? Did he fly to his nest? Ha! he knows who will take care of him. That *sacré* shoemaker it was who denounced thee. Didst thou think it was thy little *maman?* Thou didst scold me. But how didst thou get out?"

"Ah, no matter now," said François. "I have work on hand for thee. If I mistrusted thee, it is not here I should have come. Sometime we will have a little *eau-de-vie* and a pipe, *maman*, and I will tell thee all about it. Wouldst thou serve the republic, and be well paid for it? Here, take thy sticks; thou art fit for anything only when thou hast all thy four legs. Listen, now; and, to begin, thou canst read a little—enough to understand this passport, and this order from the Great Committee of Safety?"

She looked eagerly over the papers. "Yes, yes."

"And thou canst read this still better." He let a gold louis drop on the table. She put out a claw, and, failing through tremor to pick it up, drew it to the edge, and for a moment held it under her eyes; then she put it into her mouth, and, apparently satisfied, chewed on it, moving her lower jaw from side to side.

"A good purse, *maman*. It would be a bold man or a blind would steal thy head for the gold. Heads always lose in our France to-day; thy own is none too sure, *maman*."

"If thou art thinking to scare Quatre Pattes, it won't do. Ha! it won't pay." She looked as if it would not.

François saw that he had made a misplay. He laughed his best. "*Nom de diable!* thou didst like a joke once. No matter. My time is short. I expect a citizen in a few minutes. Is my old room empty?"

"Yes, and half the rest. I tell thee, *mon fils*, I have missed thee."

"Give me the key, and pen, ink, and paper. These will do. Thy ink is dry. A little water—so. I shall come down in a minute or two, and take the citizen up with me. After that I shall come down alone. The citizen will be locked up."

"Good. Will he be alive? I will have no tricks; they get one into trouble."

"Alive! Yes; he will howl."

"Ah, he will howl. What shall I get?"

"He will pay to get out."

"He will pay—how much?"

"One—two—three hundred francs."

"Pshaw! Paper?"

"No; gold. At four to-morrow—no later, no sooner—at four to-morrow thou wilt let him out; and, mind thee, Dame Quatre Pattes, this is business of the republic. What happens to him after he is let out is of no moment. He may very likely make a fuss; he is bad-tempered. Wilt thou take the risk?"

"I—Quatre Pattes? Three hundred francs! I?"

"If I return not to give further orders before twelve, thou mayst ask the municipals to be here at four.

That will save trouble.  He will then be in no way to swear thou hast his money.  That may be the best plan.  I have no mind to get thee into trouble.  Now, hold thy tongue; and remember, it will be the little cripple Couthon who will reckon with thee if in this business thou dost fail."

"This is all very well if thou dost not return; but who will pay me if thou art of a mind to come and take him away thyself?"

"'T is a sharp old Crab," laughed François.  "If I come for him, I promise thee he shall pay thee full rent; and here is his *denier à Dieu, maman.*"  He cast another louis in her lap.  "If I come not by noon, get all you can, and denounce him as a suspect; but remember—not till four."

"*Queue du diable!*  'T is a fine transaction," cried the Crab, and knocked her sticks together for emphasis.  "We will bleed him like a doctor; we will send in the bill under the door; and then—we will have some nice municipals for sextons.  Ha! ha!  It is well to have the credit on one's little *carte de sûreté.*"

François assured her that the plan was good.  At this point, however, she became suddenly suspicious.  She stood crouching over her sticks, the snake-like head slowly moving from side to side, her eyes searching the thief's smiling face.  "Why is the man to be kept?  What is it?"

He expected this.  "Ask Couthon the palsied that, thou imbecile.  I will take him elsewhere.  There are a dozen houses where they ask no questions.  Yes or no?"

"Yes, yes!"  Caution was put to sleep by greed;

or, more truly, by want, which was nearing its extremity.

He felt secure. "If he should ring before I get down-stairs, let him wait. Now, the ink and key."

"Is he to make his will? Thou wilt not be long?"

"No; I want something that I left."

"Ah! thou didst leave something?"

"Yes, and thou didst not find it, *maman*. Fie, fie, for a clever woman! Well, if thou didst not find it, few could. Wait, now."

He went swiftly up-stairs with Toto, and unlocked the door, leaving the key outside in the lock. He put the writing-materials on a table. In the chimney, just within reach of his farthest touch, he found his pistol. It was not loaded, and he had no powder to recharge it. He laughed as, putting it behind him in his waist-belt, under his cloak, he descended the stair.

"All is right. *Cordon*, if you please," he cried from the hall. He had not waited outside five minutes when Grégoire appeared, in ordinary dress, without the official feathered hat or the scarf of a functionary. He was now sober enough, but uneasy, and looked about him as if fearing recognition.

"Come," said François. They mounted the ill-smelling stairway to the attic. Neither spoke. Once they were within the room, François said: "Sit down." He took a stool, placing himself between Grégoire and the door. "To business," he said, and slipped out the famous letter from Grégoire to De la Vicomterie. He glanced at it, laughing. "There are three or more heads in this," he said. "Robespierre would pay well for it, or Saint-Just. One might put it up at auction. There would be high bidding."

Grégoire said: "I have paid for it. Give it to me —give it to me!"

"No hurry, commissioner." The thief enjoyed the situation. "Let us talk a little. Let us make things a trifle safer. Have the kindness to write a receipt for one hundred louis d'or accepted by thee as security for the head of one Louis de Ste. Luce, *ci-devant* marquis."

"Not I!" cried Grégoire, starting up.

"Ah, I think thou wilt"; and, with this, François drew his quite harmless pistol, and cocked it.

"Dost thou mean to murder me? Help! help! Murder!"

François seized him by the throat and thrust him down on to the chair.

"The devil! Fat fool! must I really kill thee? Hold thy tongue. Toto," he said, "just look at this gentleman. He is afraid, a coward—he who has killed so many—so many brave men and women, who died and showed no fear. Keep the door, Toto. There, now, citizen; write it, and quick, too, or—"

"But it is my death."

"What do I care? It is certain death unless thou dost keep faith. Once the marquis is free, and I am secure, I will burn it. That is all. Thou art forced to trust me. The situation is simple, and rather different from what it was at nine this morning. Thou art trapped."

It was true, and Grégoire knew it. He drew his chair to the table, and wrote a few lines as the thief dictated. François added a request for a date. "Thou art not clever with a pen," he said; "thy hand shakes."

" I am a lost man ! "

"No; by no means. But look out for my marquis. He ought to be very precious to thee, because—because if there should be any accident to him or to me, my friend will promptly place this harmless receipt in the hands of Saint-Just; and then—"

Grégoire sat in a cold sweat, saying at intervals: " I am lost. Let me go."

"Not quite yet. Give me ten louis."

" I—I can't. I left the money at home."

"Thou art lying. I heard it rattle when I shook thee. I might take it all. I am generous, just, like the incorruptible man with the green around his eyes, one Robespierre. Come, now."

Grégoire, reluctant, counted out the gold. "Let me go," he said. There were scarce left in him the dregs of a man. He rose, pale and tottering.

"Not quite yet, my friend. Thou wilt wait here a little while. Then a citizen hag will come up and let thee out. But be careful; no noise. The gentlemen who inhabit this mansion like not to be disturbed in their devotions. Moreover, they are curious, and generally inquisitive as to purses. Thou hast a few hours for reflection on thy sins. Pray understand that this little paper will be put in the hands of a friend of the marquis; I shall not keep it. The trap will be well set. Am I clear?"

The commissioner made no reply.

"I forgot," said François. "Here is thy letter. I keep my word. The receipt is enough."

16

The compromising document lay on the table, unnoticed by Grégoire. He fell back, limp and cowed, gripping the seat with both hands to save himself from slipping out of the chair. The sweat ran down his face. When François, calling to the poodle, left him alone, he made no motion; he was like a beaten cur.

"Come, Toto," said François, as he locked the door. "That for his wart! It is not as big as it used to be, and it is not in the middle of his nose." He went down to the room of the concierge, and threw the key of his room in her lap.

"He is very quiet, thy patient up-stairs; he hath a chill."

Quatre Pattes, standing by, nodded, and looked up. "Is he alive? No lies, young man."

"Alive? Not quite; only well scared. Imagine thyself one day on the red stair, and the basket all ready, and so neat,—thou art fond of neatness,—all as clean as thy room; and the knife—"

"Shut up that big jaw! I am Quatre Pattes. Dost thou want to frighten me?"

"I? By *St. Fiacre*, no! I only want to let thee understand how the citizen on the fourth floor feels."

"He will bleed the better, my dear." She rattled the sticks, and looked up at François, her head swaying as the head of the cobra sways. She was still in some doubt as to this too ready pupil, whom she had taught so much. "Art thou trying to fool Mother Quatre Pattes?"

"Oh, stuff! Go up and speak to the man. But take care; this is no light matter to put thy claws into. The man will rage; but a day without diet will quiet him a good bit. Then thou canst begin to make thy little commercial arrangement."

"Two hundred—three hundred. No rags, no assignats."

"Might get four hundred, Mother Crabby. There will be two sides to the question."

The old woman laughed a laugh shrill and virulent. "Two sides? I see—inside and outside. All right."

François stood in the doorway as she spoke.

"By-by, *maman*; and don't frighten him too much. Thy style of beauty is not to the taste of all men. Folks are really afraid of thee, *maman*. Don't make it a part of the bargain that he marry thee."

"Good idea, that! And when shall I see thee?"

"Possibly to-morrow; certainly within a week or so. I may have a few days' work for the committee in Villefranche—dirty country, filthy inns, not like thy room"; and he glanced at it. "I always do like to see how neat it is, and how clean. It would please Sanson. He is so particular; keeps things clean and ready—always ready."

"'T is true," said Quatre Pattes, and clattered away up the hall.

François heard her sticks on the stair, and her shrill laughter. "Thy cheese is poisoned, old rat," he said.

Once secure of the absence of his too observant landlady, François called to Toto and went out of the house. It was now about half-past one. No suspicious persons were visible. He had doubted this Grégoire. He had no mind to leave Paris, but when asking a passport he meant that Grégoire should think he had done so. He moved away, with the dog at his heels, and presently stood awhile in deep thought, at the end of the street. Grégoire was safe; he could harm no one for a day, and after that would be the last man in Paris to trouble François. Amar was to be feared, but that was to be left to chance and cautious care. Quatre Pattes? He smiled. "'T is as fine as a play, Toto. Here comes the last act. *Can* we go away and not see it?" He looked back. The shoemaker whom the Crab had wished him to denounce, with a view to the eternal settlement of her debts, was standing at his door in the sun, just opposite to No. 33 bis. It was a good little man, lame of a leg, hard-working and timid.

"It is not to be resisted, Toto. Come, my boy." He went back, and pulled the bell at No. 33 bis. No one answered. He rang three times, and became sure that, as he had anticipated, the Crab had at once gone up to see how much of truth there was in his statement.

Thus assured, he looked about him. He saw no one he had need to fear. He crossed the street, and spoke to the cobbler.

"Come into thy shop; I want to speak to thee." When within, he said: "I have been arrested, and let out—praise be to the saints! I have just now seen the old Crab. She owes thee money?"

"Not much."

"No matter. She has asked me to denounce thee, my poor friend. I came to warn thee."

The cobbler gasped. "*Dieu!* and my little ones! I have done nothing—I assure thee, nothing."

"Nor I, my friend. Now, listen. I am lucky enough

"HE PULLED THE BELL AT No. 33 BIS."

to be in a little employment for the Great Committee. I mean to save thee."

"And canst thou do that?"

"Yes, yes. Something will happen to-morrow, about four o'clock; and after that no fear of the hag. I must see it; it is my business. Can I stay a day—I mean until then—in the little room here above thy shop?"

"Why not? The children are with my sister. They shall stay till to-morrow night."

He followed the overjoyed cobbler up to the room above his shop, sent him out to buy food and wine, and sat down to await events. The cobbler came back with a supply of diet and the gazettes. François sat behind the slats of the green window-shades, and laughed, or talked to Toto, or read, while at intervals he watched No. 33 bis. He read of how Charleroi had been taken, and of the recovery of Fleurus. It interested him but little.

"They have cut off the head of the devil, and got a new god, my good poodle. *Tenez!* Hold! Attention!" He saw Quatre Pattes clatter out. It was about 4 P. M. She had no market-net. She was decisively bent on some errand, and moved with unusual celerity, her back bent, her head strained upward to get a sufficient horizon.

"It is altogether pleasant, *ami*. She will not wait till twelve to-morrow. She has gone to denounce him. Get up. Here is a nice bite for thee. She is shrewd, our snake. If she plunders M. Grégoire,—and she will, too,—she knows what he will do when he is out. He will denounce her. The play is good, Toto. The money she will have, if we know her. But, *mon ami*, if he makes her believe through the door that he is the great Grégoire of the wart, and she lets him out, and is scared, and asks no pay, Toto, 't is nevertheless a scotched snake she will be. The Wart will want to be revenged for low diet and loss of the republic's time. *Mordieu!* Toto, let us bet on it."

He read his gazettes, and waited. At six that afternoon the Crab came home. At nine François went to bed. Twice he awakened, laughing; he was thinking about Grégoire. The cobbler came in at six with breakfast, and François warned him to be careful.

At ten in the morning Quatre Pattes appeared at her door, and chatted with one or two dames of the fish-market. She rattled her sticks, and talked volubly. She was in the best of humors.

No new thing took place till three o'clock, when two municipal guards paused at her door. She came forth, spoke to them, and went in, leaving the door open. A third joined them. They loitered about. Ten minutes went by. François grew more and more eager as he watched.

"Ho, ho, Toto," he exclaimed, "there was a noise! The fool! she has gone up alone to let him out."

It was true. Grégoire had yielded in all some three hundred francs, and, as ordered, had slipped the money under the door, piece by piece, while Quatre Pattes sat and counted it with eyes of greed. She came down and hid the last of it. Now she went up again, rather liking the errand. She was absolutely fearless. She opened the door, and stood aside. "Come out," she said, "little man."

"'THE LITTLE TRAP DID WORK,' CRIED FRANÇOIS, BEHIND HIS SCREEN."

Grégoire was past restraining his rage. "She-devil!" he cried, and struck at her, in a fury of passion. He ran past her down the stairs, the terrible woman after him. She was wonderfully quick, but the man's fear was quicker. At the last stairway she found him beyond her reach, and, cursing him in fluent slang of the quarter, she threw one of her sticks at him. It caught him on the back of the neck, and he fell headlong into the hallway. In an instant he was up and staggering into the street. As he came forth two guards seized him. "In the name of the law!" Quatre Pattes came swiftly after him, screaming out: "Take him! I denounce him! He is an aristocrat!"

What she and François saw was unpleasant for her.

"*Nom de ciel!* 't is the Citizen Grégoire!" cried the third guard.

Grégoire was for an instant speechless and breathless. The guards fell back.

"Arrest me?—me, Grégoire! Have you an order to arrest me?" He was not quite at ease.

"No, no, citizen. It is clearly a mistake. We were to arrest a *ci-devant.*"

Quatre Pattes stood up, pallid.

"Take this woman!" cried Grégoire. "I will send an order. The Châtelet, and quick!"

"The little trap did work," cried François, behind his screen. "How she squeals—like a pig, a pig! She will give up the money. The citizens and she disappear within."

"This woman stole it!" roared the great man, as they came out. "Take her away."

When they came to lay final hands on her, she was like a cat in a corner.

"*Chien de mon âme!* 't is a fine scrimmage," cried François, "and the street full."

The sticks rattled; and when they were torn from her, she used tooth and claw, to the joy of a crowd appreciative of personal prowess. At last she was carried away, screaming, and exhausted as to all but her tongue.

The commissioner with the wart readjusted his garments and his dignity. The crowd cried: "*Vive Grégoire!*" and the hungry Jacobin went his way, furious, in search of dietetic consolation.

"The show is over, Toto," said François, as he sat down.

Presently came the cobbler, curious, and much relieved.

"Ask no questions," said François. "Here is a little money."

"But, citizen, it is a gold louis."

"The show was worth the price of admission. Thou art welcome. Hold thy tongue, if thou art wise. At dusk I shall slip out. Thou art safe. The Crab will denounce no more of her neighbors."

"Two she hath sent to the knife," said the cobbler.

"*Dieu!* how the *tricoteuses* will grin!"

# XXIII

*Of how François found lodgings where he paid no rent — Of the death of Toto — Of how his master, having no friends on the earth, finds them underground.*

T dusk François went out, and was soon moving rapidly across Paris. He was in search of lodging, food, and security. In an hour or less he was in the half-peopled quarter of St. Antoine. Near the barrier he turned aside, and stood considering a little house in what seemed to have been a well-kept garden. On the gate was the large red seal of the republic. It was safe for a night. If he took a lodging, he must show all his papers, and have his name set out, with his business, on a placard such as was nailed to the outer door of every house in Paris. His name, as a new lodger, must be reported to the sectional committee. He was widely known, and, alas! too peculiar to escape notice long. Now he needed time to think. He wandered awhile, ate in a small café, bought wine and bread, at night climbed the garden wall, and without much trouble found his way into the house. It was a sorry sight. The arrests must have been sudden and pitiless. The kettle stood on the dead embers. The bread, burned black, was in the oven. A half-knit stocking lay on a chair. Up-stairs and down, it was the same. The open drawers showed evidence of search. A dead bird lay starved in a cage. The beds were unmade. The clock had stopped. He found some scant provisions, unfit for use. It seemed a gardener's house. The place oppressed him, but it answered his purpose. His dog troubled him. Toto was, like himself, conspicuous, and he felt forced during the daytime to leave him locked up in the house. But Toto was sagacious, and had learned to keep quiet. For several days François lived at daylight in the streets and cafés, returning at night, to get away again before dawn. In the quiet little taverns where he went for food and shelter he made himself small, and hid in corners; nor, at this time, did he laugh much. He bought the gazettes, and read them with intelligent apprehension of the fact that change was in the air. Robespierre had never had with him a majority of his colleagues, and now he was becoming more and more conscious of his insecure hold on the Convention. As long as the ex-nobles or the foes of the republic suffered, it was of little moment to the representatives; but when the craving for blood, not justified by any political reasons, sent too many of their body to the block, the unease of the Terror began to be felt within their own hall. To be timid, cautious, or obscure had once been security. It was so no longer. That terrible master still had his way, and, one by one, the best brains of the opponents of the Jacobins were sent to perish on the scaffold. The Convention began to feel the need for associative self-defense. Revenge, fear, and policy combined to aid the enemies of this extraordinary person. Like Marat, he began to show physically the effects of a life full of alarms; for this monster dreaded darkness, trembled at unusual noises, and remained to the last the most carefully dressed man in Paris. To understand him at all, one must credit him in his early political life with a sincere love of country, and with willingness to sacrifice himself for others. It is impossible to regard him as entirely sound of mind at a later date. He became something monstrous—a mixture of courage, cowardice, blood-madness, self-esteem, and personal vanity. But there were men who loved him to the last.

It was now early in July, the month Thermidor. François began, as usual, to weary of a life of monotonous carefulness. His supply of money was ample. He was well fed and, so far, safe. He sat night after night in darkness, and thought of the lady of the château. He knew that her father was thus far secure; his name was not in the daily lists of the victims; and these were many, for on the 22d Prairial (June 10) a decree deprived the accused of counsel, and of the right to call witnesses. The end was near.

One evening about nine, as he came near to the garden, he saw lights in the house. Toto was found waiting outside of the gate. A girl came forth, and soon returned with a net of vegetables.

"*Ciel!* Toto," said François, "the poor things have been released, and thou wert clever to get out. We are glad, thou and I; but they have our house." He had left nothing at this lodging, having nothing to leave. He walked away, puzzled, and, wandering, scarce aware of whither he went, found himself at last in the Rue de Seine. It was getting late, and he began to look about him for a new lodging.

"We must find an empty house, Toto. The seal of this cursed republic is our best chance." He did not need to look far. In the Rue de Seine he came upon a small two-story shop. Beside it was a wide gateway, on which he saw with difficulty, but felt readily, the seal no one dared to violate. He concluded that there must be a deserted house beyond it, in a garden. He passed around by the *quai*, and entered the Rue des Petits-Augustines, and stood before the mansion of Ste. Luce. A light was in an upper room. Some one was in charge. On either side were railings and a garden. It was now ten o'clock, and no one visible in the long street of old houses, once the homes of the great French nobles. He pushed the poodle between the rails, and readily pulled himself up and dropped at his side. Once within, he moved with care across to the wall behind the mansion, and soon saw that he was not in the garden of the marquis, but in the larger domain of the Duc de la Rochefoucauld-Liancourt. His object was to find his way into the house which had an outlet on the Rue de Seine. As he was arranging his clothing to climb a tree near to the wall, he suddenly paused. "Toto," he exclaimed, "we have been robbed,—we—first-class thieves,—and we know not when it was. Ah, it was at that café, as we came out. Well done, too. Not a sou. Weep, Toto ; we are broken."

He lost no more time in lamentation, but climbed

the tree, looked over, came down, pulled up the dog, and descended on the farther side of the wall.

He was now in a small garden. Near him, and close to the wall, was a little plant-house. On the farther side of a grassy space stood a hotel of moderate size, with the front court, as he presumed, opening on the Rue de Seine. On each side, as he saw clearly, for the night was bright and the moon rising, there were high flanking walls. After assuring himself that the house was empty, François found a trellis covered with old vines, and, climbing this, entered the hotel by a convenient balcony. He was safe for the night, and at leisure to explore his new dwelling. He feared to strike a light, but he could see dimly that there were pictures, books, china. Evidently this had been the home of people of wealth. As the moon rose higher, he saw still better, and began to realize the fact that here were evidences of hasty flight. In a room on the second floor was a secretary, and this François readily opened.

"Toto," he said, "we are rich again." He had found forty louis in a canvas bag which comfortably fitted his side pocket. In the larder he came upon meat, cooked and uncooked, mostly unfit for use, stale bread, and cheese. Once satisfied, he went over the house, and then the garden, taking pains at last to set a ladder against the wall of the Rochefoucauld property.

The glass-house was in disorder, the plants lying about, uncared for. His foot struck an iron ring attached to a trap-door. There were staples for padlocking it, but no padlock. He concluded this to be

the opening to a wine-cave or -cellar, and lifted the
trap. It was dark below. He ventured down the
steps a little way, and then stood still to listen. Hearing noises below him, he retreated in haste. He was,
as has been said, superstitious.

"That is strange! We will look about when it
is day, Toto—not now."

Concluding to sleep out of doors, he accordingly
arranged for his comfort by taking a pillow and
blankets from the house; for now he had opened a
door below, and was in full possession. Suites of
apartments which he dared not use for sleep, and a
pretty little library, overlooked the small estate of the
garden.

No occupied dwelling was in view. Great trees in
the grounds of La Rochefoucauld and Ste. Luce par-
tially hid the houses, and, what was of more moment,
shut off the sight of François's refuge. It was, of
course, possible that at any time he might be disturbed by the coming of the officers, or, what was to
be feared less, that of the owners. But he was not
a man to be continually anxious. The outer front
door had a bar, and this he dropped into its socket.
The side walls were high. He could hear any one
who attempted to enter. His way out at the back
was made easy by the ladder he had set in place. At
dusk he began to be fully at ease, and after a day or
two was hardly less so in the sun-lit hours.

On the morning of the third day, much at home,
he sat behind the little plant-house, with Toto at his
feet, and a book in his hand, for in the library he
found several which excited his interest. Now he

was deep in a French translation of the travels of
Marco Polo. Suddenly he heard a noise of steps.
He fell back, caught Toto with a warning grasp on
the jaw, and lay still. He was so hidden in the narrow space between the plant-house and the wall of
the garden as to be for the time secure. No longer
hearing anything alarming, he rose and looked cautiously through the double glass and the sheltering
plants which were between himself and the mansion.
In a few minutes a tall man came out of the plant-
house, went into the dwelling, and by and by returning
with blankets and a basket, passed into the plant-
house, and was lost to sight. He soon came out
again with a lad, and after several such journeys to
the main house, whence each time he fetched something, they reëntered the plant-house, and came forth
no more.

This incident greatly amazed the thief. "Toto," he
said, "there must be a trap below! 'T is a lower
cellar it leads to, and there are people beneath. *Hélas*,
Toto! no sooner are we gentlemen with an estate
than, presto! a change, and it is get up and go. It
were better we took to the woods and saw far countries,
like this M. Polo." Toto regarded his master with
attentive eyes, the long black tail wagging. He seemed
to comprehend François's difficulties, or at least to feel
some vague desire to help and comfort.

"Yes, yes; it is time we settled down, *mon ami*.
Behold, we get a little money and wherewithal to
live; we hurt no one; we cultivate our minds with
travel; we start fresh, and are honest, having enough,
—which is a good foundation for honesty,—and then

—*eh bien!* my friend; let us laugh"; and he lay on his back, and tumbled the dog about.

He was in the garden, near to the dwelling, a day later, when he heard noises as of steps in the La Rochefoucauld grounds. He climbed the ladder, and, without showing himself, listened. There were voices, and now and then he caught a phrase. These were municipal guards. He beckoned to Toto, and, crossing the garden, entered the house, meaning to watch his new neighbors from a window.

He went up-stairs to the third story under the roof. As he moved toward a window, he heard a sound below. He ran down the stair, and stood on the lower landing-place, facing the front door. "We are gone, Toto!" For once he was at a loss, and stood still, in doubt what to do.

There were voices outside. The hall door had been unlocked, but the bar held it fast. After a minute or two they seemed to have given up the idea of entering. François waited a few minutes, and began to descend the stairs. Then he heard quick footfalls in the room to the left on the level of the landing above him. Some one must have entered by a window on the second floor. He turned, perplexed, instinctively drew his useless pistol, and began to go faster. Suddenly the steps above him quickened.

A man on the staircase landing behind him cried: "Halloo! Surrender, in the name of the republic!" François jumped, taking the stairs below him in one leap, but, tripping over Toto, fell headlong in the hall. The dog sprang after him, and alighted on his master's back. A pistol-shot rang out. The dog fell dead with a ball in his brain. François was on his feet. He cast a glance at the faithful friend of many a day. His own long, strange face became like that of a madman. He dashed up the stair, a second ball missing him narrowly. Through the smoke he bounded on his enemy. He caught the man by the right arm, wrested the pistol from him, and, scarce feeling a blow from the fellow's left hand, struck him full in the face with the butt of the pistol. The blood flew, and the man staggered, screaming. A second blow and a third fell. Twisting his victim around, François hurled him down the stair.

"Beast!" he cried; and, leaping over him, stooped a moment, kissed the quivering little body of his friend, and, with tears streaming from his eyes, stood still. Loud cries from beyond the wall of the garden recalled his energies. The noise at the door was heard again. He ran out and across into the plant-house, pulled up the trap, and, descending, closed it. Then he stood puzzled. It was dark; he could see nothing. He fell on his knees, and began hastily to grope about until he felt an iron ring attached to the trap-door of what he presumed to be the entrance to a yet lower cellar.

"It is this or death," he muttered under his breath, and stood reflecting, having heard no sounds approaching overhead. Thinking it better to see and be seen by those below, he struck his flint on the steel, and, with the aid of a morsel of paper and his kindling breath, soon had a light. Then he saw near by a lantern with a candle within it. He lighted it, and held it in one hand. This done, he knelt again, and with a quick movement set open the trap-doorway. What

17

he saw was a man and the muzzle of a pistol. The man cried out: "If you move, you are dead!"

"I am not a municipal, monsieur. I am only a thief. Let me come down, for God's sake! I am flying from those rascals who are in the house."

"I have half a mind to blow your brains out."

"*Ciel!* I hope you will not have a whole mind. It would only call those scoundrels. I stole a little from the house—I return it"; and he dropped the bag of louis. It fell on the head of a small boy below, unseen in the gloom. He howled lustily.

"*Diantre!* keep quiet!" cried the man.

"Oh, let him come down, duke; he is welcome." It was the voice of a woman out of the deep darkness. Tender and clear it was.

"Be quick, then, rascal! Down with you."

The thief waited for no second invitation. The duke descended; François's long legs came after. He paused to arrange some loose staves, that, in falling, they might conceal the trap. Then he blew out the candle, and was in total darkness, but where or with whom he knew not.

"Have a care how you move," said the voice of the woman. "We are in great peril. Come down quietly."

"May all the saints bless you!" said François, and sat down on the lower step. For a while all was still.

## XXIV

*Of how François got into good society underground—Of what he saw, and of the value of a cat's eyes—From darkness to light—Of how François made friends for life.*

T was dark indeed; I had never imagined such darkness," says François in his memoirs.[1] He adds that he has heard the story of this wonderful escape from the catacombs told over and over by M. des Illes. He does not consider that it did him (François), the principal person, sufficient justice. He had also heard the old Duke Philippe relate the matter, and it was incredible how crooked he got it. But, then, Duke Philippe was a man who had no sense of humor. As to his dear Mme. des Illes, when she did tell this story, the baby was the chief hero. Duke Henri,—that is, the present man,—although only a lad when these events took place, remembered them well.

"When he was seventeen," says François, "we used to fence together. I have often heard him relate to the other young fellows how we made our escape; but Duke Henri has too much imagination, and that, you see, makes a man inaccurate. I knew two very ac-

[1] See Epilogue.

complished thieves who were inaccurate. I am not.
Duke Henri's tale got stronger, like wine, as time
went on. The rats grew to be of the size of cats;
three of them pulled the baby out of madame's lap.
And as to the people we killed, it would have satisfied
M. Dumas, who is the greatest and most correct of
such as write history."

The present author grieves that he has not the
narration of this famous escape at the hands of Mme.
des Illes and the two dukes, father and son. Those
who have found leisure to read "A Little More Burgundy" have heard Des Illes's narrative as M. des
Illes related it. Those who have not read that ren-
dering may incline to hear François's own statement
of what happened after he thus found himself in
darkness with people he had never seen. I have
followed his memoir pretty closely. It tells some
things of which the other people concerned did not
know. Evidently he considered it a less tragic affair
than did they. It has been needful to condense
François's account, and to do this especially where
he speaks of his own intermediate adventures, which
were singular enough.

When, as I have said, François, obeying Duke
Philippe, put out his lantern, he sat still awhile, and
said nothing. Like the rest, he was fearful lest the
officers he had disturbed so rudely should make a
too effective search. Their inspection of the upper
cellar would be perilous enough. The anxious people
beneath held their breaths when a man overhead
stumbled across the staves the thief had set to fall
on the trap-door. After a while all noises faded

away, and in the evening the duke proposed to rec-
onnoiter once more; but when he tried to lift the trap,
it was found impossible to do so. The municipals, in
their examination, must have rolled a full barrel of
wine upon the door. This discovery was, or seemed,
an overwhelming calamity.

François during the day came to understand that
here in the darkness were Duke Philippe de St. Maur,
his son Henri, a lad, another rather older boy, Des
Illes, Mme. des Illes, and the baby, who made himself terribly well known by occasional protests in the
tongue of babyhood. As the thief became accustomed
to the gloom and the company, his usual cheeriness
returned; and when they could not open the trap he
began to propose all manner of schemes. He would
bore a hole and let out the wine, and so lighten the
barrel. He would shoot a ball through the trap and
the barrel, and thus let out the weight of wine. The
duke, who never lost respect for his own dignity, was
disgusted, and would listen to none of his counsels.

Toward bedtime the baby began to wail dismally;
the boys sobbed; and Mme. des Illes cried out to them
that they should be ashamed to complain, and then,
by way of comment, herself burst into tears; while
the duke stumbled about, and swore under his breath.
This was all very astonishing to François, who had
seen little of any world but his own, and to whom
calamity served only as a hint to consider some way
to escape its effects. He remained silent for a while,
after the duke had let him plainly understand that he
was a fool and had better hold his tongue. This
lasted for a half-hour, during which he sat still, think-

ing, with full eyes, of his dead dog. By degrees the children grew quiet, and the baby, having exhausted his vocabulary and himself, fell asleep. Then the duke said irritably:

"Why the deuce don't you do something, Master Thief? If you can get into places where you do not belong, why cannot you get out of this abominable box?"

François laughed. "Get out I would, and gladly; but how? We might wait, monsieur, till they drink up the wine, or until it dries up, or—" But here the boys laughed, and even the duke forgot himself, and said François was a merry fellow. Indeed, he was of use to them all; for, soon becoming at ease, he regaled the boys with his adventures; but how many he invented I do not know. Some were queer, and some silly; but all tales are good in the dark, for then what can one do but attend?

After a while, all being still, François lighted his lantern, on which Duke Philippe said: "Put out that light; we have too few candles as it is; and keep quiet. You are prowling about like a cat on the tiles, and twice you have stumbled over my legs."

"But I have twice said I was sorry," said François, getting tired of this duke with an uncertain temper, who repeated: "Put out that light, and sit down."

Then madame spoke: "He may have a reason to want to see and to move about."

"'T is so," said François. "If I walk, my wits walk; if I sit, they go to sleep; and as to cats, madame, I am a street cat"; and, thinking of Suzanne, he laughed.

"Ah, confound your laughing!" The duke felt
that to laugh at a joke he did not share was, to say
the least, disrespectful. "What is there to laugh at?"

François, who had been moving as he spoke, was
suddenly elated. He said it was Suzanne he was
thinking of; and when madame would know if she
were his wife, the duke was silent out of lack of interest for low company, and François began to tell
about the elders and the Hebrew maid, and of the
Amalekites who lived on the next roof. The boys
were charmed, and madame said, "Fie! fie!" but it
served to amuse. An hour later he began to move
about restlessly, and at last cried out, from the far end
of the cellar:

"This way, monsieur; what is this? A candle—and
quick!" When they all came to see, he rolled aside
an empty cask, and showed a heavy planking. He
seized the decayed timbers and tore them away, so
that as they fell a black gap was to be seen. The
air blew in, cool and damp.

"*Mon Dieu!* 't is the catacombs. My husband's
grandfather cut off this end for a wine-cave. It is
strange I should have quite forgotten it."

"But what then?" said the duke. "It is only a
grave you have opened. You might as well have
kept quiet."

The thief's feelings were hurt; he began to care
less and less for this useless nobleman.

Madame said thoughtfully: "It may be a way out.
If it come to the worst, we can but try it."

"Madame is right; and as to keeping quiet, I never
could. Sleeping cats catch no rats." He believed in

his luck. "We shall get out," he said, with cool assurance. "I always do. I have been in many scrapes. I got out of the Madelonnettes, and I was once near to decorating a rope."

"A rope!" exclaimed madame.

"Yes. *Parbleu!* I wear my cravat loose ever since. I like to have full swing, but not in that way." He was gay and talkative. The boys liked it; but not so the duke, who said:

"Well, what next?"

"We must explore. I will enter and see a little."

"But," said the woman, "you will get lost; and then, what to do?" She had come to trust the thief. He saw this, and liked it. "If we lose you, what shall we do?—what *shall* we do?"

The thief turned to her as he stood, lantern in hand. He was grave. "Madame, I am a poor thief of the streets; I have had to live as I could; and since I was a boy I can count the kind words ever said to me by man or woman. I shall not forget."

Madame was moved, and said they were all alike come upon evil days, and that perhaps now he would turn from his wicked ways.

Poor François was not quite clear as to his ways having been wicked.

"Well, if you are going," said the duke, "you had better be about it."

It was then young Des Illes said he must have a string, like people who went into caves, else he might never find his way back. The thief thought it a fine idea; and here was madame's big ball of knitting-wool. With no more delay, he took it, and leaving an end in Des Illes's hand, boldly walked away into the darkness with his lantern, and was soon lost to view.

When he came back to this anxious company, he had to report such a tangle of passages as caused him to say that to try to escape through these must be a last resort. He thought they might live on the rats if provisions gave out, but they must eat them raw.

"*Hélas!* what a fate!" said madame.

The little Duke Henri spoke eagerly, and said the Chinese ate rats.

"But not raw," cried the young Des Illes, which set them all to laughing.

Soon again they were quiet, because talk in the dark does not prosper. A little later madame called softly to the thief to sit by her, and would hear of his life. François related his exploits with pride. She made no comment, but said at last: "Your name, my friend?" And when he replied, "François," she declared that he was no more to be any one's thief, but always François; and this was a hint to the duke, who took it in silence, and was evidently depressed.

After this, madame bade the boys say their prayers; and soon all were asleep, except François, who sat against a cask, and saw Toto's brown eyes in the darkness.

At last the morrow came. The provisions were shared, and, as usual with François, his spirits rose as he filled his stomach. He held the baby, and was queerly interested in this mystery of unwinking eyes. Might he give it of the bottle? He satisfied the child, who seemed fearless of that long, good-humored face.

Might he hold it longer? It would relieve madame. He sang low to it a queer thief-song, and then another none there could understand.

" *Ciel!* " said the duke, who had slept off his splenetic mood; " you have a fine voice."

" Ah, would it were a hymn," said madame, " or a psalm of Clément Marot!"

" I know no hymns," said François, " but only some old choir chants."

Upon this he began to sing, low and sweet, one of the old Latin songs:

> Salve, mundi salutare,
> Salve, salve, Jesu care!
> Cruci tuæ me aptare
> Vellem vere, tu scis quare,
>   Da mihi tui capiam.

The rich voice which in his boyhood days had soared like a lark up among the arches of Notre Dame had come again. He heard himself with wonder and with sad thoughts of the chances his boyish haste had forever lost for him.

" And you a thief!" cried madame. " Where— where did you learn—"

But at this moment noises overhead put an end to all but listening. At last François said: " They move the casks. It were well to take to the caves." And this was hastily agreed to, when, of a sudden, the noises ceased.

François still urged instant flight; but the duke said, " No; we must wait," and gave no reasons. The thief did not agree, but held his tongue, as Mme. des

Illes said nothing, and since, after all, this was a duke.

An hour later he started up. "By Heaven, they are at the trap!"

The duke was no coward. He ran up the steps, pistol in hand, and gave his second weapon to François, who stood below. The trap was cast wide open, and a big municipal was seen stooping over the open space; for beyond him the cellar was well lighted up. The duke fired without an instant's indecision.

"By St. Denis! 't is a man, this duke," cried François, as the officer pitched head down into the cave. The thief set a foot on him as he lay, and reached up the second pistol to the duke, while young Des Illes, too curious for fear, crawled up the broad stone stairs to see. The thief heard a second shot, and followed the lad. There were several candles set on casks, and through the smoke he saw a municipal in a heap at the far end of the upper cellar. He was groaning piteously.

"Load again, monsieur," cried François. "Quick! there may be more." He himself went past the duke, and young Des Illes after him. He turned the officer over.

"He is not dead," he said. "Best to finish him."

But here was madame at his side, saying: "No, no! No more—I will not have it. *Mon Dieu!* it is bad enough. I will have no murder."

"Then let us go back; he is as good as dead."

"*Mon Dieu! Mon Dieu!*" cried the woman; and so in haste the upper trap was closed, and all went again down to the cave.

The officer below was dead, with a ball through his head. Mother and children huddled away in the far corner, scared. The duke said:

"What now must we do?"

"We must go, and at once," said François. "They will soon come back, and then—"

"Yes, yes," cried madame; "you are right. You were right; we should have gone before, and saved all this bloodshed."

The duke made no comment, except to mutter, "I suppose so"; and at once began to assist François's preparations for flight.

And now the thief's readiness and efficiency were shown. He arranged every one's loads, filled baskets, laughed over a shoulder at the boys as he strapped blankets on the duke, and at last loaded himself with all that was left. They took the arms of the dead man, and soon trooped out into the darkness. The duke, who at once went on ahead, carried a lantern.

At the first turn, François called out to wait, and ran back. The duke swore. He was now eager to go on, and declared that the thief would deliver them up, and save his own head. But madame was of other mind, and so they stood expectant. At last came François, laughing.

"Ah, monsieur, this comes of honest company. I forgot the bag of gold. And these—these are priceless. I have the fellow's clothes. When a man does not resist, the temptation is great; neither did he assist."

"Stop that talk, and come on. Are we going to set up a shop for old clothes?"

François fell behind. "The duke would make a poor thief," he said to the boys. Young Henri de St. Maur said: "You are insolent. My father a thief!"

"*Tiens!* There are times when to steal is virtue. *Allons donc!*" and he strode on, laughing, and telling the boys stories.

There were many little incidents that day, but the worst was at evening, when they found a great cave, lofty and wide, where had been cast, long before, the bones out of the overfilled cemeteries. Here it was that skulls fell from the great heap, and rolled away on every side into the darkness, while the rats ran out in armies. The thief was of all the most alarmed, and stood still, saying paternosters and aves by the dozen. After this they went on aimlessly, now and then hearing overhead the roar and rumble of wagons. Their nights proved to be full of sore trials. The rats assembled, and grew bolder. One bit the baby, who cried until the thief lighted a candle and watched while the rest slept, or tried to do so.

The dismalness of these underground labyrinths was such as no man could imagine. One day they walked a half-mile through a wet cave-passage so narrow that two persons could not move abreast. It ended in a blank wall, and they were forced to go back, over shoe-top in water. Or, again, they went up rude stairs, stumbling, but hopeful, only to descend once more into the depths of the earth. Now and then a putrid rain fell on them, and at every turn the rats fled by them, now one and now a scurry of countless troops. Twice a mass of rock fell in some distant passage, and strange echoes reverberated in cavern spaces, so that the boys cried out in terror, and even François shivered at the thought of how they might be buried alive by one of these downfalls. Each sad day of weariness had its incident of terror or disappointment; and still, with lessening hope, they trailed on after the dim light which the duke carried as he led them—none knew whither. Each morning they rose cold, wet, and unrefreshed, ate of their lessening food, and after some little talk as to how this day they should keep turning to left or to right, set out anew, the duke still in advance, with an ever-changing mind as to where they were or what they should do. As day followed day, their halts became more frequent. They lingered where the dripping rain from the sewage of the great city overhead was least; or at times paused suddenly to listen to mysterious sounds, or to let the rats go by them, splashing in the noisome puddles underfoot. The night was as the day, the day as the night. They had no way to tell the one from the other, except by the duke's watch.

So confusing was this monotonous tramp underground, the days so much alike, that at last these sad people became bewildered as to how long they had wandered. Their food was becoming less and less, and on the evening of the fifth day the duke and François knew that very soon their stock of candles would be exhausted. These had, in fact, been of small use, except to keep the scared children more cheerful when night came on and the rats grew bold.

This evening of the fifth day, and earlier than usual, Mme. des Illes declared of a sudden that she could

go no farther, and must rest for the night. The duke
had a new plan, and urged her to go on. She cried
over the baby on her lap, and made no answer. They
sat down to pass another night of discomfort. After a
little talk with the boys, François drew apart from the
rest, and began to think over the wanderings of the
day. Their situation this evening was somewhat better
than it had usually been, for they sat in a dry end of
one of the many excavations, and did not feel the
cold, moist winds which howled along these stony
caves, carrying a changeful variety of unwholesome
stenches. A silent hour went by in utter darkness.
At times François rose to drive away adventurous
rats. At last he lighted a candle, and set it at the
open end of the cul-de-sac. When he saw that the
rats would not pass the lantern, he whispered to
madame of this, and that he meant to explore a little,
and bade her have no fear. The duke had thus far
had his own way, and it had not been to François's
taste. He took a second lantern, and moved off around
a corner, resolute to find a means of escape. The duke
ordered him to return and to put out the candle.
François made no reply. He counted the turns as he
went on, and listened for the noise of vehicles above
him.

"A pretty duke, that!" he said. "I should have
made as good a one. I like better that devil of a marquis; but *diantre!* neither is much afraid—nor I, for
that matter."

Sometimes he turned back, at others went on boldly,
noting whence blew any current of warmer air. At
last he came upon an enormous excavation. In the

middle was a mass of partly tumbled stone, laid in courses. This broken heap was large, and irregularly conical. He moved around it in wonder, having seen nothing like it in his explorations. He turned the yellow and feeble lantern-light upon the heap, and at first concluded that the old makers of these quarries had here built for themselves a house, which had fallen to ruin.

But where was he, and what part of Paris was over his head? He remembered at last to have heard that these catacombs were once used as receptacles for the dead, in order to relieve the overpeopled graveyards. Had he been less alarmed, he might have guessed where he was when they came upon the bones; for that must have been near to the cemetery of the Church of the Innocents. But while the duke had led, François had taken less than his usual active notice, and had been content to follow. Here, now, was a new landmark. This before him could be no dwelling of quarriers, but must be a house fallen into the great cave. He had heard of such happenings. To be certain where and on what street so strange a thing had occurred would afford knowledge as to the part of Paris under which he stood. He would ask the duke; he might know. Thus reflecting, he began to walk around the tumbled mass. A vast amount of earth must have come down with it. He pried here and there, and at last found a gap in the ruin, and crawled in between fallen timbers until he could stand up. On one side was a wall and a wide chimney-place, and on the top of this wall the great beams of the ceiling still rested. Their farther ends lay on what seemed the wreck of the opposite wall, thus leaving a triangular space filled in at each side by broken stone. Amid this were the crushed steps of a staircase, quite blocked up. The lantern gave little light. Only close to the fireplace could the tall thief stand erect. He turned his lantern, and cried out:

"Ye saints!" Close beside him were the remains of a high-backed chair, and on these, and beside them, portions of the bones of a man. Two great jack-boots lay beside him, gnawed by rats. His skull was broken, and lay where the eager animals had dragged it.

Few could have stood here alone, and not felt its terror and its mystery. François stood a moment, appalled, and unable to think or to observe. At last he began to study the place with care and increasing interest. A rusty sword, sheathed, was caught in the arm of the ruined chair. Here and there lay bits of gold lace. He picked up the rusted clasp of a purse, gnawed by the rats. Near it lay scattered a number of gold and silver coins, a rosary, and a small ring set with red stones. He put them all in his pocket. There was scarce a remnant of the man's dress.

François looked at the tumbled bones. "*Mon Dieu!*" said he; "am I like that?" and turned to see what else was here. On the lowest stair was a glint of yellow—a cross of gold. "Good luck!" he cried. On the hearth was a copper kettle, green with rust. Soon he began to see better, and at last found a fragment of wood less damp than the rest of the floor and what lay upon it; for a steady, slow, irregular rain fell in drops, with dull patter here and there. He shaved off some slivers of the wood, and, getting at

18

the drier inside, soon, with paper from his pouch, made a fire on the stone pavement. Presently he had a bright little blaze, and in the brilliant glow began to shed his terror. He found other wood, and nourished the flame. But when he saw that the fragments were from the end of a crushed cradle, he ceased to use them; because here were little bones lying scattered, and the man guessed at the extent of the tragedy, and was strangely stirred. He moved to and fro in the tent-like space in awe and wonder, in thought reconstructing the house, and seeming to share in the horror of its story.

Before leaving, he looked again at the overturned chair, the stones lying about it, and the moldering remains of the man. He must have been asleep, and died instantly when the house fell into the great cave. There was no more to be seen. "God rest his soul!" said the thief, and crawled backward out of the tangle of broken beams and stones.

In a few minutes he was again with those he had left, and, saying only, "'T is well, madame; we shall get out," fell into a peaceful sleep.

The next day every one dragged on wearily, the duke still leading, and François hoping that he would be asked advice. The water rained on them a noisome downfall, the rats came out in hordes; and still François cheered his companions, now carrying the baby, and now encouraging the tired boys.

I have not given in full detail all the miseries of these weary days and sorrowful nights. They have been more fully told elsewhere by one who felt them as more serious than did François, whose narrative I now am following. These unhappy victims of the Terror had been altogether six days in the cave, but François not so long. By this time their spirit was quite broken. The thief alone remained gay, hopeful, and even confident, but saw clearly enough that these people, used to easy lives, could not endure much longer the strain of this unguided wandering in the dark and somber alleys of this horrible labyrinth of darkness and foul odors. The duke seemed also to be of a like mind, for on the morning of the seventh day he awakened François at six, and, of a sudden grown sadly familiar, whispered low to him:

"Is there any hope? Madame and the boys are failing. Soon we shall have to carry them."

"We shall get out," said François.

"But how? how? Why to-day any more than yesterday? Do you think of any way to help us?"

"If monsieur will permit me to lead—"

"Good! Why did you not say so before?"

François made no direct reply, but asked: "Did ever a house fall into these quarry-caves?"

"A house? Why do you ask? Yes; it was long ago. The house of the lieutenant of the guard it was. I do not recall the date. A house in the Rue des Pêches."

"Will this help to know when it was?" and François showed his coins and told his story.

"Yes, yes; I see. How wonderful! These are of the time of Francis I."

"Rue des Pêches?"

"Yes; it is now the Rue des Bon Secours. It is close to the Asile des Innocents."

"*Dieu!* monsieur, then I know. I think we may get out to-day; but it may be well not yet to tell madame. I think we are still near to the fallen house."

"Then you shall lead," said the duke. "*Tiens!* a queer fellow, this thief," he muttered, and went to waken the sleeping children. No word was said as to the house of the lieutenant of the guard, but François refreshed the tired party by promising a speedy glimpse of day. For, now that the candles were few, they thought more of this than of the perils which the daylight might bring.

The thief led, and all day long they went on and on. Once he was quite dismayed to find that he had lost his way, and once came to the very entrance of the cave he had left the night before. The duke again became querulous and dissatisfied; but François only laughed, and, resolutely concealing his mistake, retraced his steps. It was near to seven o'clock in the evening of July 28 when the thief bade them rest, and he would be back soon. The duke said something cross; but François made no reply, and, turning a corner, lost sight of his party. He took careful note of the turns and windings of this maze, and now and then found himself in a blind alley, and must of need turn back. At the far end of one of these recesses he saw in the gloom two great, green, phosphorescent eyes. Like mighty jewels they were, set in the darkness. They were soon lost to view, and came and went. "They are cats," he murmured; "and what a hunting estate they have! Ye saints! if I had here my poor Toto!" He began to move toward these eyes, which shot back the light his lantern gave. There were three sets of the pale-green jewels, and now their owners were manœuvering to escape. He began to use caressing cat-talk, such as had won the heart of Suzanne, and, falling on his knees, crept closer. Then there was a quick rush past him of his feline game; but one cat was indecisive, and he had her by the leg. He paid well for his audacity, but held on, and pretty soon began to exercise the curious control he had over all animals. At last pussy lay still and panting. When the scared animal grew quiet, he set her down. For a moment she hesitated, and then began to move away. As he followed she ran. He cast the lantern-light before her, and pursued her with all speed. Once or twice she was nearly lost to view. Then she turned a corner, and another, and of a sudden fled toward a distant archway, through which he saw the light of day. A great rush of warm air went by him. He stood still, murmuring aves. To his surprise, he was near to the place where he had left his companions. He stood a moment in deep thought. "We are out at last," he murmured. "But *ciel!* there is much to think about. We may have too much light."

He went back and told of the discovery, but of the cat not a word. The duke said: "I thought we should soon get out; come, let us be off."

Madame said gently: "Let us kneel before we go, and thank the good God for this friend he sent us in our trouble." Then they all knelt, and she prayed, speaking her thankfulness to Heaven, with at the end a word as to her husband, and also asking God's mercy for him who had led them forth out of darkness into light. When François heard her, he was disturbed as he had never been in all his days. When a man like François sheds tears, it is a great event in his life. He rose from his knees, and asked the duke and the rest to go with him; and thus it was that in a few minutes they stood fifty feet from an open archway, through which came the level light from the western sky.

The duke was moved at last to say how clever François had been; and how had he managed it? The thief declared it had been easy; but the cat got no credit, and never was praised, then or ever, for her share of their escape. Set in this rocky frame before them was a picture as it were of a disused quarry, and beyond it vineyards, with yet farther a red-tiled housetop. Here it was, as they paused, that madame said solemnly, with tears in her eyes:

" ' God said, Let there be light: and there was light. And God saw the light, that it was good.' "

After the duke and François had peeped out, and seen no one, the duke began to set forth a variety of schemes as to what they should do. None of these was very wise, and at last madame turned to François. He had disappeared, but presently came again, dressed in the clothes of the dead officer. He wore his sword and pistols, and now, as seen clearly in the light of day, was certainly a queer enough figure. The garments were too short below and too wide above, and over them rose the long face, the broad mouth, and the huge ears. The boys, who looked on their troubles as at an end, set up a shout of laughter.

"The deuce! I shall arrest you, citizens," cried

François.  "And first, monsieur."   He explained that
he proposed to tie the duke's hands behind his back,
and with, as was usual, one end of the rope in his
hand, would conduct the *ci-devant* into Paris by the
Barrière d'Enfer.   The weeping widow would follow,
with the two children, to see the last of their poor
papa.

The duke was disgusted, but pretended to be much
amused.   "Well, it is a pretty comedy," he said, as
Mme. des Illes insisted.

"*Dame!*" said the thief, "but the tragedy is not far
away."

"And what is to come after?" said she.   "Had we
not better wait till night?"

"No.   The guards are doubled at night.   It is bold-
ness which will win."

"And what then, François?"

"I must find for you a refuge while I go to see if
M. des Illes may not have returned; for, madame, you
have assured me that he would be released.   Pray
God it is so.   And what better is there?"   The duke
was forced to consent.

A rope found in the officer's pocket made part of
François's spoil.   He tied the duke's hands, and
showed him how, at need, a pull would release them.
The gold was divided.   All else they left.   François
reported the way clear, and they set out.   But the
boys giggled so much at the duke and his indignant
face that François paused.

"*Dame!*" he cried, "madame must weep."   She was
already doing that, her mind on the fate of M. des
Illes.   "If you boys are fools, and laugh, we are lost.

Cry, if you can; but, for the love of Heaven, do not look about you, or smile.  Take a hand of madame— so.  Cry, if ever you mean to get away safe."

The road beyond the quarry was little used, and they went on, the duke furious.  When they met any one, François cried: "Get on, aristocrat!  Pig of a *ci-devant*, march!"

Duke Philippe muttered: "*Sacré*, thief!" and got a smart jerk of the rope, and more abuse, until the fun of it nearly upset the thief, who could scarce contain himself.  At the Barrière d'Enfer were but two guards; nor were there as many people in the streets as usual.

Suddenly François halted at the summons to leave his prisoner with one of the two men, and to enter the little office and exhibit his papers, as was needful.

"*Dame!*" muttered the thief, "one cannot know all things.  I forgot about the papers."  He showed, however, no indecision.  "Guard this wretch, citizen," he said.  "Here, take the rope.  He is a returned *émigré*."  The man took the rope.  "I shall not be long."  So saying, he went in after the second guard, closing the door behind them.  The man sat down at a desk, and opened a blank-book, saying: "The order, citizen."

"I am afraid it is lost," said François, eagerly searching his acquired pockets.  "The mischief!  What to do?"

"To do?  Thou must wait till the lieutenant comes back.  He has gone to see the fun."

"Fun!  What fun?"

At this moment the man rose hastily.  "*Diable!*

thou art François! I thought I knew thy voice.
There are orders to arrest thee. Citizen Amar desires thy society. Best make no fuss. I arrest thee.
I am in luck. It is sure promotion. What trick art
thou up to? And those folks outside, who are they?"

"But thou, an old thief, to arrest a comrade! Surely
thou wilt not."

"No use. Come! no nonsense."

François put out a pleading hand. "But they will
kill me, comrade." He looked all the alarm needed.

"Bah!"

In an instant the strongest grip of the Cité was on
the man's throat, and closed as a vise closes. A faint
cry escaped as the man struggled. François threw a
leg back of the fellow, and as he fell dropped on his
chest. It was brief. The man's heels clattered on the
floor; he was still. The thief rose. The man was to
appearance dead. He would revive, perhaps. "*Peste!*"
cried François, "it is hard to keep one's head."

Seizing a paper from the table, François went out of
the door, closing it after him, and coolly caressing a
cat on the step. He said to the guard that his comrade would be out by and by, and that it was all
right. As he spoke he waved the paper, and, taking
the rope, went on, crying: "Get up, *ci-devant!*" As
they got farther away he hurried the duke. "Death
is behind us. Get on. Faster—faster!" He twisted
and turned, and was not at ease until they were deep
in the sinuous, box-hidden paths of the Luxembourg.

Very few people were to be seen, and these looked
at or after them with curiosity.

"We must be a queer party. Get on, citizen. Thou

art lazy. Thou wilt soon have a fine carriage." He was terribly anxious. "*Sacré*, monsieur! For the love of the saints, go on, and quicker!"

"What the deuce is it?" said the duke.

"That beast at the barrier knew me. He was an old thief."

"And what then? Why were we not stopped if he knew you?"

"He does not know me nor anybody now."

"*Foi d'honneur*, but you are a brave fellow!"

"Thanks; but make haste."

At last they were in the long Rue de Varennes, where they saw a great crowd filling the street, and were soon in the midst of a mass of excited people.

François cried out: "Room, citizens, room!"

An old woman shook her fist at him, yelling furiously: "Cursed Jacobin!"

The people were wild; and presently a man hustled the supposed officer. Others cried fiercely: "Hang him!" Another screamed out: "Robespierre is dead!" and the crowd took up the cry. A dozen hands seized on François.

"What the deuce is all this?" he shouted. "Take care, or the law will have you."

"Robespierre is dead! *À la lanterne!*"

Upon this, the duke exclaimed: "Let him go; it is a good fellow, and not an officer"; and then, amid a maddening tumult, succeeded in hastily explaining enough to secure the release of the officer.

"*À bas la guillotine!*" cried François. "Down with the Terror!"

The crowd thickened, and went its way with wild

cries.  Meanwhile the boy Des Illes was lost, and madame in tears.  They went on, asking questions, and hearing of the execution of Robespierre, Couthon, Saint-Just, and the rest.  The thief said : "Let us go straight to M. des Illes's house."

At the door madame fell into her husband's arms ; and soon after dusk the boy came running back with his father, who had gone out to search for him.

Then all was hastily made clear, and the long story told of Des Illes's release, and how he had found the dog, and in the cave the Jacobins both dead, and of his vain efforts to discover his own people.  They were fed and reclothed ; and now, it being ten at night of this 10th Thermidor, François rose.  "I must go," he said.

"You ?  Never ! " said madame.  "Our house is your home for life.  You will wander and sin no more."

On this, François looked about him, from one kind face to another, and sat down, and broke into tears.

"It shall be as madame desires.  I am her servant."

And this is the end of the adventures of François, the thief.  Let who will judge him.

# EPILOGUE

*Wherein is some further account of François and of those who helped him.*

I N a little book which has found many friendly readers I related a strange story of the
French Revolution.[1] In it was promised
some further account of the most remarkable of the personages concerned. I
have now fulfilled my desire to relate the adventures
of François. The singular incidents I record are not
without foundation.

In the story above mentioned I have told how I
chanced to meet François and those with whom he
spent his days after the stormy period during which
they first came together. My acquaintance with M.
des Illes and the old Duc de St. Maur slowly rip-
ened into friendship. I was a lonely student in the
Latin Quarter, and felt deeply the kindness which
never ceased insisting that their house should be to
me a home. In the summer, and often after that, I
was a guest at Des Illes's château in Touraine. There
I came to know François, as one may know a French
or an Italian servant. During these visits he acted

[1] "A Madeira Party," The Century Co., which contains a tale
called "A Little More Burgundy," to which the reader is referred.

312

as my valet, serving me with admirable care, and never better pleased than when I invited him to talk about himself. He had long since shed his thief-skin, but I fear that it was only the influence of fortunate circumstances which left him without excuse to be or to seem other than as honest as the rest of the world about him.

I have known a great variety of disreputable folk in my lifetime, but never one who had so many winning qualities, or who was so entirely at his ease. A scamp in the company of men of better morals usually becomes hypocritical or appears awkwardly aware of breathing an atmosphere to which he is unused. François had no such difficulties. For half a century he had been for Des Illes something between friend and servant. His former life and habits were well known to the few who came to his master's house. He was comfortable, with some forty thousand francs in the *rentes*, for his old acquaintance, the marquis, had not forgotten his services. He had no necessity to exercise what he still tranquilly called his profession. Like a clever street-dog adopted by a respectable family, though for a time uneasy, he ceased by degrees to wander for the joy of stealing a bone, and became contented with the better and less perilous chances of a dinner at home.

I learned from M. de St. Maur, the duke's son, that while Mme. des Illes lived François remained the most domestic of animals. Her death caused him a grief so profound that for a time his master was troubled lest his reason might suffer. She herself would never hear a word against him. Unlike her husband, she was a fervent Protestant, and had now and then some vain hope of converting François. While she lived he considered himself her special servant, but after her death transferred his regard to young Des Illes, the son. For many months François pined, as I have said. He then became restless, disappeared for a week at a time, and it is to be feared that once, or more often, he courted temptation. When I knew him all this was in a remote past. At the château he usually came to my bed-room an hour before dinner to set out my evening dress, and was pretty sure, when this was done, to put his head in my little salon and ask if I needed anything. Perhaps, like M. des Illes, I might desire a *petit verre* of vermuth for the bettering of appetite. As I soon found what this meant, I commonly required this sustaining aid. When by and by he returned, carrying a neat tray with vermuth and cognac, it came to be understood that he should be led into talk of himself over the little glass, which would, I am sure, have paid toll before it got back to the buffet. Pretty soon I got into the way of making him sit down, while I drew from by no means unwilling lips certain odd stories which much amused me. With an English or Irish servant such familiar intercourse would have been quite impossible; but François, who had none of the shyness of other races, soon came to be on as easy terms with me as he was with M. des Illes. When I asked him one evening to tell me his own story of the famous escape through the catacombs, he said, "But it is long, monsieur." When I added, "Well, sit down;

I must have it," he replied simply, "As monsieur wishes," and, taking a chair, gave me an account of their escape, in which he drew so mirthful a picture of the duke's embarrassments that I saw how little of the humor of the tale M. des Illes had allowed himself to put into his recital.

François's long life amid people of unblemished character had by no means changed his views. Yes, he had been a thief; but now he was out of business. He had retired, just as M. des Illes had done, there being no longer any cause why he should relieve his own necessity by lessening the luxury of others; monsieur might feel quite secure.

As for politics, he was all for the Bonapartes, who, he said, were magnificent thieves, whereas he had never been able to rise to the very highest level of his business. M. des Illes objected, and the last time he had indulged himself in a prolonged absence — monsieur would comprehend that this was many years ago — there had been a serious quarrel; and how could he annoy so good a master, even though they disagreed as to matters political? If monsieur were still curious as to his life, he had a few pages in which he had set down certain things worth remembering, and would monsieur like to see them? Monsieur would very much like to read them. Thus came into my possession this astonishing bit of autobiography, which at last I had leave to copy. It was oddly written, in a clear hand, and in a quaint and abrupt style, from which, in my use of it, I have generally departed, but of which I fear some traces may yet be seen.

Two evenings later, and before I had found leisure to read all of it, François said to me, "Does monsieur think to give my poor little account to the world?" I said I did not. At this I saw his very expressive face assume a look which I took to mean some form of regret. As he spoke he was standing in the doorway, and was now and then mechanically passing a brush over my dress-coat. Presently he said: "I only desired not to have set forth in France, when I am gone, such things as might give concern to M. des Illes, or trouble him if he should outlive me."

I replied that it should never be published; and when, after this, he lingered, I added, "Is that as you desire?" It was not. His vanity was simple and childlike, but immense.

"Monsieur will find it entertaining," he said; and I, that this was sure to be the case, and that it were a pity the world should lose so valuable a work. At this his lean face lighted up. Perhaps in English it might some day be of interest to monsieur's friends; and as he understood that the English were given to stealing whole countries belonging to feeble folks, it might seem to them less unusual than it would to people like those of France. But monsieur was not English. He asked my pardon. I kept a grave face, and inquired if it were a treatise on the art of theft.

This embarrassed him a little, and he made answer indirectly: did monsieur entirely disapprove this form of transfer? He seemed to regard it as merely a manner of commercial transaction by which one man alone profited. I returned that as to this nations held diverse opinions, and that some Oriental people considered it a creditable pursuit, but that personally it did seem to me wrong.

M. des Illes was distinctly of that opinion; but, after all, his (François's) account of what he had seen and been was not limited to mere details of business, and I might discover his adventures to have other interest. When he heard at last that some day I might, through his writings, enlighten the nations outside of the pale of Gallic civilization, he went away with the satisfied air of a young author who has found a publisher with a just appreciation of his labors — a thing both rare and consolatory.

His personal history, as I have said, was well known to the entire household; nor did he resent a jest now and then as to his disused art, if it came from one of a rank above his own. The old duke would say, "Any luck of late in snuff-boxes, François?"

"M. le Duc knows they are out of fashion."

"*Eh bien;* then handkerchiefs?"

"*Diable!*" says François. "They are no more of lace; what use to steal them? M. le Duc knows that gentlemen are also out of fashion. M. le Bourgeois is too careful nowadays."

"True," says the duke, and walks away, sadly reflective.

This François was what people call a character. He had a great heart and no conscience; was fond of flowers, of birds, and of children; pleased to chat of his pilferings, liking the fun of the astonishment he thus caused. Had he really no belief in its being

19

wrong to steal? I do not know. The fellow was so humorous that he sometimes left one puzzled and uncertain. He went duly to mass and confession, but — "*Mon Dieu*, monsieur; nowadays one has so little to confess, M. le Curé must find it dull."

When I would know his true ethics as to thine and mine, he cried, laughing, "*Le mien et le tien;* 't is but a letter makes the difference, and, after all, one must live." It seemed a simple character, but there is no such thing; all human nature is more complex than they who write choose to think it. If character were such as the writer of fiction often makes it, the world would be a queer place.

He is dead long ago, this same François, as my old friend Des Illes wrote me a few years later. He was very fond of a parrot he had taught to cry, " *Vive Bonaparte!* " whenever the aged duke came by his perch. One morning Poll was stolen by some adroit purveyor of parrots. This loss François felt deeply, and vastly resented the theft,— in fact, he described himself as being humbled by the power of any one to steal from a man bred up to the business,— and so missed his feathered companion that for the first time he became depressed, and at last took to his bed. He died quietly a few weeks after, saying to the priest who had given him the final rites of the church: " M. le Curé — the gold snuff-box the duke gave you —" "Well, my son?" "The left-hand pocket is the safer; we look not there." Then, half wandering, he cried: " Adieu, Master Time! Thou art the best thief, after all"; and so died, holding Des Illes's hand.

I learned from the duke and his son, as well as

from M. des Illes, many more facts as to François than he himself recorded; the good old Curé Le Grand, who was a great friend of mine, also contributed some queer incidents of François's life; and thus it was that, when years had gone by, and I became dependent on my pen, I found myself able to write fully of this interesting product of Parisian life.

After considering the material in my possession, I soon discovered that it would not answer my purpose to let François's broken memoirs tell his story. There were names and circumstances in them which it were still unwise to print. Much of what I may call the scenery of his somewhat dramatic adventures was supplied by the singular knowledge of the Revolution which the curé delighted to furnish. The good priest was by far the most aged of this group, and yet to the last the most clear as to memories of a tragic past. Thus it came that I was led to write my story of François in the third person, with such enlightening aid as I obtained from those who knew him better than I.

In his defense I may be permitted to quote the curé's cautiously worded opinion:

"Oh, monsieur, no man knows another, and every man is ever another to himself. For you François is a thief, strangely proud of an exceptional career and of his victories over the precautions of those from whom he stole. Is it not so, monsieur?" I said it was. "But the *bon Dieu* alone knows all of a man. I was not a priest until after the great wars. God pardon me, but I like still to tell tales of Jena and

Austerlitz, and of what we did in those days of victory. To kill men! The idea now fills me with horror, and yet I like nothing better, as monsieur well knows, than to talk of those days of battle. And François —'t is much the same. How could one live with these dear people, and get no lesson from their lives? Our gay, merry-minded François loved to surprise the staid folks who came hither to visit us; but I know that — ah, well, well, priests know many things."

I thanked him, but still had doubts as to whether the moral code of our friend François was ever materially altered by precept, example, or by the lack of necessity to carry on his interesting branch of industry.

Before telling his story I like to let him say for himself the only apologetic words I could discover in this memoir:

"I have no wish to write my whole life. I want to put down some things I saw and some scenes in which I was an actor. I am now old. I suppose, from what I am told, that I was wicked when I was young. But if one cannot see that he was a sinner, what then? The good God who made me knows that I was but a little Ishmaelite cast adrift on the streets to feed as I might. I defend not myself. I blame not the chances of life, nor yet the education which fate gave me. It was made to tempt one in need of food and shelter. 'T is a great thing to be able to laugh easily and often, and this good gift I had; and so, whether in safety or in peril, whether homeless or housed, I have gone through life merry. I had thought more, says M. le Curé, had I been less light of heart. But thus was I made, and, after all, it has its good side. I have always liked better the sun than the shadow; and as to relieving my wants, are the birds thieves?"

I noticed on the margins of François's memoirs remarks in a neat female handwriting, which he told me were made by Mme. des Illes, who alone had read his story.

At the end I found written: "If ever another should read what is set down in these pages, let them have the comment of charity. He who wrote them was by nature gifted with affection, good sense, and courage. He had many delicacies of character, but that of which nature meant to make a gentleman and a man of refinement, desertion and evil fortune made a thief and a reprobate. She who wrote this knew him as no one else did, and, with God's help, drew him out of the slough of crime and into a long life of honest ways. CLAIRE DES ILLES."

www.ingramcontent.com/pod-product-compliance
Lightning Source LLC
Chambersburg PA
CBHW020939030726

47496CB00005B/1265